© 2023 Joe Murtagh. The rig be identified as author of thi asserted by him in accordance with sections 77 and 78 of the Copyright, Designs and Patents Act 1988. All rights reserved.

PREFACE

Lancashire, England 1958

Liverpool's Scotland Road was typically busy and noisy, and yet now it was eerily quiet. It was almost as if the locals were expecting something to happen. In a side street down near the docks, shadowy figures flitted along, silhouetted against the walls by the meagre glow of streetlamps. Occasionally other shadows moved behind curtained windows. A few windows were in complete darkness.

Suddenly, a piercing whistle blast sounded, and five burly figures launched themselves against a door which flew open under their onslaught. The light from a hall lamp showed the intruders as uniformed police. Two moved quickly through the ground floor rooms while the others rushed the stairs, burst into a bedroom, and were surprised to see a young girl on a bed and an older woman bathing the girl's thighs.

"What the hell is going on here?" asked a police sergeant.

The girl screamed and covered herself with a sheet.

The older woman cursed, "Bloody coppers! Can't get a minute's peace for you lot."

"Nothing in the other room," said a police officer joining his colleagues from a second bedroom.

The sergeant gave the women a hard look and asked his question again, but with greater force. "What bent games are you two playing?"

"I didn't want to have it done, honestly officer," the girl blurted out in an obvious Irish accent.

"Have what done?"

"This thing, this termination. My mother insisted on it. We couldn't live in our village for shame if I didn't. The church would cast us adrift."

"Are you saying this woman is bringing about an abortion?"

The older woman replied, "Yes and I'm helping her in a desperate situation. Can't you see she is terrified?"

"Terrified or not," said the sergeant, "you know the law as well as I do. You are both under arrest. We're taking you to the police station where you'll be held in custody pending a medical examination and formal charges." As the police team left the building, the youngest and newest asked, "Does this often happen? A brothel raid turns out to be an abortion?"

"Expect the unexpected in this town son," replied a colleague. "It's all happening here. And often."

The subsequent police investigation into the affair closed after charging the arrested pair and the mother of the girl. Besides discovering that the girl and her mother had travelled from Dublin for the abortion, no further information was unearthed, or arrests made.

In fact, a wide network of illegal terminations was in action, across Liverpool and Manchester, conducted by maverick midwives and supported by transport, accommodation, sophisticated communications processes, and client movements. All masterminded and controlled by a ruthless and highly organised individual. Paradoxically, the Scotland Road arrest had come close to bringing down the network, albeit accidentally. Instead, the criminal controller handed over the operation of the network to two trusted lieutenants and moved away from the area.

South-West Coast of Scotland 1959

The long, and low, ranch-style building set back high on the hillside above Dunure harbour presented uninterrupted views across the Firth of Clyde and spectacular sunsets over the Isle of Arran. Built after the 1939-45 war as a holiday home, the five-bedroom villa gave easy access to the beaches and town of Ayr, five miles to the north, and to the world-famous golf course at Turnberry, a similar distance to the south.

A driveway from the main coastal road wound up to the red roof tiled, brick-faced building where two black saloon cars and a small coach were parked near the entrance.

In the heavily carpeted main drawing room, four men were sitting in comfortable armchairs drawn around a blazing log fire, talking animatedly and occasionally laughing.

Each held in hand a glass, whisky or brandy according to personal taste, and a lone smoker enjoyed a cigar. The tallest of the group was Crawford Baxter, nursing a large measure of scotch as he sat chatting to an overweight silver-haired man in his early sixties. Across from them on the other side of the fireplace, the smoker shared a joke with a man with a balding head and florid complexion. An unusual gathering of individuals brought together for a weekend of playing, planning, and plotting.

The smoker was Charles Palmer, a prominent Glasgow businessman. Next to him was balding Martin Harrison, the assistant chief constable of Glasgow police. The foursome was completed by Baxter, a consultant gynaecologist, and Oliver Woodhouse the Lord Provost of Glasgow, chairman of the city council, and the greater Glasgow development committee.

The four, who had earlier that day played nine very windy holes on a links golf course at Turnberry, knew each other well. All were freemasons in the city centre masonic lodge and arranged the weekend retreat to take in some golf, relaxation, and attendance at a Burns Supper evening in Ayr. They had also allowed time to discuss future business opportunities away from prying eyes or curious ears.

The villa at Dunure supplied the perfect setting for all this.

After some time, the police chief stood up, walked across the room to the huge panoramic windows, and gazed down on the harbour lights of Dunure, then across the wide expanse of water to the twinkling lights of Whiting Bay on the Isle of Arran some fifteen miles away. He glanced upwards and spotted the navigation lights of a plane, heading further north to Prestwick airport he guessed. "Clear night tonight," he said." Little cloud to speak of. Frosty start in the morning, I expect. Glad we got some golf in this morning."

"Well, some of us played golf," laughed Baxter. "I just had a good walk."

"Yes, we noticed Doc," said Palmer to his golf partner of the day," but tonight we all need to be on our game. In the dining room, after we've finished eating and the staff have cleared off, each of us will receive a numbered and sealed pack of information. Please note and obey the secret and confidential headings."

The pack he referred to contained the very latest plans for the next phase of the reincarnation of Glasgow - a detailed and comprehensive programme for the eradication of the remaining city slums and their preferred replacements, the ground works for further new housing estates beyond the existing city boundaries, and the infrastructure needed to support the people exodus. This view of the future was complemented by the latest motorway, highways and routing proposals from the teams who had been planning this for years. A forecast budget went with the information.

Rising from his armchair, Woodhouse, the Lord Provost, leaned his arm against the mantlepiece of the inglenook fireplace, then addressed the others. "Gentlemen, as chairman of the city corporation, it is my pleasure to present and share with you the vast opportunities that are open to us if we play our cards wisely. In the coming years there will be an even greater demand for materials, manpower, and capital. A fortune waits for any business group that establishes itself to take advantage of this. It's our intention to be that group and benefit from the inside knowledge that we have at our disposal.

"My existing companies are geared to providing demolition, road building and transport," announced Palmer. "And with the cooperation of the police, the city chambers, and the development executive, we're well positioned to launch today."

"What you have now is merely the start, Charlie," said Woodhouse. " Read and absorb the information packs and after breakfast tomorrow we'll convene in the dining room to discuss the extent of the challenge and agree specifically how we take advantage of the knowledge and positions we have."

Baxter listened with interest but kept his thoughts to himself; thoughts on why he was getting involved with a businessman and two senior city figures who appeared beyond reproach and planned to control the issuing of contracts and licences for infrastructure, gambling and impending new alcohol laws which were on the horizon. And they were doing all this purely for their own financial benefit.

CHAPTER ONE

Each step she took on her journey to her parents' home that day moved her closer to an ordeal she could not have imagined; each passing hour drew her into a nightmare she was ill equipped to handle. But she didn't know what she was moving towards. If she had, she probably would have turned back.

Anybody would have done the same. If she knew what lay ahead, and how much her world could change in the coming days, a step forward would mean that she was knowingly capitulating to a horrific transformation of her life.

Her world in Glasgow was ordered, predictable, and safe. Most days she faced life with a smile, was helpful, and went out of her way to be considerate to other people. Although somewhat naïve, even a little gullible, she was nevertheless a decent well-balanced individual who lived by her innate values of honesty and truth. Nightmares didn't happen to her. Until now.

A cold winter wind tugged at her coat as she left the ferry behind her and hurried along drab Glasgow streets. Grey sandstone tenement buildings - blackened by the ravages of soot, smog and industrial grime - loomed above and around her. The tram lines on the cobbled road glistened with the earlier rain.

She sensed more rain in the morning Clyde-side air, pulled her coat tight around her and quickened her step towards her parents' home close to the sprawling shipyards.

Twenty-seven years old and strikingly attractive, Alice Walker was a State Registered Nurse and spent off duty days like this visiting her parents. Most of the visits went into helping her mother in the home, running errands for her and generally keeping her company. This day she expected to be much the same, but she had also planned a little bonus for herself. To make the most of her day off she had arranged to later meet her boyfriend and spend some time with him in the city centre.

Her mother and father had moved to Scotland from the north of England during the hard 1930s depression, with the promise of work for her father as a labourer in an admiralty shipyard in Glasgow. He had previously worked in the drawing office of a small shipbuilding company in Sunderland which had gone to the wall in the turbulence of the depression. Labouring had not come easily to him, and the physical demands of being a ships' plater's helper had taken a toll on his health, leaving him bitter and quarrelsome.

As she neared her destination, she felt blessed and guilty that she now lived in nursing accommodation elsewhere, and not in this part of the city.

Many years before, her parents had applied to the housing authority for a move away from this area but had heard nothing more They rented a two-room ground floor tenement flat in this Govan area of the city. The property was run down, damp and cramped, with a central building entrance, communal outside toilet and a shared back yard, which regularly smelled of cats' urine, and was often home to illegal bookmakers and *pitch and toss* gamblers. Their tenement building had been earmarked for demolition for some time, as had many others in that area. Born and raised in this area, she had unhappy memories of the place.

She strode past the school where she'd once hoped to gain a ticket to higher education, and a career as a schoolteacher which would take her away from her slum surroundings. Hopes which had turned out to be elusive.

The winter air nipped at her face as she passed the red police box opposite the Salvation Army church hall, the familiar row of local shops, and the childhood homes of friends. Friends whom she envied, who were now married with children and had moved away to lighter, brighter futures.

She crossed the noisy Langlands Road, with its assorted collection of busy hardware, bakers, butchers, clothing and tobacconist shops, and well patronised pubs. Pubs like The Boars Head where, together with many other shipyard workers, her father had drunk heavily on Fridays. And then came home and took his frustrations out on his wife.

Trudging past the familiar milestones seemed to her like a rough trek through a gloomy memory lane.

Her mother, Martha, was a gentle soul and a woman of her time - subservient, compliant and obedient to the wishes of a husband whose thanks often came in the shape of a verbal onslaught, or back handed slap. There were many women like her in the community who had lived through similar experiences and offered her mother a sympathetic ear and a neighbourly arm around the shoulder.

Martha had worked as a French Polisher before developing severe arthritis in her hands. Now in her fifty-eighth year, the disease had spread to other joints in her body and severely limited her movement. This also constrained her ability to carry out her share of the communal tenement chores such as sweeping, washing and generally cleaning the cold stone hall and walls. She looked to her daughter to help with these tasks on her visits.

James, her father, had for most of his life lived and worked in a male dominated environment, and been conditioned by the harsh realities of years labouring on exposed and dangerous ships' gantries. Working life in Govan shipyards was for the brave and hardened. In his time there, he had seen five fatal accidents and thought nothing of the fact that severe injuries and worse never brought work to a halt. Just a fact of shipyard life, or death. Over the years he'd become blind to his wife's needs, increasingly argumentative and oblivious to his own behaviour. Yet, she and Alice were virtually all the family he had left. He had lost touch with his younger brother in England and regularly cursed the move to Glasgow.

Over the years his health had deteriorated, his breathing had become laboured, and had forced him to give up his beloved cigarettes. This deterioration had further sullied his moody and turbulent attitude.

Increasingly, as his treatment of her mother worsened, Alice's dislike of her father intensified, and their relationship descended to a just about bearable low. She had promised herself that she would find an opportunity to leave Govan whenever it was practical. Her parents however had remained together, and life had gone on much as ever.

To bring some extra income to the family, in her teens she had taken part time shop assistant work at weekends. Later, she had given up hopes of further education and left school as soon as possible to take up full-time shop work. She became ever closer to her mother, and worried for the future and how her parents might cope financially.

Martha had repeatedly urged her to think of herself and pursue some kind of career. She'd assured her daughter that there would be enough money for her parents to live on. They would get by, as she put it.

After many months, and a great deal of soul searching, at eighteen she had eventually applied for and secured a position in England as a trainee nurse, living and training in the hospital. That had been almost nine years ago.

The grim memories of those past earlier years were revived on the journey to her parents' home. Now, after a very long night attending to her duties, she was going back to visit her folks at the miserable accommodation they called home.

She turned a corner into the street next to her parents' and was shocked to see a house flat eviction in progress. She joined a small group of onlookers watching the proceedings.

"This is the third eviction in a week around here," said an elderly lady in the group to no one in particular. "Oh, those wee weans. Look at them, poor wee souls."

A bed, table, kitchen cabinet, some chairs, suitcase, and a child's cot were being piled onto the pavement next to a child and a woman cradling a baby in her arms.

Two men in trench-coats and holding clip boards stood beside a policeman and watched as neighbours sought to spread a tarpaulin over the pathetic belongings, while a man she assumed to be the husband harangued the officials. The child had tears streaming down its face, was wailing, and shivered as it clung to its mother's dress. It began to rain heavily. The baby cried even louder.

Dear God, she thought. This is what happens when the landlord doesn't get his rent paid. This could be my parents on the street. What would I do if that happened?

She hurried away from the dismal scene, acknowledging some passing neighbours who recognised her, until she reached the ugly tenement building which housed her parents' address. She paused for a moment: gathered her thoughts, putting behind her any everyday concerns or pressures. She wanted to be bright and outgoing, this was important. She entered the tenement building and knocked on her mother's door.

"Come in, come away in my dear," her mother said as she opened the door. "You look frozen. Take your coat off and sit by the fire, I'll put the kettle on for tea. Your father is at the doctors' surgery looking for medication to ease his bronchial troubles. It'll be a while before he's back."

12

Alice entered the small flat and looked around the sparsely furnished but scrupulously clean room. It was always spotless. Her mother, despite her arthritis, had to maintain it that way to keep the peace. She noted the scant furnishings in their familiar places, the outmoded sideboard with the framed wedding photograph on top, and next to that the centre of her parents' entertainment - a large radio set. Televisions, though widely on sale, were beyond her parents' means.

She kissed her mother, asked how she was, and passed her a small brown paper bag containing the sugar, tea and butter she had brought to supplement the larder stock. Bringing a few provisions with her on visits to her mother was a habit, almost a duty, she had developed. Post war austerity had generally eased, but an economic hangover still affected many families. A wider range of food items were now much more available, but the means to buy them among poorer working-class families such as hers were not. Her parents had barely enough to keep the roof over their heads and feed themselves.

"Yes, I'm fine, love," answered Martha in response to her daughter's earlier question. "You know how it is. Some days just getting by. Others are better, if not great." She momentarily glanced towards a window. "I could do with seeing the weather brighten up so I could get out for a while." She smiled as she returned her attention to her daughter. "Looking at four walls every day can feel like prison. Still, I'm thankful we have a roof over our heads, a good fire, and a warm bed." She laughed. "Could also do without this wretched arthritis playing up with the rain and damp. Anyway, enough about me. How are you? What's going on in your world? You look tired."

Alice hesitated before answering, knowing that her mother was putting a brave face on things. It was ever thus and served no purpose to dwell on her plight. What *did* matter to her mum was hearing news about her daughter. "Oh, I'm alright, Mum, really. I'm busy as ever. Never seem to be enough hours in the day at times, but that's the life of a nurse, you know?" Or the life of a downtrodden wife for that matter, she thought. "I was working late last night and have some sleep to catch up on. Maybe that's why I look tired, but I feel fine. I know what you mean about being within four walls, but you're probably better off indoors for now. The weather doesn't seem to know what it is doing - wind and rain, sunshine for a bit, then sleet. It'll be snow next." She nodded. "Coming across the river on the ferry today was miserable. The old sailor who pilots the ferry was predicting snow before the week is out."

Her mother screwed her face up and said, "Well it is winter, so I suppose we shouldn't be surprised. And it could be worse. I had a letter from my cousin in Canada last week, she said they are snowed in for days at this time of year."

"Is that your aunt Mary's daughter?"

"Yes, her mother, my father's sister, died just before Christmas. There are not many of the family left, not in Scotland anyway."

"All the more reason for you to stay out of the cold, Mum," Alice chided. "I would really like to be able to help more. Maybe when the weather changes I can take you out to the botanical gardens or for a picnic in one of the parks."

"You do help us a great deal, Alice. You don't have to worry about us. We get by."

Her daughter thought to herself, yes, they did manage, but only just, and there were no reserves to fall back on. The eviction scene she had seen came into her mind and she was on the verge of relaying this to her mother, but decided to keep the conversation as light as she possibly could. She busied herself with a few household jobs, ironed a few sheets and pillowcases, then joined her mother at the kitchen table.

As they chatted over tea and home baked scones, Martha asked about her daughter's job in the women's hospital, a job she had taken the previous year, and the third hospital she had worked in. "Are you enjoying it, Alice? You don't seem to get much free time, other than when you come to see us. I don't hear you talk much about your job. Don't you have time to get out and enjoy yourself, meet other people?"

"I'm happy there and as busy as I've ever been," she assured her mother. "My free time is sufficient to give me a break, I've made some friends among nurses, and we occasionally go out shopping in the city centre when we can."

"Isn't there a special friend you have, other than your nurse friends?"

Alice smiled to herself. It was inevitable that at some stage today her mother would start probing about her love life. "Maybe I'll meet someone special, sometime. If it's to be, it will be. Don't you remember, before your arthritis got so bad, the song you used to sing to me when you danced me around the floor? You know, que sera sera?"

That's all she wanted to say. She had no wish to encourage a further conversation that led to a discussion about her mother's desire to become a grandmother or be reminded that Alice's biological clock was ticking.

Her parents had not met her boyfriend, Phil Groves. Alice had only vaguely mentioned having had occasionally seen a boyfriend. He was not a topic of conversation. Discussing her nursing job within limits was safe territory and so she brought the topic back to that. "Mum don't worry, I'm really enjoying my job, though the hours are a bit tiring. The word in our hospital is that there is a major shortage of nurses right throughout the national health service. There are lots of changes going on due to losing nurses while they're still in training, I hear."

"What, they are not finishing their training?" Martha asked.

"That's right. Around half of those in training don't finish their course. Which puts a greater burden on those of us left to cover gaps in exposed areas."

"Why don't they finish their training? It's a good job, well respected, and we'll always need health workers, won't we?" her mother asked.

"Mainly, it's because of trainees leaving to get married. But nursing training is no walk in the park, Mum. Both mentally and physically, it's regimented and demanding. Some just don't like it and leave. There were times during my training I had doubts about carrying on. I'm glad I stuck it out."

"I'm glad too, Alice, and proud of you. How will this shortage affect you?"

"At present I'm working in a general ward," Alice said, "but will get moved around the hospital. I don't mind that. It gives me wider experience. The nurses' accommodation isn't exactly spacious but it's comfortable enough. I've recently moved rooms and now share a room with Frances McEwan, a senior midwife who has been there for some time. She's bright, cheery and chatty, and she's helped me settle in."

"Where is she from?" Martha asked. "Is she Scottish?"

"She's originally from Scotland but has worked in different places. The nurses' quarters are like being in the army - a bit regimented, formal rules, weekly inspections, and strictly no males. But I like it, and it's a far cry from here."

Alice moved their talk on to the ever-present challenges in making financial ends meet, and how her parents were coping.

Matha explained there had recently been an unexpectedly high increase in their rent, and this added load, together with the cost of every-day utilities and groceries, was a problem they confessed to having no answer to. "It's a bit unexpected and more than we can afford without cutting corners elsewhere," Martha added.

"What corners, where?"

"We'll manage, dear. We'll get by."

This news alarmed Alice. She wondered where it would all end if her parents could not pay the rent. The earlier eviction again loomed large in her mind. Her father's poor health had occasionally caused him to take unpaid time off work, and the news of a rent increase meant matters were unsustainable. "How has Dad been this past week?" she asked her mother.

In a faltering voice, Martha said, "Things have gone downhill, since the doctor delivered some very unwelcome news." She stared at her daughter and seemed to be making some kind of calculation. "He… he said that recent tests have shown your father has developed early Alzheimer's disease and they are sure of the diagnosis. He'll shortly have to consider giving up work. It'll be too dangerous to continue working in the shipyard or, it seems, anywhere else. Time will tell." Martha's gaze dropped to the floor and her shoulders sagged. She appeared scared and demoralised, her eyes tearing up.

Alice moved beside her, put her arm around her and held her close. Although taken aback, she was not entirely surprised at this news. It seemed to confirm fears she held about his condition and some of his most recent behaviours. She knew full well the effects of this disease and how quickly it could deteriorate, and she also feared for the additional impact it would have on her parents financially. As much and as deeply as she felt for her mother, it was difficult to feel the same degree of sympathy for her father when she recalled his worsening domestic behaviour over the years. She kept that thought to herself. Her mother had no need to be reminded of her husband's conduct. She held her mother's hand and counselled her as best she could, trying to sound optimistic about medical advances which might help delay the disease. "We need to be positive, Mum. Things are changing for the better in medicine and every day new treatments are being found and brought into use." But she knew this was a forlorn hope, and that her mother knew this too.

She stayed with her mother a little longer, talking of neighbours and relatives, birthdays and anniversaries, but soon their conversation petered out. The news of her father had severely knocked her spirits, and shortly after she took her leave of her mother, much sooner than she had planned, and before her father returned from the doctors' surgery. This was a visit she wished she had never made. Her normally bright outlook was now engulfed with a heavy black cloud.

CHAPTER TWO

As Alice emerged from the gloom of the tenement building, she ran into a rain shower. Typical Glasgow weather, she thought. She had paid particular attention to her hair before she left the nurses' quarters that day in anticipation of meeting her boyfriend, and although she wore a headscarf it would provide little or no protection. Without an umbrella she could get soaked. With an hour or more to pass before her meeting with Phil, she ducked into a nearby busy café where she ordered coffee.

The air in the café was laden with cigarette smoke, and the noise of early lunchtime workers' chatter competing with Little Richard belting out Baby Face from the juke box. She found a seat by a steamed-up window, sat down, stirred her coffee and pondered on the news of her father's health and the bleak outlook for her parents, which in turn led her to think about her own life path and her hopes for the future.

Her mother's news had greatly increased the concern she felt about her parents' plight and what lay ahead. Their need for financial help had already been prominent in her thoughts. It would now be a constant nag. Her overriding thought was, how could she lighten that burden? She wondered if there was any way she could increase her nurses pay. And that prompted her to think about her work. She was inwardly proud of her progress as a nurse. The hard slog from student nurse to where she now was had followed the traditional path of menial tasks that included bedpan scrubbing, sluice room duty, and bed and laundry change. And the hours were very long. In the early training years leading to her gaining enrolled nurse status, there were times when she had wanted to give it all up. Life then was regimented, highly controlled, and severe discipline was all-pervasive. And yet the rewards seemed at best patchy and at worst non-existent. Practical training was erratic, many shift hours were overnight and required working on grave matters better suited to the professional attention of far more experienced nurses, other work had to be completed out of scheduled hours, and lectures had to be attended in her own time. All this while receiving a pitiful wage. However, she had been proud to have a real job helping others and had an innate sense of duty. So, she had stuck it out.

In fact, alternative life-choices for unqualified young women in the 1950s were few, and time to pursue other opportunities had been very limited.

Having now reached state registered nurse level, she felt a strong vocational satisfaction, and her sense of social responsibility and community spirit was fulfilled. She now had a career.

However, the hours were still long and the financial rewards meagre.

This had been her life path until now.

As she looked around the café and at the lessening queue, she smiled as Pat Boone singing *April Love* started playing on the juke box, a song she shared with her boyfriend Phil. "Their song," she liked to call it.

She wondered what the future held for them.

Deep in her heart she longed for marriage and to have a family, to be like her schoolfriends. In Phil, she felt she had found someone who could provide the perfect answer to her dreams. She warmly remembered their first meeting at a private hospital summer gala the previous year. She had been on volunteer duty at a first aid tent and Phil had driven his boss and his wife, who had been a patient, to attend the event. Two years younger than Alice, Phil was chatty, slim built, smartly dressed and darkly handsome, with thick black hair, an easy-going manner and a broad smile which had immediately attracted her to him. He also exuded social confidence which she admired and lacked herself.

He worked as a waiter, barman and general factotum at The Regency, a city centre private members club. His working hours were irregular, but during the past year or so they had managed to meet up for dancing, cinema, coffee bar meets, and an occasional meal where he met the lion's share of the costs. In that time, she had grown ever more attracted to him and had suggested marriage. She felt she could live the rest of her life with this man. By contrast, he had so far only joked about being too young to die, and not yet ready for such a commitment.

What Alice didn't know was that Phil Groves was perfectly content with the status-quo in their relationship and didn't aspire to anything more than taking her out, being seen with her, and doing more of the things they'd already enjoyed. Her striking good looks, light brown hair, blue eyes, and tall shapely figure were something of a capture for him, and for the time being he was happy to continue the relationship so long as it was without obligation.

He valued his freedom.

Besides, he liked to play the field and had often had two girlfriends on the go at once. He kept his cards close to his chest, particularly concerning his past. His school days had been marked by stealing from other school kids and teachers, regular clashes with school masters, frequent dressing downs for truancy, and afternoon and evenings were spent in dingy snooker halls. Eventually he was expelled at age fifteen. Thereafter he took a job in a whisky bond warehouse. Within weeks he became part of a group stealing full, but unlabelled, bottles of Scotland's finest export. By his seventeenth birthday he was known to the police for petty theft. He was housed in a young offender borstal for a year, well on his way to becoming a criminal, and a confidant of some of the city's gangsters. As well as valuing his freedom, he needed time to carry on his involvement with some of the Regency Club's private members.

The Club was located on the top floor of a five storey Victorian building, reached by elevator from a discreet ground floor entrance. Heavily carpeted, oak panelled and richly furnished, it housed a restaurant, a games room and member's bar, together with a few smaller function rooms, and an entrance attended by an imposing doorman. The clientele, exclusively male, were a cross section of some of Glasgow's comfortably wealthy commercial merchants- small business owners, car dealers, metal traders, clothing manufacturers, a smattering of professional card players, and several nouveau riche with dubious backgrounds and uncertain sources of wealth.

Managed by a former international football player, the club attracted the sports minded fraternity who enjoyed its privacy to conduct their business over a meal and a drink.

It also attracted some of the city's hardest and most ruthless characters.

Groves had worked there for almost five years and had quietly gained a reputation for a willingness to help members with difficult problems, particularly in recycling questionable assets, and for keeping his mouth shut. When occasionally invited, he joined in members late night card games. The problem was, he was currently three hundred pounds in debt to a club member. A pressing debt he could not pay.

His past was entirely unknown to his girlfriend. As was his gambling debt.

In the café, as the hubbub had subsided, Alice ordered another coffee, and her thoughts returned to the latest news of her father's health. Its dire, soon to be felt effect on family finances weighed heavily on her mind. Her parents were living in a crumbling building, with no savings, paying a punitive rent and still some time away from receiving a state pension. Money was a pressing and major concern, and it would only get worse.

Her gloom lifted a little when she thought of her boyfriend, very much the brighter side of her life. She wiped the condensation from the café window and peered out into the street as though trying to see into the future. The rain had stopped.

She glanced at her watch, realised it was time to go, finished her coffee, and left.

After breakfast, the four associates gathered in the villa at Dunure to discuss the information they had received the previous evening.

"The amount of work the city will require in the next five to ten years is absolutely enormous," the Lord Provost began. "This you should have gleaned from your confidential packs. The contracts for the works will be awarded to the winners of applicant bids, but not necessarily to the lowest cost bid. The awarding committees will have discretion and the final say. They will assess the bids based on quality and time, as well as cost. We're well placed on the appropriate committees to steer the awards of those contracts to the holding company we are about to set up. Martin and I will ensure the successful contract awards from our respective committees. Charlie, you must devote all your energies to gathering the necessary people, equipment, materials, and skills to deliver the desired outcomes. It is critical that you have the resources required to meet the changes. Our capital investment will support you in this respect. The initial phase will involve the mass demolition and clearance of tenement buildings in the remaining city slum areas, following the resettlement of the occupants to new peripheral housing areas. Similar clearance actions will be needed in the city centre to provide for planned commercial development there, and a rerouting of highways and arterial roads will be necessary. Not revealed in the pack you were given, but in top level discussion currently, there will be a motorway driving through the heart of the city, from west to east, which will provide an eventual link to the motorway planned from Edinburgh. Additionally, a ring road round the city is envisaged, which will enable mass movement to and from the centre for commuters, commerce, and travellers. Gentlemen, this is no mere tinkering with a small housing problem. It is a vast programme of change which will alter the face and heartbeat of Glasgow for decades to come. We will take advantage of the opportunities it will offer. Any questions so far?"

"When can I start recruiting the resources I will need? As you say, I don't have anywhere near enough at the moment," said Charlie.

"You should already be planning your strategy and organisation; the leaders, and the skills you will need to bolster what you already have. The financial resource is available through the holding company. We will meet weekly to develop this and prepare for the first contract."

"What's to be my contribution, Oliver?" asked Baxter.

"We will need a non-executive director on the board who outwardly has no obvious interest in the commercial dealings. Rather, a respected public figure balancing the interests of the board were they to be scrutinised."

"Isn't what we are doing somewhat improper, maybe even illegal, unlawful?"

"The organisation of the group, the holding company, is not illegal. Having said that, the awarding of the contracts could possibly be seen as sailing close to the wind," The Lord Provost looked stern." But the role you are asked to play is one of an even-handed professional face in the board room. No more, no less. And of course, your share of the start-up capital is required. Happy?"

"I understand, thanks Oliver," Baxter confirmed. Inwardly Baxter was not at all sure that what they were embarking on was entirely legitimate. But if the Lord Provost, Assistant Chief Constable, and a celebrated businessman such as Palmer were behind it, he would go along with the business venture. They surely would never risk their positions and reputations. Besides, he would enjoy the money.

"If there are no other questions, we meet again as agreed in a fortnight. Charlie will get the Holding Company registration under way, and then we launch the enterprise," the Lord Provost ended.

CHAPTER THREE

The weak winter sun occasionally poked through clouds as Alice Walker left the café and moved along the bustling main dockside road towards the Govan Cross underground station. From there she intended to travel three miles on the subway train to the city centre where she would meet Phil. From the shipyard on her left came the staccato thud of riveters' hammers and the sing song sound of caulkers' tools providing an industrial accompaniment to the squawks and squeals of seagulls overhead. She noted a tall crane manoeuvring a steel plate into position high above the outline of a ship under construction, and her eyes were drawn to a stream of sparks from another high gantry where welders were working. She had recently heard on the radio that new ships were being lost to Glasgow yards through orders being given to lower cost shipbuilders abroad and wondered how long the work would be available on the Clyde. Particularly, and regardless of his health concerns, she wondered how much longer there would be work for her father and men like him.

She descended the steps to the station platform. The warmth and familiar smell of the underground greeted her as she joined a small throng of passengers waiting for the next train. The journey to St Enoch station in the city took less than fifteen minutes. In that time her mood had lifted a little at the thought of seeing Phil, and she hoped she could find another chance to turn the conversation to marriage, children and family life.

After leaving the city centre underground station, dodging tramcars, cars, trucks and buses, she crossed the crowded Argyle Street and made her way to the rendezvous at Marco's, a trendy basement café come restaurant. This was a mecca for fashionable young Glaswegians, and during the day attracted mainly office and shop workers. Until Phil introduced her to it, she had never heard of the place.

The Victorian buildings along her route were indicative of the wealth of the city. There were richly carved figures above doorways, elaborate designs around windows leading into high ceilinged rooms and offices, and above many of the streets, regiments of starlings were perched on the edge of roofs targeting unwary pedestrians.

She reached the entrance to the café: and made her way down a spiral staircase. As she did, she could see right across the room. There were few customers. Phil was already there, at a corner table and waving to her as she entered.

She made her way around mostly vacant tables, took off her coat, and moved in beside him.

"Hi" he said as he hugged her. "Did you have trouble getting here? You're a bit late."

A hurt expression spread over her face. "That's a nice greeting. *Hello you're late.* Nothing about 'nice to see you', or 'how are you'?"

"Oh, sorry. Can I get you a drink?"

"Yes, you can, and maybe bring back a smile and a warmer welcome,"

Phil shrugged, avoided eye contact, stood, and started moving around the table. "I see you're not in your nurse's uniform. Why's that?"

"Excuse me," she responded. "I…I know you like my uniform; you've said that before, but it's nice to have a change of colour. I wear uniform day in and day out. You liked this when I wore it before. Have you gone off it?" She smoothed out her pretty pale green patterned dress and gave him a puzzled look. He grimaced, mumbled a low response which was lost against the hum of background noise and piped music, and left the table to order drinks.

She sensed a tension in Phil that was new, almost as if he was preoccupied with something else that was bothering him. This was new to her because so far, he'd always come across as laid back and open.

On his return with the drinks, she described her morning visit to her parents' home, the heart- rending eviction she had witnessed, and the news of her father's health. She confessed that she was now very worried about the family finances and what lay in store for her parents.

His response was a flat, unsympathetic and almost disinterested "Oh, that's too bad" "

His lack of empathy in her news unsettled her, almost angered her and after finishing their coffees she steered the conversation around to asking why he was in such a strange mood.

"I'm not in a mood, just have a lot on my mind," he said. "I've been busy. And things have been getting on top of me."

"What things?"

"Just things at work, you know. People and things."

"That's not like you Phil. What's happened?"

"Nothing's happened," he snapped.

"Hey, take it easy. It's obvious something has happened. You're not like your normal self."

"Is that right? And what's my normal self?"

"God's sake Phil, what's got into you?"

"Nothing. Everybody has off days, don't they?"

"Oh, this is an off day, is it?" queried Alice with some concern.

"Give it a rest, I just have things on my mind at work."

He continued to be evasive for some time, but when at length her insistent questioning outran his patience, he gripped the table, his voice rose, and he snapped, "I'm in trouble. I need money. quite a lot. and soon." Then, with a pleading look he said, "You need to help me. Please, can you help? I have no one else to turn to."

"Why do you need money. How much do you need?"

He glanced at the ceiling, around the café, then looked back at her and lied. "I've broken some very expensive equipment at work and am forced to pay the equipment replacement cost or lose my job. No job means I lose my accommodation and I'll be out on the street. My boss is raging."

Further questioning about the damage and the cost was met by vague and ambiguous answers, until angrily he finally blurted out that he needed "hundreds of pounds."

Coming on top of her family's financial woes this was a bombshell. "Are you kidding? What have you done, for God's sake? Can't the equipment be repaired?" she asked, her voice rising.

"The equipment is completely beyond repair and needs replacing, and if I am to keep my job, I have to find the money to pay for it," he replied." I need the money and quick."

"Just like that? Hundreds of pounds, what the blazes is the equipment?"

Phil ignored the question and again asked for help.

Marco's Café was beginning to fill up and her voice carried to other tables where people were taking notice. Phil asked her to keep her voice down and tried to change the subject, but to no avail. She continued for some time to press Phil for answers but received no responses that satisfied her. Her head was spinning with this latest financial demand, and Phil was clearly upset about his job. She was getting nowhere with her questions and eventually she ran out of steam.

But she'd made a decision. Despite receiving the vaguest of answers to her questions, her thoughts were to share his plight and help the man she loved.

The rest of their conversation was flat, desultory, conditioned by the money problem, and eventually after an hour, Phil excused himself saying that he had to get back to work. They walked to her bus stop, where he kissed her on the cheek and left her with a pleading reminder that he needed help and quickly.

On the bus ride from the city centre, along the north bank of the river toward the nurse's home, she turned over the disturbing events of the day in her mind.

Finances, money, or *the sordid topic of coin* as her mother sometimes referred to it, now loomed massively in her life. Her own wage rate of less than 4 shillings an hour yielded just over 9 pounds a week for her 96-hour fortnightly shift work schedule. A great deal of this income went towards her food and accommodation at the hospital, clothing, fares, and personal items. She helped her mother with food as often as she could, particularly when her father was off work ill. Her savings amounted to less than £25 which she'd earmarked to help buy a second-hand motor scooter. She was long tired of catching buses and trams to visit her folks and a new vehicle would enable her to go wherever and whenever she wanted. Regardless, £25 was nowhere near enough to meet her parents' probable future needs, and certainly not enough to get Phil out of trouble. Finding the money to solve her parents' and her boyfriend's problems seemed hopeless.

She sat upstairs at the front of the crowded bus and stared out the window at the darkening evening, her thoughts submerged in a confusion of issues, hopes and emotions. A few fellow passengers were smoking which annoyed her, but the lower no smoking deck was full, not even standing room. She wanted to be back at the nurses' home in time for tea, so she had to put up with the upper deck or wait for another bus. The passenger sitting next to her opened a newspaper and she caught glimpses of news about the singer Buddy Holly's death, Hawaii becoming a state in the US, and an item about Fidel Castro and Cuba. She had only a vague idea where Cuba was and concluded that, wherever it was, it was probably much warmer than Glasgow. The upper deck was almost full, and the bus windows had steamed up, prompting constant wiping of the condensation to see outside and into the darkening streets.

"Fares please, any more fares." The sound of the bus conductor came closer as Alice fished the correct change from her purse. The conductor braced herself against the lurching of the bus, punched out the required ticket, and gave it to the nurse, who pushed the ticket into her glove. Alice looked up at her, took in her dark green jacket and trousers with red piping, the leather bag of coins around her waist, and the silver ticket machine looped around her shoulders and perched above her chest. She wore a thin tartan tie tightly knotted at the neck of a white paper collar, set off by a tie pin depicting the trade union she belonged to. Coin blackened fingers protruded from the ends of fingerless gloves and a peaked hat completed the working uniform. Alice wondered if bus conductor was the kind of work she could do if she had to. But no sooner had she thought it than she dismissed the idea, it was not for her. She hated wearing trousers, didn't look good in dark green, and was sure Phil would hate the look. Besides, working in a smoky atmosphere would remind her of her father, and the polluted air that caused his lung condition. She smiled her thanks to the bus conductor who moved back into the bus and continued her chant, "Fares please, any more fares."

It had started to rain again, and the pools of light from shop interiors and neon signs cast an eerie glow on the pavements. Passing tramcars and buses occasionally added a light show to the scene. Yesterday had been for her, a routine, bland, easy to forget kind of day. Today had turned into a bad dream. So much to grasp, to find answers to. She had to find a way to help her parents, and now Phil.

Her thoughts centred on Phil and his need for so much money. She looked back at the months of their relationship and wondered how much she really knew him. On their infrequent outings he always seemed happy-go-lucky, attentive, and caring. He was well paid, generous, and always smartly dressed in the latest styles. He shared accommodation at the Regency Club with a co-worker George, whom she had never met but Phil had often talked about. Phil had no family, being an only child of deceased parents. Other than the little she knew of his job, precious little more was known of his background.

They had been intimate a few times on countryside trips to Loch Lomond the previous summer when Phil had borrowed his boss's car, but their respective living arrangements precluded overnight stays and regular lovemaking. And hosting men in nurses' rooms at the hospital was expressly forbidden. This did not bother her because though she wasn't a prude, nor was she promiscuous. Alice simply had old fashioned values that urged her to marry before engaging in regular sexual activity.

Having seen most of her contemporaries marry and have children, she dearly longed for the same. It was the one overriding ambition in her life. In Phil she believed she had found her man, but he was in no hurry to take the plunge. She wondered why. Was he just stringing her along? Did she dream too much?

She knew she was naïve, but wondered was she being too naïve. Was he everything she thought he was? Was he the right one? Certainly, she had never felt as drawn to any of the few earlier boyfriends she'd had. But his behaviour in the café had been a major surprise, and his less than forthright answers on his need for money worried her. There seemed to be a different side to him that she hadn't seen before.

Was her dream of a long-term commitment with Phil just a dream, she wondered? Or was all this days' bad news simply depressing her and piling up negative thoughts? As glimpses of the hospital appeared through the evening gloom, the bus slowed to a halt and stopped.

She brought her thoughts back to the present, made her way downstairs and alighted at her destination, together with a handful of passengers who were heading to visiting times at the hospital. She entered the solid stone-built nurses' home of Ardengrange Hospital for Women in time for tea in the staff room. She paused at the resident's mailbox, picked up an envelope addressed to her, read the contents, raised her eyebrows, then moved to a small dining room and joined nursing colleagues. The latest hospital gossip of the day was in full flow and her companions seemed not to notice the fixed stare she had as she turned over in her mind the information contained in the letter she had just received.

CHAPTER FOUR

Phil Groves had said his goodbyes at the bus stop, but his destination was not his workplace as he had said.

He'd lied.

He walked a few streets further on, then turned into a bar on Renfield Street. Through the cigarette smoke and at the end of the long, polished bar, he spotted a man he knew as Doug.

"How's things Phil? You're early. Everything OK? Fancy a pint?" said Doug, offering his hand.

Groves shook the outstretched hand, and with a wink replied, "All hunky dory." He looked around the bar and motioned Doug to a seat in a far corner. It was early evening, and the pub was busy with pre theatre drinkers, some formally dressed, with partners, others more casual, and alone.

In his mid to late fifties, Doug was overweight, balding and bearded, and was wearing a well-worn grey suit and dark blue raincoat. He had the air of a man who knew this location well and was entirely at ease in the surroundings. He picked up the drinks, moved to join Groves, and sat down beside him.

Groves completed another look around the room, was satisfied he recognised no one else in the bar, leaned across the table and asked, "You have the money?"

"Yeah, of course," said his companion. "As we agreed. Two hundred and twenty pounds". He patted his coat, indicating it was in his pocket, and started to take out a brown envelope.

"God's sake, you silly bastard, not now," hissed Phil. "Use your brains. Wait until the bar clears a little. You don't know who's in here."

"What're you worried about mate? It's not as though we are public enemies, is it?" Doug said. "We're not handling guns, drugs, or false passports."

Groves gave him a querying look and asked, "Drugs?" The challenge didn't seem to bother Doug. "Drugs are big under the counter sellers at the minute my son."

"What do you mean? What drugs? Under what counter? Not the shop, surely?"

"Drugs, like uppers. You know, bennies. Pills that give you a high." Doug explained, "There's apparently a big demand for them among students, party goers and night clubbers. They give you energy, keep you awake and focussed."

"Are you and your brother handling them? What are they worth?"

"No, our shop is clean. And we're not in that game. Not yet anyway. But pills are being passed on for ridiculous sums, as much as a quid for a single tablet. It's something we might consider."

They swapped opinions on one or two of the lone drinkers dotted around the bar, concluded that they saw no one paying them any attention, then turned their attention to discussing football and the previous weekends' results.

"No surprise who's heading for the league trophy again this year," said Groves.

"Still a lot of games to go, so I wouldn't bet on it," Doug responded.

"Can't imagine you betting on anything, Doug. You're too tight."

As they finished their beer, Groves asked, "How's your brother doing? Haven't seen him in quite a while."

Doug's face screwed up. "His ticker is still a bit dodgy, and he has to take three different tablets each day." He waved a hand. "And not the kind of tablets I was just talking about. But he's as sharp as he ever was, despite that. He keeps the business legit and trouble free."

"Which is good for us eh?" said Groves rubbing his hands together. "No sniffing around from the law is just what we want."

Doug chuckled and nodded emphatically.

The business in question was a pawnbroker's shop, owned and run by Doug and his brother. The shop sales front proved an ideal vehicle for moving on jewellery of dubious origin, much of which was channelled there via Groves acting as the go between for Regency Club patrons who had every reason to keep their hands seemingly clean.

Groves thought of his present companion as *Doug the Fence*.

The £ 220 pay-off was from rings and watches Groves had left with Doug the previous week. He needed Doug to value the jewels on behalf of a club client. The club member had in turn agreed to Groves' reported valuation of just two hundred pounds, and in reward had promised him ten percent as commission for his part.

The under-cutting of the valued goods was a common trick Groves engaged in and had proved lucrative over recent months. He used the money he skimmed as stake for poker games and keeping up his well-groomed appearance. The cost of the latter, when asked, he explained through success at the former, but was careful not to be seen to flash money around. The need to dress smartly was an ingrained part of Groves' make-up and the man-about-town image he fostered. It helped him to impress the ladies. Italian suits, Crombie overcoat, custom-made button-down shirts and Cuban heeled winkle picker shoes were all part of his wardrobe. He saw himself as something of a trend setter in a city of the fashion conscious.

After some time, and a final look around the bar to confirm they were not being watched, Doug passed the envelope under the table to Groves who stuffed it into the back of his trousers and buttoned his jacket.

They completed their business, drained their glasses, said their goodbyes, and left the bar.

Groves walked the few streets back to the Regency Club, changed clothing, and took up his usual place behind the members' bar.

An hour or so later the club manager called him into his office and bluntly reminded him that a gambling debt he owed to a member was outstanding. Unless he arranged to pay it, he would be looking elsewhere for employment. "You are in hock for three hundred notes," he rasped. "I don't need club members banging on my door and telling me that my staff, who shouldn't even be at the card table, owe them money and demand that I do something about that."

Groves promised that within a month he would repay the debt.

To which the manager responded, "You've got ten days, no more. If you don't, you'll be looking for a new job, as well as looking over your shoulder in case the guy you owe lives up to his reputation. Now get back to your job while you still have it."

Later that evening, a small, middle aged dapper man approached the members' bar and ordered scotch and water. He placed a copy of the Racing Times on the bar top and glanced at the front page as Groves poured his drink. Groves put the whisky and water on a tray, took the newspaper from the bar and placed it on the tray, then followed the member to a quiet empty ante room where he placed the tray on a table, closed the door and left.

The man opened the newspaper and counted out the banknotes inside. Satisfied, he sipped and savoured his malt whisky and water, then peeled off ten pounds and returned to the bar. Groves helped him put on his coat and bade him goodnight. The man disappeared into the chilly night.

The waiter took the crumpled notes the man had left on the cloakroom table, put them into his pocket and smiled.

Everybody needs money, he thought.

The business he had just completed had been simple. This club member asked no questions and took things at face value. All Groves knew about him was that he had five or six large coaches which he hired out for day trips and holiday weekends away.

Tonight's transaction had gone smoothly. Things were not always that easy.

In the past, he'd carried out similar jobs for club characters who were anything but *smooth*; vindictive people with violent reputations; people not to be crossed.

Sammy Quigley was one such person. And he was the man to whom he owed the gambling debt. Quigley was thirty-four years old and ruthlessly controlled east end and city centre gangs in a range of illegal and criminal activities. His forte was burglary, theft, gambling, illegal drugs, extortion, money lending, and assaults across the city. Loud, arrogant, and unforgiving, he aimed to extend his activities across a wider area of the city.

A gambler with a volatile temper to match his sadistic streak, Quigley had a partners' stake in the Regency Club, and was a regular at poker games at the club where he had invited Groves to occasionally sit-in on games. One game too many for Groves where he ended up three hundred pounds in debt to Quigley, and on a short timeline to repay the cash. Quigley encouraged him to settle his debt quickly, very quickly in fact, by describing how he had, in similar circumstances, nailed the hands of a debt defaulter to the floorboards in a hotel room.

Shaken by this example, Groves needed no further encouragement. But, his prospects of repaying Quigley were perilously slim and time was not an ally.

There was always more than one way to obtain ready money though, he believed. For the rest of his evening shift he considered various ways to obtain enough to clear his debt.

He could not confess to Alice that he owed money from gambling. She was a looker, and that's all that mattered to him. She had set values on the right versus wrong stuff. As pathetic as the excuse was, better that she believed he'd broken some equipment rather than owed notes to a bloke who liked hammering nails through human flesh. It was a longshot that she could help him, given she'd been prattling on about something to do with her parents and rent. But she was still an option. She was, after all, gullible. And then there was Doug The Fence. He'd been very interested to learn from Doug that the quick money on the street right now was to be had from selling drugs. According to him, there was a ready market in Glasgow and surrounding areas. Specifically, there was an increasing demand for Benzedrine "uppers" from students and club goers, and for heavier drugs such as heroin from foreign sailors on the docksides. This was a world outside Groves' understanding and network, but he wondered if there was any mileage in sounding out how his girl felt about it. As a nurse Alice would almost certainly have access to drugs, and she certainly needed money to help her parents. Those damn values of hers remained the problem. He pushed the idea to the back of his mind. For now. Longshot or otherwise, he'd see if he could strip her of her savings. And if that didn't work, then he'd up the ante.

CHAPTER FIVE

After tea in the Ardengrange nurse's staff room, Frances McEwan spoke to Alice about the latest news of nurse departures, minor scandals, petty jealousies and romantic rumours of doctors and nurses. She stopped when she realised that Alice was paying her scant attention. "Alice, you're miles away. Have you heard anything I said?" she queried.

"I'm sorry, I've had a rotten day. Can't really believe it," She blurted out the events of her day, her parents' and boyfriend's woes, how the need for money was crushing her, and finally confessed she was seriously considering leaving nursing to find better paid work.

"You wouldn't do that would you?" asked McEwan, in disbelief. "You'd be mad. What would you do? What other experience have you? Where would you live? How could you give up years of hard-won experience and respect?"

There were no immediate answers to her roommate's questions. But with what she was going through, she desperately needed to earn more money, and was prepared to consider pretty much anything.

The pair moved back to the twin room they shared in the nurses' home and continued their conversation. They discussed at some length whether there might be an opportunity to obtain a post in a different hospital, but the chances of increased pay were very slim, SRN posts were not plentiful, and nurses pay rates were usually national-agreed levels for roles with specified qualifications. After nine years in the profession, with no alternative skills, qualifications, and experience to take elsewhere, they both agreed it appeared absurd to quit her job. Thus, leaving nursing was no practical solution to the escalating problems in Alice's world.

When commencing work at Ardengrange, Alice had been accommodated in a large barracks-type bedroom with five other nurses but had recently moved in to join Frances McEwan in smaller accommodation. The two of them shared a twin room, with two beds, a small wardrobe and dressing table each, and an adjoining bathroom. Alice thought it was a perfect palace.

McEwan, a senior and very experienced midwife, was employed freelance. She had a peripatetic role which regularly took her away to various parts of the district, training and coaching trainee nurses and midwives. This often left the accommodation solely to Alice for days on end.

In the many conversations between the roommates, they had openly talked about their backgrounds and lives. Frances MacEwan, nee Gardiner, admitted to being nearly thirty-six, was attractive, willowy, and fair haired. Her high boned face carried a broad smile which exposed a tiny glint of gold in some expensive dentistry work. She had been nursing for more than sixteen years. With some sadness, she told Alice how she had married a soldier when she was nineteen and had been widowed the following year, when her husband lost his life fighting in World War II. She had remained single since then and threw herself into keeping herself occupied. She recalled how she had trained and worked as a nurse in Edinburgh, moved to Dundee where she worked on maternity wards for six years or so, before taking up her present appointment. She admitted to no steady love interest when they talked about boyfriends, romance, families, and love life, as they did quite often. She did go out regularly to see various relations across the city, when she had time off. Her duties took her to wider parts of Glasgow and the West of Scotland, and sometimes included overnight stays. Off duty, she dressed in the latest fashion, and had an up-to-the-minute knowledge of city centre life and what was happening. Alice thought that she had a wisdom beyond her years and in many ways talking to her was like swapping notes with an older sister. As a result, she felt relaxed about sharing confidences, including her love life such as it was, and asking her advice on most things.

Due to some nurses quitting their jobs, Alice had recently been scheduled to cover a six-month gap at the hospital's small annexe. She'd begin in a few days. She knew little of the role of the unit to which she had been assigned but expected to be briefed on her duties by the matron the following day.

The main hospital, situated in the more affluent and leafy western suburbs of the city, supplied private general support and medical procedures for female patients, and had a separate gynaecological wing of which the annexe was a small part. Set some distance from the main hospital in a tree screened corner of the grounds, the isolated annexe was a two -storey brick building built during the second world war. Initially used for housing convalescing, and recovering sailors and pilots wounded in action, it was taken over post-war by the main hospital.

Alice asked McEwan what she knew about its role.

Her roommate answered, "The annexe is mainly used for ante and post-natal private outpatients as far as I understand. I don't know much more than that I'm afraid. When you are briefed tomorrow, you could also ask Matron Hardcastle for more shift work. She is hard but fair. She authorised the move of accommodation for you. The managing consultant is Crawford Baxter who specialises in gynaecology. He's the clinical head of the wing. I've worked with him in the past and he does a good deal of private work. Both have offices in the building."

"That sounds something of a possibility. I'll try to bring the subject up with Matron if I find an opportunity," Alice said.

In the Matron's office on her first day at the gynaecology wing annexe, Alice sat across a wide desk from Edith Hardcastle, and listened intently as she had her job role explained to her. The matron was rumoured to be a fearsome personality, commonly called *Hardcase* by the junior nurses, but was in fact very welcoming and friendly. As a result, Alice felt quite relaxed about the temporary duty.

"There is nothing in the role that you haven't encountered and managed before, Alice. All the duties and responsibilities are straightforward, and the atmosphere here in this small unit is a little less formal than in the main hospital. I think you'll fit in well."

Towards the end of the briefing in matron's office, they were joined by Crawford Baxter who recalled that he'd met Alice before at a seminar he'd addressed. He smiled at Alice and said, "hello again Nurse Walker. Welcome to the annexe. I look forward to your help here. And my goodness we need all the help we can get because we're always busy."

Alice smiled. "Thanks Mr. Baxter. Nice to see you again."

In concluding her briefing, Hardcastle asked Alice if she had any final questions.

"Not directly related to the responsibilities here, but I do have a question on working hours." Alice explained her need to help her parents and was looking for the opportunity to work extra shifts if available. The matron was understanding enough in her response but regretted that the scheduled shift rosters were all complete and she could not help. Alice thanked her, said goodbye to the matron and Baxter, then left.

As the door closed, Baxter and Hardcastle looked at each other.

Hardcastle nodded.

Quietly, Baxter said, "I agree."

The following morning the matron unexpectedly approached Alice in a hospital corridor and told her that - despite there being no other regular shifts available - there was extra work she might want to consider: helping Crawford Baxter with private outpatients in pre-natal care. The added work would be outside normal shift hours, sometimes in the evenings, and occasionally at weekends.

If she was interested, the matron would let Baxter know and he would contact her.

Alice didn't hesitate. She tried to hide her excitement and relief when she said she was very interested.

Just before her break that day, Baxter called Alice into his office. He outlined the work involved which was to provide nursing support for examinations and clinical procedures associated with early pregnancy. This could be once, or sometimes twice, a week. Because the work dealt with private patients, he explained there was a need for absolute confidentiality, and she must not discuss with anyone the identities of patients or their treatments. There would be no formal or published schedule of times, and Alice would be expected to make her services available at short notice, subject to fulfilling her normal shift duties in the annexe. Finally, Baxter told her that payment for this private patient work would be outside the normal routine, and straight into her hands.

Payment could be as much as she ordinarily earned in a month.

Alice was stunned, a little bemused, but delighted and wanted to know more.

But Baxter waved away any questions she had until she considered his offer and confirmed it back to him. Stressing the confidentiality of the subject, he suggested Alice think it over, and let him know the following day.

CHAPTER SIX

The annexe managing consultant Crawford Baxter was English, forty-nine, divorced, and lived in a luxury flat near the hospital grounds. He had built an excellent reputation for clinical expertise and patient care and was highly regarded for external charitable work in support of women's causes. He'd joined and become a regular at an elite golf club where he developed a network of influential associates and been welcomed into the city centre masonic lodge. A late model sports car underlined his success credentials.

His life however had not all been plain sailing.

Some years before his arrival in Glasgow, a serious charge of inappropriate behaviour with a patient in the north of England had been alleged. Baxter had been admonished by the regional governing board, but not struck off. As a result, his marriage had foundered, and eventually ended in divorce. Much of his misdemeanour was covered up, not publicised. He successfully sought a new appointment far from the scene and moved to Glasgow where he'd obtained a position at Ardengrange Hospital. In the past year, he had taken over the operational control of the hospital's annexe where many of the private outpatients attended for treatment or advice, on pre- or post-natal issues. Some of his appointments were women seeking information on termination of unwanted pregnancies.

The British law forbade abortions except in very exceptional circumstances, such as life-threatening conditions of the mother, and was only to be carried out in accordance with strict rules under the control and authority of the appropriate medical authorities. The penalties for illegal abortions were severe. Nevertheless, these so called "back street abortions" had been carried out for as long as anyone could remember, despite the threat of imprisonment for those undergoing, conducting, or aiding these illegal acts. There were obviously manifold reasons why women elected to choose the tragic and extremely dangerous procedure of having a back street abortion. By contrast, there was typically only one reason why surgeons and their aides carried out the task: cash.

And there was plenty of cash to be made because the illegal abortions were very expensive, with some individuals performing them often having only minimal medical training and using unsuitable or non-sterilised instruments. Whether qualified or not, all hired back street abortion practitioners were greedy parasites by nature. The prices they charged drove many poor women to self-abort, contributing significantly to female ill-health and in many cases death. Like many of his profession, Baxter had sympathy for the plight of women, who for many reasons, medical, personal, and social, found themselves with an unwanted pregnancy. In principle he favoured termination under wider circumstances than currently allowed, but only in proper conditions with trained medical staff. He certainly knew the boundaries of the law in respect of terminations, and the dangers of being struck off the register if found to have been illegally involved in any. Despite this, a year ago his actions had overridden his sense of legalities, and he had arranged a termination for the relative of a very influential client, an associate from his golf club. He'd carried out the termination procedure himself, in the appropriate surroundings of a private room in the hospital annexe and with medically trained assistance. He had taken a substantial fee. And this was not the only time he had done so. Within a short time, that wealthy client had passed the information about Baxter's assistance to a senior politician who also had pressing need of the service. Baxter's help for a similar arrangement was sought, and the gynaecologist carried it out for an equally hefty fee. Providing such a service was extremely lucrative Baxter knew, but if his actions were made public his career would be brought to an abrupt halt, he would face criminal charges, imprisonment and professional ruin. However, he also knew from previous experience that if managed properly, the rewards outweighed the concern of discovery. If managed very carefully, the risk- reward ratio was favourable, considerably so.

Crawford Baxter was, above all, an opportunist. Prior to moving to Glasgow Baxter had worked in gynaecology in two hospitals in the Liverpool area, one public, one private. In the latter he had been exposed to the temptations of the murky world of illegal pregnancy terminations and he had succumbed. He became indirectly involved with a small group of maverick midwives in the area who carried out abortions for cash. The group was highly organised, and had set up a network of contacts, transportation, and premises. They used information he fed to them, via third parties, on patients at the private hospital who were seeking terminations.

The group had used much of their proceeds to buy small flats where the abortions were carried out. That made sense to Baxter and for a while the illegal operation ran smoothly. That was until the group became greedy and rented out the same flats to prostitutes.

The operation came crashing down when the police raided a flat believed to be a brothel and found an abortion in progress. Following a short investigation, some but not all the group were arrested and prosecuted. Undeterred, within months the rest of the group had restarted its activities.

Fortunately for Baxter his name wasn't mentioned by those arrested. He was too smart for that to happen, having taken the precaution to provide his information to the network controller through a series of third parties.

His luck ran out later when the relationship he was having with a patient was revealed and considered to be inappropriate. He was censured, but not struck off.

Within weeks of taking over the control of the Ardengrange annexe, he was shocked to be contacted by the mastermind of the Liverpool abortion network with whom he had been involved. He was forcefully reminded of what he had done there, and how it was not too late to inform the police.

He was threatened that if he wanted to safely continue his career, he must set up a similar abortion service using the hospital he now worked in, under the remote direction of a *Network Controller*.

The Liverpool experience was very much in his mind in his Ardengrange dealings. He continued to see patients who sought information on unwanted pregnancies but was very circumspect in his responses to requests for terminations. And he didn't involve himself directly in further terminations. Instead, he planned and set up a third-party network, a special service unit, to cater for only the wealthiest and most confidential of clients he personally vetted.

He needed a centralised site for the illegal abortions, and he needed staff for the procedures - preferably former midwives, recruited externally, who would have no problem operating in this twilight world of crime.

Without doubt, in his mind the ideal base of operations was the annexe.

But, to get the annexe he had to engage and secure the support and agreement of Edith Hardcastle. She was the site's matron. Nothing happened in the annexe without her approval. Plus, she had access to nursing staff who might be used to assist. And, she had control of staff accommodation, supervised many aspects of patient care, ran the cleaning and supplies regime with a rod of iron, and personally guided nurses and other annexe staff through their training and development.

She had a powerful position of responsibility, and an imposing presence.

She also had a past.

Hardcastle was a sadistic bully to her juniors. As a staff nurse, she had been formally reprimanded for her behaviour twice. But, the dire shortage of qualified nurses, her bribe to a disciplinary panel member, and a move to a different hospital had salvaged her career.

On the pretext of reviewing the effectiveness of the services in the annexe, Baxter had called the matron into his office, where he had deftly moved the conversation from existing services to something he said was much requested by his patients, but sadly lacking. The provision of private terminations. Baxter spelled out his plans to the matron pitching them as being essentially a humanitarian service to women, conducted in a private and safe environment. He assured her that they would lie well within the existing laws governing abortions, and he would ensure all medical permissions and sanctions were obtained.

Hardcastle was sympathetic to the dilemma women faced in unwanted pregnancies, and in principle was not difficult to convince of the value of the proposed service. However, she refused to get involved in agreeing arrangements with clients, or directly scheduling nursing staff to participate.

Having seen a green light of sorts, Baxter then persuaded Hardcastle that the service he would arrange would be infinitely safer than back street abortions, entirely confidential and conducted by qualified midwives, out of normal hours.

Aware of some of the moral ambiguities surrounding the law and the application of thoroughly professional medical treatment of unwanted pregnancies, Hardcastle warmed to Baxter's positioning of his proposition. Still, she was hesitant.

And so, Baxter decided to be more forthright with her.

He told her he knew about her past disciplinary hearing and the bribe. He also told her he knew she had forged references.

His bombshell got her attention.

The final clincher had been the money.

Baxter knew that Edith Hardcastle needed money. She was three years away from normal retirement age and tired of the regimented life she led. She had never married and had no living extended family. Being a matron was her life, and she had become disenchanted with the way things were.

The climb to the top of the nursing pyramid had not been easy for her. Wartime nursing in England was where she had shown her mettle, and she was rewarded by increased responsibilities in a post in her hometown - the heavily bombed and damaged Liverpool. Post war she had remained in that city until a tragic event almost convinced her to abandon her profession. Her fifteen -year- old niece fell pregnant. The equally young father denied responsibility. Hardcastle was asked by the girl's mother, her only sibling, to arrange a termination. She did this through people she barely knew, who offered the service no questions asked. Apparently, these people had had been doing illegal abortions for a long time.

The procedure was very badly handled.

The niece died of septicaemia within two days.

Hardcastle's sister never accepted the loss of her only child, and within a year had taken her own life.

To this day, Hardcastle hated the boy who impregnated her niece, hated her sister for asking for help, and hated herself for being so cavalier in arranging the termination.

But most of all she hated the individual whose bungling had taken two lives. Not a day went past in her life that she didn't think of the tragedy. The guilt she had from employing a charlatan still raged and burned her soul.

As a result, she was twisted out of shape and bridled with a cruelty that only constant pain can sometimes induce in people. Her attitude manifested itself in poor treatment and bullying of nurses under her control. Such treatment bordered on sadism. Eventually, the reprimand for her behaviour happened. The bribe and relocation had to happen. And all that Hardcastle had left was a job of sorts with little chance of progression.

Initially, she moved to a post in Newcastle on Tyne and stayed there for three years. The job was fine but dead-end. After all, Newcastle was still in England and some gossipy snippets of her reputation had drifted this far north in the country. But then an opportunity arose for the position of matron at Ardengrange in Glasgow. She half-heartedly applied, expecting to be rejected. But a miracle happened. It seemed that the Scottish border was enough to stop wagging tongues. More likely, the bureaucratic inefficiencies within data transfer between the English and Scottish healthcare professions meant that her reputation hadn't preceded her in Glasgow. She got the job and the promotion that she thought was permanently barred to her.

However, her happiness was transient. After time, the responsibilities at Ardengrange became stressful, and the brief rekindled joy of nursing she had once felt in her youth had quickly evaporated. All she now had was her daily desire to buy the small flat she currently rented. If that happened, she'd retire early.

Which is why Baxter's mention of cash fully sucked her in.

This was her solution.

She agreed in full to his proposal.

And she told him that there was no time like the present to get organised and set up and run the special service unit in the annexe.

CHAPTER SEVEN

In the Regency Club, Phil Groves was arranging to receive a package from a member which he guessed were the proceeds from a burglary. He had passed on items for this man before and, with his outstanding debt in mind, was mentally assessing how much he could get from selling on this latest package. He realised the money would not be enough. Unless he could do this every day, it would take more than the ten days his boss had given him to pay off his gambling debt.

He called the nurses' home from the club bar telephone and left a message for Alice to call him when she finished shift. Perhaps she could get enough money to help him, he thought, or maybe he could sound her out on the outside possibilities of obtaining the quick sale drugs he had heard about. The following lunchtime he intended to go across town to meet Alice in the hospital grounds, if she could manage the time. With luck he would have received the package and deposited it with the pawnbroker in the morning. Groves thought about how he could broach the subject of drugs with Alice. It was something of a wild flier. He knew she had a very pressing need for money, but also had a set of principles. Maybe if he gave her a strong enough incentive.

Later that evening, Alice returned his call and agreed to meet him outside the nurses' home lodge the next afternoon during her break.

Groves had spent some time considering how far he thought Alice would help and realised he would have to be very careful if he wanted to explore the idea of amphetamines with her. As desperate as she was for money for her parents, and naïve as she could be, Alice was not stupid and would not jeopardise her future. He would have to offer her an incentive for the future, an incentive he knew she would swallow.

The following day, he was still dwelling on what that incentive could be. His mood was not helped by the fact that his morning pawnbroker meeting had been called off. And when he met Alice at the main door of the lodge, he had to endure an inane and somewhat nosy chat with another nurse whom Alice introduced to Groves as her room-mate Frances.

When he and Alice were alone, his temper was at best irritable and at worst foul. Still, he had work to do and that included extorting his so-called girlfriend. So, he continued his questioning on her ability to help him out. They walked together round the grounds of the hospital until a rising, bone-chilling wind drove them into the public cafeteria.

Alice watched Groves while they sipped their coffee, in a quiet section of the cafeteria. He still seemed to be tense and edgy and all he seemed to want to talk about was his need to pay the money he owed for the broken equipment. As they talked, her head was pounding, and she struggled to focus on what he was saying. It seemed that he had a desperate need for hard cash, but she could not entirely understand the urgency. She asked why, if he had broken equipment in his work, couldn't his employer take back the repayment cost from his pay at a certain amount each week. It just didn't make sense. She also asked him what the equipment was that cost so much. She continued to quiz him, and the less she received as an explanation, the more she questioned despite her aching head and the worry she had about her parents' turmoil.

People around the cafeteria began to look across at them.

The questions were too much for Groves. The meeting with Alice had not gone as he had hoped. The real reason for his need for cash was off limits and he'd had absolutely no opportunity to develop the conversation on to the riskier topic of drugs. He decided that this was the time to offer the incentive. And that incentive was a veiled ultimatum.

He dramatically ended their meet by asking her why she asked so many questions, why she apparently had no faith in him, and how could he go ahead and marry her when she had no belief in him.

And then he stormed out of the building.

A dumbfounded Alice watched him disappear out the cafeteria door into the chilly afternoon. Had Phil Groves just proposed to her, albeit in the strangest and borderline aggressive way? She thought he had. Wasn't sure, though. Wasn't sure about much of anything as she made her way out, too preoccupied to be embarrassed by the stares that other customers were giving her. She went back to her shift in the annexe and throughout the rest of the day her mind was consumed by the annexe offer Baxter had made, by Phil's latest strange behaviour, his urgent money needs, and his parting reference to marrying. He could not marry her if she had no belief in him. That's what he said. That meant he wanted to marry her. Had thought about marrying her. Wanted her. And all he wanted in return was her belief in him. She shook her head as her thoughts hammered the inside of her head. Belief. That's all she had to give him. But, was she too late? Had he changed his mind about marriage, she wondered. She had to find out. She also had to get to the bottom of the money issue he had. She didn't know what to make of it all. Money had seemed to be at the root of everything. And it seemed to be spoiling everything, including her parents' life and the opportunity to have a blissful marriage. Altogether it had been a crazy day. She was looking forward to finishing her shift when she could telephone Phil at the Regency club and bluntly query his parting shot on marriage.

Groves had taken a taxi back into town from the hospital, gone directly to his room at the club and waited for the phone call he was sure would come. He knew that Alice wanted marriage, felt certain she wanted him, and he planned to make the most of that situation and turn it into what he hoped would be a very useful opportunity. He was called to the club staff phone later that evening and heard Alice's voice ask, "Have you calmed down yet?'

"Yes, I'm so sorry my love, I've too much on my mind and it's getting to me," he replied.

"What did you mean when you mentioned marriage today? Are you serious, or just having me on?"

There was a long and deliberate pause for six or seven seconds, then he said, "I've never been more serious in my life."

He could hear Alice's intake of breath, and he smiled as she exclaimed, "My god, are you proposing? Say that again. Is this really happening? When did you change your mind? Why?"

"Whoa, take it easy. One thing at a time. Yes, it's happening. It's about time I settled down and I want you to be the one. Will you?" he asked.

"Yes, yes, yes! Of course, I will, eh, when?" Alice gushed. "Where? Oh! There's so much to think about."

"All in good time. Let's meet again as soon you can get time off and we'll plan it out."

She sounded breathless when she said, "I'll be free for most of the morning the day after tomorrow, before my afternoon shift. Is that, OK?"

Groves told her that sounded perfect. He ended the call, smiled, and decided he had Alice hook, line, and sinker.

Next morning, after a sleepless night thinking of Phil and their future together, Alice returned to her shift in the annexe. From his office, Baxter watched her walk past to attend to her duties in the ward. He finished the call he was on and allowed a satisfied smile to spread across his face. He had finalised arrangements with a retired midwife for her to perform an abortion in the annexe. Now he only needed an assistant for the procedure.

He and the matron had discussed the suitability of Alice Walker for the role they needed to fill, and were completely in agreement that Alice's almost naïve, mellow openness and desire to please would provide the perfect fit for the role that they had in mind. It involved a new patient and one that would bring the annexe a lot of money. The matron would ensure the availability of a room, and the wealthy mother of the patient had agreed the terms.

He called Alice into his office and asked if she had further thoughts on the extra work, now that she had had time to think it over. Her few questions were skilfully met by Baxter. Not that it was difficult, given it appeared to him that the nurse seemed distracted.

She confirmed to Baxter she would take the extra work.

"Good" said Baxter, "You won't be disappointed, I'll let you know when you're required."

Alice was on an emotional high when she met up with Groves in the Kelvingrove Art Gallery and Museum. It was his idea to meet there. He'd told her that, as well as being close to the hospital, he felt it would lend a little artistic, perhaps even romantic, atmosphere to his plans.

The truth was more mercenary. Groves had read somewhere that Da Vinci and Salvador Dali, neither of whom he knew anything about, had exhibits there, and were said to be evocative. He felt that any help he could get to impress and convince Alice to accept his plans was to be grabbed with both hands. Ordinarily he would never set foot in the place, but it seemed to be what he considered a posh location and free entry at that, so he went for it and hoped to God, Da Vinci, and Dali that it worked.

They met in the museum's cafeteria and Alice excitedly asked what had changed his mind about marriage.

"Why now? What's changed Phil?"

"I told you it's about time I got married, I'm almost twenty-six, and won't ever find anyone like you again. You are the one I want. I want to make you happy."

"Oh Phil! I'm so very happy, really. Can we make plans? Can I tell folks? Where will we get married? When. Where will we live?"

"Slow down, we have plenty of time, let's get engaged first then set a date eighteen months to two years ahead."

Alice frowned. "Why so far away?"

"We need to be practical Alice. It will cost a lot of money, which we don't have. I have a big problem right now, remember? It's short term but needs to be sorted out."

All the gloomy thoughts about money that Alice had had in the previous days came surging back as she thought of their earlier conversations, and the difficult financial problems her parents had. Traditionally, a bride's parents would foot the bill for wedding expenses, but that was out of the question Alice realised. It occurred to her

67

now that announcing to her parents that she was engaged would be the equivalent of rubbing their wounded faces in salt. They were proud people and would feel more shame about their inability to pay for her wedding than they would about not having money to buy food.

They continued a lengthy chat which ranged from his urgent cash need, possible impending loss of job and accommodation, to Alice's meagre £25 savings which she had already offered Phil, and to her parents' precarious future. Even borrowing money was impossible because without collateral, the possibility of a loan now and in the future was remote.

She made a decision and decided to confide in Groves about the extra work opportunity offered by Crawford Baxter. She could not be specific about when the extra work would be available, or exactly how much she could receive, but it would be considerable. It would certainly help Groves if she got the job. Groves, eager to know more, asked how quickly it would happen. The ten-day ultimatum his boss had given him was now down to six.

"I can't be sure. It might be this week," replied Alice, "or next week, or whenever, I just don't know. It's not a regularly scheduled programme as I understand it."

Groves huffed. "I could well be out on my ear by then, no job, out on the street."

"I'm sorry Phil but I can't control it." Alice explained." I'd do anything to help, you know that, but I can't force it."

Groves pulled a smiley face, and with a wink said, "Maybe you could find the odd pills lying around. That could get both of us some hard cash."

"Pills, what pills, what do you mean?"

"Oh, you know, pep pills." Her stomach wrenched.

"Amphetamines! Where would I get those, and what would you do with them?"

"Sell them. There's a big market among students and clubbers, I'm told. Keeps them awake and buzzing."

"I couldn't, even if I knew how to get them." Alice squeaked, "I'd get into a great deal of trouble. No, I won't do it. I could lose my job and career. And… and, well, it's just so wrong, Phil. It would be theft. Of drugs. And drugs that would be illegal if they were sold on the streets" She shook her head in disbelief. "Honestly, Phil. How could you ask me? How could you. No, definitely not."

"Well, that's it I suppose. I am back at the beginning then. No money and I'm heading for the exit," moaned Groves. "No job, no accommodation and what next?"

In the space of a few seconds, Alice's emotions had dived from on high to the depths. How had things gone so much awry in so short a period? She had no appetite for further discussion, and left Groves in the museum. She caught a bus to the hospital to start her shift, her mind rattled by the turn round in events.

Groves remained behind for some time in the cafeteria and wondered if his incentive had just been holed below the waterline. Should he follow it up? Was there any further mileage in the pretence, he asked himself. He decided he would give it a day, a day he didn't really have, then ask Alice again, after starting with references to them getting married. He knew he was running out of options and Quigley was coming to the club for his money anytime.

That evening, Phil Groves was anything but happy to see the face of Sammy Quigley at the end of the Regency Club bar.

"Where is it?" asked a smiling Quigley.

"I don't have it all just yet Sammy, but I will in a few days."

The smile transformed to a vicious, searing stare and an accompanying promise of a very shortened life span if the debt was not paid in full, in two days. Groves grunted his understanding and felt a mixture of relief and abject fear as he watched the thug leave the bar.

CHAPTER EIGHT

Alice Walker lay awake for much of that night trying to get her thoughts in some semblance of order. The day had opened with so much promise but gone downhill as it moved on, Marriage? Maybe or maybe not. Money? No answers. Extra work? Odd set up. And Phil?

Next morning, she telephoned Phil at the Regency Club and came straight to the point. "I've thought very hard about taking this extra work at the hospital and have had second thoughts. I'm not sure it's something I want to do. I'm sorry but it's not something I want to get tied up in."

"What d'you mean, *tied up*?" Groves sounded groggy.

"I think there could be a possibility that the work might not be authorised, and I don't think I want anything to do with that."

"You're a nurse, what could go wrong?"

"Plenty could go wrong. If it's complicated medical procedures I am not experienced in, or unofficial, or unauthorised."

"Unofficial? What do you mean?"

"Under the table, you know, unofficial."

"Why would you think that?"

"Well, it's outside normal annexe hours, private patients, security and privacy heavily emphasised, cash paid directly, and as much as I earn in a month. It just seems too good to be true."

"Maybe, but you're a very experienced nurse, more than competent. The money is considerable, isn't it? Is it not worth the risk?"

"What?! I could lose my job and even be jailed if it was illegal. Sod the money."

"Don't be daft. It wouldn't be illegal. We both need money, and quickly. Don't you remember what we said yesterday?"

"You need money Phil. It's all you have talked about this past week or so. I am happy to wait and save for a wedding. Why can't you?"

"You know my problem. I need cash now. Have you had any other thoughts about getting me some pep pills then?" He did not tell Alice just how quickly he now needed the money having had the threatening visit from Quigley the previous evening.

"I don't believe you. You don't seem to care how you get money so long as you get it. Don't you see that? Don't you care if I'm put in danger to get it? It's wrong, and dangerous, and I just can't do it."

"Maybe you just don't think enough of me to help me. Maybe you're too wrapped up in being Florence Nightingale. What's the real problem with the extra work you've been offered? You're in a hospital, you're a qualified senior nurse, the people you work with are doing it. So, why can't you? Where's the danger? But, if you won't do that, what's the big problem with the pep pills? A couple of boxes of pills going missing, who's to know? Are

72

you really interested in clearing our immediate problems before we get married?"

"Our problems? Our problems!" she yelled. "They're your problems, not mine. I have enough problems without this, I've had enough I want no more of them, or of you."

Alice's body shook with anger as she slammed the telephone receiver into its cradle.

She sat for a long time and in her mind replayed their conversation over and again. Should she stick it out and do what he suggested or keep her values? Inwardly, she knew the answer.

When she later returned to the nurse's home at the end of her shift, she was met by an excited lodge porter who pompously informed her that there were two gentlemen in the staff room who had asked to see her. "They look official and important," he cautioned.

Alice's immediate thoughts were that something had happened to one of her parents.

She crossed the reception and entered the staff room, which was unusually empty, and was met by two young men in raincoats. Both appeared to be in their late twenties, or early thirties.

"Good evening," said the taller of the two, "Are you Nurse Walker, Nurse Alice Walker?" he asked.

"Yes," replied Alice. "Can I help you? Who are you?"

Showing Alice his police warrant card, the tall one said, "I'm Sergeant David Morton. This is my colleague, Constable Michael Watt. We would like to have a chat with you, in private if that's possible?"

"Is it about my parents?" she croaked.

The senior policeman assured her that it was not, then rocked Alice by telling her they wanted to ask her some questions about her boyfriend.

"Phil?" she queried.

"Is your boyfriend called Phil?" asked Morton.

"Yes, that's right," answered Alice. "Phil Groves. What do you want to know? Is he in trouble?"

The sergeant asked how she knew Groves.

Alice recalled how, and when she had met Phil, what she knew about him, their relationship such as it was, and confirmed that she had talked to him on the phone that afternoon. "What's all is this about?" she asked. "How did you know he is my boyfriend?"

Morton explained that they were part of a team investigating stolen property and other incidents across Glasgow, and routinely following up leads to eliminate individuals from enquiries. Groves' name had been raised as someone who might have information to help them, and the police were talking to anyone who he associated with, and who they thought could help them.

Alice was shocked and blurted out, "Just wait until I see him."

Watt told Alice that although she was not under any suspicion, he recommended that she didn't say anything about their visit which might in any way frustrate their investigation. He explained that they knew Groves was Alice's boyfriend, based on work carried out by a surveillance team. The Regency Club where Groves worked had, for some time, been suspected of possibly being linked to criminal activity. The club, including some of its members and its employees, had been watched, and since Alice had been seen meeting Groves, the police needed to know more about their relationship. Alice gulped, then spat out, "I'm not a criminal, and I don't think Phil is."

"You're not accused of anything, Nurse Walker. Nor is your boyfriend." said Morton. "We just want to ask you a few questions. Has your boyfriend ever asked you to hold money for him at any time?"

"You're kidding me, no he definitely has not," replied Alice.

"Ever given you rings, watch, bracelets and so on?"

"Absolutely not."

"Do you have access to drugs, Benzedrine for example?"

She looked askance at the policeman and replied," Yes of course, nurses sometimes do."

"Has your boyfriend ever asked you for any?" Watt asked.

Alice stared hard at the detectives as the penny dropped. She didn't confirm or deny anything, but couldn't bring herself to any response until she had confronted Phil. "Is he involved with drugs?" she asked. Then her voice rose as she gasped, "You suspect me of helping him?"

"Calm down, we are simply following up possibilities at this stage. You are not suspected of anything." The policeman re-emphasised she was not suspected of any wrongdoing, but if it turned out that she had anything to hide it might be the worse for her.

Alice was shaking, "I've done nothing wrong, I never would."

"Pleased to hear that nurse Walker," Morton said. "But you should be aware that this conversation shouldn't be discussed, at all. We will possibly continue it another time, and meantime, if you remember anything which might help our enquiries, please call me on this number." He handed Alice a card with his name and telephone number of Northern police station.

They left, and Alice slumped into a chair. She wanted the world to go away right now.

What David Morton had not told Alice was that the Regency Club was suspected of running illegal high stakes gambling games, operating as a hub for receiving and selling on stolen goods, and lately had come under suspicion as a potential source of illegal drugs. Further, a stolen diamond encrusted brooch had been identified when put on display in the pawn-brokers sale window, and Phil Groves had regularly been seen meeting the pawn-brokers brother, in pubs and cafes.

Nothing damning, but sufficient to be followed up.

When Alice had recovered a semblance of composure, she left the staff room and returned to her shared bedroom where she found McEwan in her dressing gown, ironing her uniform, her freshly polished shoes by her bedside.

"Hiya you had a good day?" asked her roommate. "Mine's been lousy."

Alice tried to answer but couldn't contain her tears. She sat down at the small room table, put her head in her hands, and sobbed. After a good deal of comforting and persuading by McEwan, she eventually stopped crying, and voiced all her concerns about her parents, her major doubts about Phil, his touting for amphetamines, and the visit by the police.

"What did the police want to know about drugs?" asked Frances. "Were they suggesting a problem in this hospital? Why did they ask you?"

"No, they didn't mention the hospital. It was just a general question I think." She made McEwan solemnly promise not to repeat the details of her interview, then looked at her room- mate and cried some more.

"There's really nothing you can do at the moment," McEwan offered, "When do you expect to see Phil?"

"I don't want to see him ever again," Alice wailed. She felt betrayed and ashamed. "The same applies to the bloody police."

"Tomorrow is another day, Alice. Things will brighten up, you'll see," McEwan assured her.

The rest of the day passed without incident, but she couldn't stop fretting about how she could manage the issues she faced.

Later that evening she lay in bed and stared at the ceiling. Things had just seemed to get worse and worse, problems multiplied day by day. Her parents, her boyfriend, marriage, Baxter, and his possibly unofficial work, all closing in on her mind.

All linked by money. The lack of money. Or the pursuit of it. Where was her life heading?

She realised she was now at a critical point in her life and had to resolve these issues, or at least bring them to an acceptable conclusion. The difficulties her parents faced had no immediate answer but might over time be resolved. She would just have to continue to provide support and act as opportunities arose.

Phil Groves however had now become a quite different prospect. Her deep dreams of marriage to him had disintegrated. She had seen another side to him in their recent meetings, a side she distinctly did not like. An almost threatening attitude, and the interview with the police had added further doubts about him. With his obscure reasons for needing money, he was clearly hiding something, and his attitude towards her had changed in an unacceptable way. She'd had more than enough of the emotional roller coaster.

The idea of marriage was a non-starter to him it appeared, and she could not elicit any response from him which might indicate a longed for, oft dreamed of future. He was stringing her along and she was being as naïve as she had ever been, she concluded. She finally decided she would put her marriage hopes behind her and split from him.

End of romance.

In the morning over breakfast, she shared her thoughts and conclusion with Frances McEwan.

"Wow, that's definite? Goodbye boyfriend?" her roommate queried. "What about your parents? What will you do?"

"I'll just have to keep an eye on them and help as much as I can until I get a solution. Money is the major problem."

"So, what about extra work at the annexe? Any luck with that?"

"There is an opportunity, but I'm wary in case it's under the table, unofficial work which might drop me in trouble. I have accepted it but have some doubts." She explained a bit more about what was on offer.

"Your worries are nonsense Alice, that's just complete nonsense. It's just out of hours private sessions. Mr. Baxter and Matron would never allow anything untoward. They have important positions and reputations to protect. Think about it seriously, it would certainly help you out."

The recommendation that McEwan gave her convinced Alice that she was imagining problems which didn't exist, and that the extra work would be straightforward and helpful.

Her routine in the annexe was mundane everyday nursing. On shift she was in control of the reception area, managing patient schedules and a small four bed ward, none of which stretched her. She had settled in easily. But *easy* didn't pay the bills. She made her mind up to take the extra work offered. When Baxter arrived at the annexe that morning, she confirmed that she would like to take his offer of additional private work at the annexe.

"Delighted to hear that Nurse Walker," he beamed. "We'll work well together. I'll let you know when I need you."

CHAPTER NINE

That afternoon Alice was called into Matron Hardcastle's office where a phone call was on hold for her. She queried the Matron, "Who is it?" and was stunned to be told it was her mother.

"Hello, Mum what's wrong, why are you calling?" asked Alice.

There was no disguising the palpable emotion in Martha's voice. "We're losing our home, Alice! Losing our... our home! Dear God. We... we have to be out in four weeks."

Alice felt like she'd just been pushed off a precipice. "What! For God's sake why? What's happened? When were you told this?"

Her mother was breathing fast when she replied, "Just this morning. Your father has let the rent slip into arrears. Not... not his fault. Not really. I think. We are being put out."

Alice looked at Hardcastle who was staring at her. She fixed her eyes on a blank wall and blurted, "How much arrears? Can you get more time?"

There was silence for a few seconds. In a tone that sounded calmer, yet utterly resigned, Martha broke the silence with, "The rent hasn't been paid for three months and we have no more grace, or money."

"God almighty. This is so cruel, Mum." She tried to think, but right now her brain felt like it was being gripped and vigorously shaken by something very strong. "I'll find a way to help." It was all she could say right now. "Don't worry. I'll help."

"Sorry dear." Martha was sobbing again. "So sorry to trouble you." The line went dead, either because there was nothing more to say or because her money on the payphone ran out.

Alice's hand was shaking as she put the receiver back into the cradle. Her stomach was in knots and skin felt cold and clammy. She glanced again at Hardcastle. The matron was still staring at her but seemed unable or unwilling to speak. She mumbled thanks to her and moved out from her office and into the corridor. She stood with her head against the wall and inwardly wept.

A passing porter asked, "Are you okay, nurse? Do you need help?"

It took all her mental fortitude to try to haul herself back into the here and now. "Thanks, no. I'll be fine. It's just a little moment I've had. A moment. It… it will pass."

The porter smiled sympathetically and continued onwards with his duties.

But she remained where she was, her body taught, and mind seemingly locked in some kind of fear-driven stasis. *Fight, run, or just roll over and die*, she'd once heard her father say about life. He'd said that upon return from a Friday evening night out with his work pals at the local pub and his words had been slurred and brimming with bitterness. Still, the comment had at the time resonated because it had given her an insight into his tortured soul. But now his comment seemed apt for her plight. And the problem was she didn't have anywhere to run to and wasn't sure if she had any fight left in her. That left the option of submitting to everything. Being weak. Facing up to the reality that events were beyond her control. Whatever she did next, she was sure of one thing: she was starting to think that suddenly life was becoming just too much to cope with.

She closed her eyes, decided that all she could do right now was focus on the next thing in her day, breathed deeply for a while, opened her eyes, and walked back into Hardcastle's office. She said that she urgently needed to see her parents and needed time to go back to her accommodation first so that she could change.

Hardcastle's response was cold, but she agreed to the early departure. She added that Alice would either need to make up the lost hours or have her next pay packet accordingly deducted.

Thirty minutes later, Alice entered her accommodation room.

Frances McEwan was there and instantly recognised the distress on Alice's face. "Back early and with that look. What's happened?"

Alice slumped into a chair and held her head in her hands. "My parents have had notice to quit their home. It seems the rent hasn't been paid for months. More than that I don't know. I'm going to see them now."

"Dear God, that's awful? How are they taking it?"

"I won't really know until I get over to see them in Govan, I've only talked briefly on the phone."

Frances urged her to keep her chin up and promised to give her any help she could to find a place for her parents to go to.

When she reached her mother's address in Govan, a visibly distraught Martha Walker opened the door to her daughter. Alice immediately put her arms around her mother and promised, "We'll sort something Mum, don't worry." She had no idea how she'd be able to stick to that promise.

Martha nodded towards the vast expanse of Glasgow. "Your father's out there somewhere, and I don't know when he'll be back."

"Let's hope he stays out for a long time."

"Alice!"

Though she didn't regret the thought, she regretted blurting it out to her fragile mother. "I'm sorry, Mum. Don't…" she shook her head, "don't know what to think. Or say, for that matter. Trying to make sense of everything. What's happened? How did you get into this state?"

Martha gestured her inside, closed the door, and then said quietly, "Your father has always managed the rent money; I didn't know he hadn't been paying it. Its beyond fixing. We owe more than three months back rent plus this current week. And we now must get out because a new tenant is ready to move in."

"But how?! Why?! Where's the money Dad's been earning gone?"

Martha didn't seem to want to answer that question. But it was clear her mind was working on many levels, perhaps dragging up manifold memories. Finally, she looked her daughter in the eye and said, "I knew your dad liked to bet on the greyhounds but had no idea of the losses he had made."

"God almighty!" Alice now didn't care how her words came out. "The dogs?! Idiot!"

"Alice – you mustn't speak of your father in that…"

"Mum! Wake up! You're going to lose your home. And because of what? A husband who treats you like… well, you know. Spends money on a dog rather than you. This whole thing is crazy!"

Martha sighed loudly though her subsequent words were meek. "I know. But what am I to do?"

Alice made no effort to hide her anger when she replied, "Well, I'm not going to stay until he comes back because I will go for him, Mum. But, I promise you we will get this fixed. Somehow. Four weeks you say? Something must be possible. Something *has* to be possible. And one thing's for sure – Dad won't be part of that solution."

"Don't be hard on him Alice. He's been through a great deal, and I don't know if he can face into this latest difficulty."

"Don't be hard?! How easy has he been on you, Mum? How thoughtful? How helpful? We'll get something arranged, and quickly I hope, but don't expect Dad to be included in making the arrangements."

Alice left her mother with a promise to get back to her as soon as she had an answer to the problem, and certainly by the next weekend. When she reached her nurses' room, there was a note on her bed from McEwan telling her that she was meeting a friend who might be able to get her parents alternative accommodation. She would know later that night.

Alternative accommodation? Alice desperately tried not to let relief take hold. Kept telling herself that it might not happen. But still, it *could* happen. And at this precise point in time, she needed all the hope she could get. Her dear roommate had arranged her move out of the barracks style accommodation to the snug yet charming room they shared. And now she just might, might, be a lifeline for Alice's parents. The warmth she felt for McEwan was all-encompassing. And what her roommate was doing for her gave her faith that there were still good people out there.

That afternoon, as Groves was starting his afternoon shift in the Regency, Sammy Quigley appeared again. His presence sent a chill down the barman's spine.

Quigley leaned over the bar and whispered, "You can do something for me that will clear your debt."

Groves blinked and croaked, "Er, yes? What's that?"

"I need to send a message to someone who has been cramping my style." He smiled. "And he only understands action."

"What action?"

"Put a fire under his arse, or more to the point, his business." Quigley outlined the plan, the location and the set-up but omitted the owner's name. He wanted a particular car burned, and soon. He gave Groves the address and the option. "Your choice - the fire or your debt."

Groves gulped. "When?"

"Do it tonight."

"And my debt is cleared?"

"Correct." Quigley checked his watch and looked impatient.

Groves swallowed hard, thought for a moment, and agreed.

"I have some good news Alice," an elated McEwan gushed as she bounced into their room later that night. "My friend has completed the purchase of some flats and will be happy to help you out by renting one to your parents, at a reasonable rate. She's looking for respectable tenants, so it will help her too. It's on this north side of the River Clyde and will be so much easier for you to get to see them."

From despair to this, in a matter of hours. Alice reeled from the news and could feel her heart walloping her chest as she stuttered, "That's wonderful news! I... I don't know what to say. To thank you. To... When can they move in Frances?" She laughed, more out of utter relief than anything else. "Is this real?"

The laughter was infectious, and McEwan joined in. "It's real alright. They can move in within a week, I believe. Isn't that great?"

Alice felt the tears welling up in her eyes and poured out her grateful thanks. "What about the rent? Is it weekly? Monthly? How much will it be? They have very little coming in."

"Don't go worrying about that now, Alice. Something can be arranged. And you can help with their costs from the extra work with Baxter."

"I can't thank you enough Frances, I don't know what I'd do without you, you are a true friend."

McEwan downplayed her role in arranging housing for Alice's parents but was happy to hear Alice voice her indebtedness.

It was music to her ears.

However, her explanation to Alice on how she arranged the flat was considerably less than factual.

In fact, a great deal about Frances McEwan wasn't truthful or altruistic.

McEwan was a woman of many talents, none of which were for the wholehearted benefit of her fellow citizens. Least of all for Alice Walker. McEwan was ambitious, ruthless, powerful, and a cold calculating user of people and circumstances. A qualified nurse and midwife, McEwan had in the past manipulated her role to establish and run illegal abortion operations, in respectable clinical practices in cities in the North of England. She controlled a network of abortion cells in four major areas and, motivated by money and power, decided to expand her operational model into Glasgow. Having left her criminal networks in England under the control of trusted associates, she moved to the city of her birth.

Her re-introduction to Glasgow was eased using Crawford Baxter.

She knew Baxter of old, having had him embroiled in the networks she controlled in the Liverpool area. On occasion while working there, he received enquiries for abortion. He passed details of the more interesting abortion enquiries to McEwan, particularly if prospective clients were wealthy and nervous about a procedure being pursued through official channels. After he moved to Glasgow, McEwan lost touch with him for a while. That didn't matter to her because she knew he might prove useful again at some future point. That proved to be the case when she decided to move to Scotland. Knowing he'd have no choice other than to be compliant, she instructed him to employ her within his organisation as a freelance peripatetic midwife. And she ordered him to develop his current operation within the hospital into an abortion factory.

The new peripatetic role would provide cover and enable McEwan to come and go as she pleased. Using her experience and money gained in England, the objective was to develop her plans to target the influential people she needed to consolidate her criminal intentions. And her ultimate objective was to position herself as the nameless controller of all illegal abortions in England and Scotland.

Almost everything she has told Alice was a lie.

Moreover, her name was not McEwan.

She was single, in her forties, and never married. Her boyfriend disowned her after she became pregnant in Liverpool, while he was abroad fighting in France, from where he was later rescued at Dunkirk. Through her nursing contacts she arranged an abortion, which started a long association with maverick midwives in the Liverpool area. And she constructed a life-story far removed from reality to avoid awkward questions about a chequered background.

She first met Alice when attending a welcome meeting for new staff. She warmed to the newcomer., noting her friendly, open, almost simple manner. She knew she would make a respectable 'front door' for the house of horrors she was working on. She used Baxter to arrange a change of accommodation for Alice, to join her in the twin room she presently occupied by herself. She convinced him that Alice would be the perfect addition for the annexe abortion operation, and perhaps in time she'd be able to do more than just be a smiling meet-and-greet receptionist.

The flat that was available to Alice's parents was not obtained from a friend but had been purchased by McEwan herself, together with three other properties. She needed insurance for the properties, the kind of insurance that would protect her flats from interference. Insurance which she knew from experience she could buy from villains. Her plan was to use the flats as drinking dens, brothels, or occasionally as overnight recovery wards post abortions. Just as she'd done in Liverpool.

The property developer who sold her the flats steered her towards the insurance provider he used for some of his other properties - a man called Arthur Burns.

McEwan and Burns agreed a deal to protect her assets, and she was pleased to find these included police protection and a short notice taxi service across the city.

She guessed that Burns was a serious player in the criminal world and made a mental note to find out as much as she could about him and develop him to her own ends.

CHAPTER TEN

In the austere post-war decades, the City of Glasgow was a behemoth struggling to find its economic and social balance. While searching for likely replacements for its once global shipbuilding and heavy engineering industries, the city attempted to resettle many of its population from squalid, overcrowded and dilapidated housing, into hastily constructed and utilitarian housing estates on the perimeter of the city. These estates were being built many miles from work locations, with little or no facilities for shopping, leisure, or entertainment. Due to significant resultant expansion of its patch, the city's police force couldn't cope. Its under resourced police force faced a rising wave of criminality across a widening geographic area, which was an open goal for home bred and incoming criminals.

In a red brick Victorian town house on the outskirts of the city, a tense atmosphere was building. Four criminals were sitting at a rectangular table in a high-ceilinged room, cigarette smoke drifting around their heads, and the conversation was punctuated by the clink of bottle and glass. One of the men was Arthur Burns, the insurance provider on McEwan's payroll. On the other side of the table was Charles *Charlie* Palmer, a heavy-set man in his late forties who glared at his companions as he toyed with a paper knife.

Next to Burns were Mathieson and O'Hara. Like him, they were in their thirties, lean and wiry, fashionably dressed, sporting various items of gold jewellery. The three had known each other from what could be called childhood but was actually a wild, vicious, and mainly lawless gang upbringing in the East End of the city. And that gang lifestyle was not unusual. Though the number of gangs had slightly lessened in Glasgow since the end of the second world war, they were still active. They were, however, different in nature. The notorious gang warfare of the Thirties was mainly conducted by unemployed and disaffected grown men who'd been hit by the depression and lack of opportunities. Their prime motivator was fighting similar gangs for the kudos and notoriety it brought. By contrast, the post-war gangs concentrated on solely using their efforts for material gain. Extortion, theft, blackmail, gambling, and money lending became the main elements of some gangs' activities, and the three who sat before Palmer had served apprenticeships in those gangs. Palmer had noticed their rise in various parts of the city and over time recruited them to his group. He directed their abilities to control and develop the varying strands of his criminal enterprises, particularly in the northern and southern areas of the city. Until recently, these activities had proved very lucrative and had satisfactorily lined his pockets.

To the outside world and by comparison, Charlie Palmer was a successful self-made businessman. He owned demolition and construction teams, car salesrooms, supporting maintenance workshops, and property development operations. He was a member of his local church, regular public donor to hospital charity drives, family man, freemason of long standing, had a network of local politicos, and was a prospective city councillor.

He was also a close confidante of Martin Harrison, the Assistant Chief Constable of Glasgow City Police.

Palmer's large stone-built villa, in the exclusive Kilmacolm area to the west of the city, completed the impression of successful respectability. But, behind that facade was an intelligent, ambitious, cold, calculating thug who controlled a web of crime; a violent man with a vicious temper, which was forecast by his tugging at an earlobe and his nostrils flaring. His present legitimate business portfolio had been funded by a successful twenty-five years of crime. A large part of this success had come from him courting the asst chief constable. They had known each other since each started out on their respectively polar-opposite careers. Beginning with small bribes and tip offs to the police, Palmer ensured the survival of his own operation by helping Harrison scale the heights of police promotion by whatever means he could, in return for police turning a blind eye to his activities. He now had plans to step back entirely from his Mr Big crime boss role, hand it to a chosen successor, and focus on his ambition to become a city councillor.

His gang supervisors - as he called Burns, Mathieson and O'Hara - managed the daily activities which brought him his illegal income. In turn, the income helped Palmer fund the different parts of his criminal estate. Dozens of cafes, independent pubs, tobacconists and confectioners, small traders and shopkeepers, cinemas and even dance halls were their targets for extortion. A visit from a supervisors' gang of thugs was enough to convince most that a weekly insurance payment would keep their businesses free from mishaps such as accidents, fires, and vandalism. If that insurance payment was still not forthcoming, a second visit and some unfortunate accident typically brought the recalcitrant into line. Illegal bookmakers, very vulnerable to extortion, were also targeted, with a weekly pension payment being enough to stop the police being tipped off. Small hotels were viciously encouraged to provide the necessary space for the gangs to sell liquor and spirits, mainly stolen and at hugely inflated prices, after legal trading hours ceased at 9.30 pm.

Palmer aimed to extend his criminal activities beyond the present areas he controlled, and viewed the restaurants, small shops, and pubs in the city centre as fair game.

However, two immediate problems existed. First, the areas he wanted were the territory of Sammy Quigley. Second, Palmer's own rackets in the north were providing less income than before, with police being more active and victims becoming more confident as their fear factor reduced.

Now, Palmer held the gaze of each of the three others for a moment then stated, "Right, that's enough of your fucking excuses. The weekly take is down. What are you going to do about it?"

"It's Quigley's doing," O'Hara said. "He's giving the beat police information. We should put him in a box."

Palmer locked eyes on him. "Don't be as stupid as you look, O'Hara. Where's that going to get us?"

"Tit for tat boss," Burns said. "We know Quigley's team, their game, and locations. Give the bogies the inside track on them."

"That'll start a turf war. It's not what we want, is it?" Palmer growled.

"Sooner or later there will be a war with what we plan to do," Mathieson chipped in. "Might as well be in the driving seat when it erupts."

"Hmm, maybe," Palmer replied. "Get your heads together, work out the details of it, and get back to me here, tomorrow. Burns, stay behind. I want a word with you."

When they were alone Palmer asked Burns how he felt about stepping up and taking control of all the operations now, rather than in a year as he had previously planned.

"What's up Charlie, why the rush?" Burns queried. "You're not ill, are you?"

"Weary maybe, but not sick. I've always intended to step well back from running our business and lead a more, shall we say, straight life. You know that." Palmer breathed out slowly. "I've had quarter of a century in this game. I now intend to try my hand at politics. City-level, least ways."

Burns grinned and asked, "There wouldn't be something in that for your other businesses would there?"

"Maybe, maybe not, Arthur. What I want most of all is our present set up managed well, low key, no publicity and scandal free. You get my meaning?"

"I'm ready Charlie. Let me know when, and I'll take over."

Palmer nodded. "Low-key remember, and by the way, that's not exactly helped by that flash new car you've bought."

Later that day, O'Hara, was still smarting from his put down by Palmer. And he had other ideas about his future, and low key was not among them. He had been a supervisor of a part of Palmers criminal enterprise for several years, but had never subscribed to his beneath the radar, behind the scenes modus operandi. He was old school, an eye for eye, retaliation was mandatory. He had control of more than a score of thugs in his cohort, and now decided to aim them at Quigley. To hell with constraint, he thought. Quigley was screwing up his business.

Sammy Quigley was a creature of habit. Cunning, ruthless, demanding, and vicious, but dangerously habitual in some ways. He regularly used the same tavern, on the same night, to drink. This was well known in gangland circles. O'Hara decided to make Quigley's habit his downfall.

Cigarette smoke circled lazily into the air in the crowded bar of the Calton Arms tavern. The almost entirely male drinkers, who ranged in age from twenties to men in the twilight of life, gathered at a long-beaten copper bar, or seated themselves at tables spread along the walls. The buzz of serious conversation, and clink of glasses were only occasionally broken by the opening of either of two doors that led onto the street outside. New arrivals were scrutinised carefully and greeted with a nod of recognition, or a hard stare that conveyed mistrust and suspicion. This was a watering hole for local regulars, no more than a hundred yards from Glasgow Cross. Its atmosphere spelled out no visitors, no football fans, no young bloods, and leave if you are ignored. Over ninety years old, the tavern was no mecca for out-of-town revellers or seasonal tourists, it was noted for its clientele being working class, hard drinking, and no nonsense.

It was also noted as being regularly used on a Wednesday evening by Sammy Quigley. Bracketed by two of his gang he sat ensconced at the end of the bar near the washrooms, and occasionally sipped at a glass of Guinness stout. His eyes were directed at the evening newspaper, and an account of the city council's latest demands for the police force to crack down on, as they saw it, American-style organised crime.

Quigley gave a chuckle. They haven't a clue what goes on, he thought.

At the same time, outside the Calton Arms a large grey van emerged from a thickening fog and stopped at it the pub's doors. The van's rear doors opened, and four youthful men emerged out of the gloom, each dressed in a raincoat and flat cap. Leaving the van doors open, they moved purposefully toward the tavern entrances.

Led by O'Hara, they unveiled a variety of weapons, threw the doors of the Calton Arms open, and burst in. Brandishing an open razor, O'Hara headed for Quigley at the end of the bar, striking the face of one of Quigley's men in the process. The would-be defender reeled back, hands and face reddening as he attempted to stem the flow of blood from the vicious slash. Behind O'Hara, his team threatened any one in their path with bayonet, hatchet, hunting knife and short sword.

The regular drinkers were no strangers to violence and adopted their own strategy for the occasion. Some went beneath tables, some rushed for the open doors, others pushed tables and chairs in the path of the attackers, a few moved to protect Quigley and produced their own weapons. The space between the invaders and their quarry became blocked. More of the tavern regulars became involved in denying O'Hara and his troops access to Quigley, and some serious stabbing injuries were inflicted. A chair crashed down on the shoulders of O'Hara as he was in the process of throwing a hatchet at Quigley. The chair spoiled his aim, his intended missile sailing into the gantry and smashing bottles and optics which in turn added the unmistakeable crash of breaking glass to the cursing and shouting.

Quigley recognised O'Hara.

And he recognised the significance of this attack.

He believed that revenge could be eaten hot or cold, and opted to run and fight another day. He leapt over the bar and exited to the rear of the premises through a storeroom, on to a service lane that ran the length of the street.

O'Hara could do nothing as Quigley escaped. He and his men withdrew to the main doors on to the street and clambered through the still open doors of the van. He shouted at the driver, "Fuck off, and fast."

Two days later Arthur Burns and Charlie Palmer were still looking for O'Hara. They presumed he had gone to ground following the Calton Arms attack. None of their criminal organisation knew where he was. After the attack on Quigley, he'd dropped off two of his men at a hospital for treatment to their wounds, then had the driver drop him off near the main Edinburgh-Glasgow Road.

He never reappeared, but Quigley knew exactly where he was, and where he would forever stay.

CHAPTER ELEVEN

Like most major cities, Glasgow had a very dark aspect. Murder, rape, burglary, extortion, fraud, and assault were commonplace if not rampant. And as the city council moved communities away from condemned housing to new estates on the outskirts of the city, law enforcement took to harnessing new ideas and practices to combat these challenges. The Central Police Station set up a police information room, using telephones, teleprinters, facsimile machines and radio equipment to provide rapid, and up to the minute information to radio patrol cars across their widening area of responsibility.

For some time, the city had been divided into seven divisions - Central, Marine, Eastern, Northern, Southern, Govan and Maryhill - each having a well-defined area of control. A new approach in the recent past had merged uniformed police from a number of those divisions into a cross regional mobile group, which quickly gained the public's moniker of the *Flying Squad*. The squad's remit covered all areas of the city, and its role was to combat all major crime. This so-called flying squad had achieved some limited successes in bringing individual murderers to justice, but the police commission office was convinced that a great deal of burglary, extortion, prostitution, bribery, and drug theft was connected, organised, and run by a Mr Big.

Illegal drug distribution had been identified as the number one criminal activity across Glasgow and the wider

West of Scotland. Corruption was rife and increasing, and drug theft and abuse had become pervasive.

The head of the snake could not be found.

Whitehall in London had noticed and acted.

A small and specialised group of five London detectives were sent to the city, tasked with identifying, penetrating, and halting the prevalent drug problem. To achieve this, the group were given almost unfettered power, and answerable only to a faceless commissioner in Whitehall.

This move had been leaked to the press and had become a hot topic among the public and police alike.

It was known that Inspector Norrie Carse led this team, consisting of Inspector Johnny Harper, and Sergeants Gus Bailey, Spike Kelly, and Jake Airlie. All had exemplary records and commendations for past actions, and all were noted for their very unconventional approach to policing.

What wasn't common knowledge was that Carse was now thirty-five years old and had finished the war as a highly decorated special forces sergeant, hunting on-the-run Nazis in France. On the disbandment of his specialist unit, he had retired from the army and joined the police force in London. There, he'd distinguished himself - first as a beat copper, then in plain clothes as a detective. Unmarried, he had devoted his post-military life to his work as a law enforcer.

In many respects it was an odd decision to join the massed ranks of the Metropolitan Police, given he wasn't tribal by nature and preferred his own company or that of a small and select group. Though, like many of his generation, he was not university-educated, he was by nature a cerebral gentleman, with manners to reflect that disposition and a penchant for reading books during down time and for taking off his hat when in the presence of a lady, no matter what her status in life.

He was quietly spoken, never blasphemed or swore though didn't worry if others did, was handsome to some ladies, less so to others, and off-duty liked to wear his herringbone tweed jacket when out and about, even though the garment was probably more fashionable in the 1930s. Not that he socialised that much. He was rarely asked out, and that was probably because people sensed that he needed some time to be alone. Many men like him were the same after they'd returned from overseas.

But, reserved or otherwise, he was not a complete loner and revelled in having amiable contact with good comrades. Perhaps, he'd often wondered, that's why he'd joined the police. It wasn't the work itself that he was drawn to but rather knowing that the true potential of humankind is always exposed when confronted by extreme circumstances. He'd seen people for whom they truly were happy in war. And he had a notion that in peacetime the nearest he'd get to similar, was within law enforcement.

Deep down, he and others knew that wasn't the only reason he'd joined the police. He was asked to join by his former commanding officer turned superintendent in the Metropolitan Police Force. And that happened after the officer had to get him released from Kensington Police Station when he'd rescued an elderly Chinese greengrocer from being beaten up by three pent-up and drunk navy men. The men thought the greengrocer was Japanese. Carse had tried to explain he wasn't. The men didn't care what he had to say. They hit and kicked the Chinese man. Carse did worse to them. And he'd have done the same if the victim had been Japanese. His former commanding officer had referenced that event when talking to him in the London cell. And he'd referenced Carse's renowned contempt for discourteous behaviour. Now was the time for Carse to join the Met, be better than most others who served, lead by example, and once again go after the bad guys. Carse had accepted the offer, very minded that he was probably unemployable elsewhere.

It had proved to be the correct decision. His career soared. And after successfully leading an assault on drug dealing in London, he'd been hand-picked to go to Glasgow and replicate his success there. And he was given considerable autonomy to get the job done in whatever way he saw fit. He decided that the small team he needed around him had to comprise intelligent men who had proved themselves in extraordinary circumstances, and crucially were people he trusted with his life. Without doubt, those men were Harper, Bailey, Kelly, and Airlie. Like Carse, they were all in their thirties and didn't suffer fools gladly. Carse and his team had almost unlimited power to do what they had to.

The top floor of the Glasgow Central Police Station was reluctantly given over to the group. They named their floor the Central Research and Examination Wing. The rest of the station immediately referred to the area as the C.R.E.W. room, and unsurprisingly the group became known as *The Crew*.

After finishing unpacking boxes, Carse summoned his team's attention. All of them sat on desks and watched him as they drank their hot drinks and smoked.

He looked and nodded at each man, his expression the same firm yet knowing expression he'd always adopted when briefing his troops in the war. "The top bosses down south believe that there is a Mr Big behind most of the crime across this city. As importantly, they think that there is a spy in the local camp. The prevalent issue is drugs. The streets are flooded with amphetamines. It's probable that the source of these amphetamines is one or more hospitals. The so-called local Flying Squad and other local police are trying to keep these hospitals under surveillance. But they are understaffed and lack the expertise to keep rigorous tabs on what goes in and out of each medical facility. Too often, raids have been met with nothing to show for it except red faces. It much worse than sheer incompetence. It's come to my attention that there are coppers on the take." He paused, ensuring that every man was capturing not just what he was saying, but equally what he was leaving unsaid. "We cut through that corruption, without mercy." He pointed at a window. "Out there, hospitals are our number one target. Our first objective is to understand what the local police have been doing and where and when. We need to know where the hits and the misses have occurred. To get that data, Kelly and I will take the city area north of the river. Johnny - your team take the south."

"Right boss," said Harper.

"We'll pull in all the existing police information available covering those areas from wherever we can get it, and fashion it into something we can work with. We have authority to go where we like and do what we like."

"Any limits? asked Airlie.

"Short of Armageddon, no," replied the leader. "The local boys are not very happy at our arrival and interference as they see it, but let's try to ignore that unnecessary fight. If problems arise, let me know and I will sort. I have a line into the chief constable.

A few nods and a grunt confirmed to Carse that his message had been received.

"How long have we got to deliver a result?" asked Bailey.

"I've put the word out among the various cop shops in the city that I want all existing and available intelligence on major crime north and south of the city here within three days. We'll analyse and evaluate it, then decide what actions we take. We have another issue to consider." He tossed a couple of folded newspapers towards his men. "The Glasgow City Press has a daily column on crime. Some bastard has leaked the news of our arrival. Today's column says that our first major target will be the drugs explosion across the region. It mentions our focus on theft of amphetamines from hospitals. It also says we know the drugs are widely distributed nationally and internationally."

The CREW team looked at the newspapers.

"Looks like the local rags have been reading our mail," said Airlie. "Still, should be a quick fix up here and then back to the London for a decent pint of beer."

"We have our work cut out before that pint." Carse gestured towards the papers. "City Press report is pretty accurate, and I'd dearly like to know who's feeding it scraps. It's not the data that bothers me, not yet, but rather than articles like this will encourage senior cops up here to press us for a result. Takes the pressure off them obviously. But where the press is wrong is that we actually don't yet have any evidence that the drugs are being sourced from hospitals. We need that evidence."

Kelly asked, "Do you reckon the local cops have given up, now that we're here?"

Carse shook his head. "Their flying squad coppers are still active and pursuing leads. If anything turns up in those enquiries we'll be in the loop. Our priority is tracking the drugs." He breathed in deep and looked around their new base of operations. "First, let's get the domestics sorted out here - phones, secure cabinets, transport, maps, and all the other stuff. You know the routine - anything we do here must be invisible to all but ourselves."

The men stood and were about to commence their tasks.

Carse held up a hand and said, "As soon as this place is assembled in the way we like it, we get ourselves into the action on the streets. Jake, Gus - get yourselves dressed for the occasion of getting among the cafes, bars, clubs, pubs and dance halls, particularly near the docks, the university and the art college. You are buying whatever is available, the end game being the sources. Don't waste time on pushers and pimps."

Bailey laughed. "Take the only two Scots in your team and toss us into the grubby vipers' nest." His expression steeled. "Let it begin."

Carse smiled, then looked at the others. "Johnny - I want you and Spike to pin down the other end of the supply chain. There are written reports from earlier cops' investigations into pharmacies, healthcare distribution warehouses, hospitals, and drug manufacturers. I'll chase up those reports myself. Any questions?"

"Back here when?" asked Bailey.

"Keep it fluid. But, at the latest, here for a review in three days unless something breaks. And if there is a development before then, call it in for an immediate parliament."

While his men were busy sorting the wing and preparing for their deployment, Carse poured over the reports the city police had written up from their investigations. He was looking for anything out of the ordinary, something that didn't sit right with his copper's senses. He delved into the intelligence compiled over the previous year, looking for anything that might connect a particular surgery, hospital, or drug manufacturer to possible amphetamine leaks. He found nothing but *low-level noise*, as he called it. He decided to review past interviews with individuals. He eventually unearthed the report of Sergeant Morton's interview with Alice Walker. The contents piqued his interest. A nurse working in a hospital, with a boyfriend linked in the past to criminal offenders? On the face of it, nothing said during the interview excited him, but Morton's post interview comments recommended a further interview based on her nervousness, her non-committal response to questions on amphetamines, and her link to a known past offender called Phil Groves.

He called Morton to find out more, only to find he was on leave. He told the voice at the other end of the line why he wanted to speak with Morton and was delighted to hear that Alice Walker had also tried to speak with Morton with information about drugs.

He decided to meet the nurse.

Frances McEwan also read the Glasgow City Press report with great interest. It had serious implications for her. If the new police team was focused on the drugs epidemic, they would certainly be poking around in hospitals, and she needed to have them diverted well away from the activities in the Ardengrange annexe.

She met Baxter at a quiet restaurant in a village just outside Glasgow and spelled out her instructions. "The police hot shot squad that's up from London apparently has drugs as its main target. We need to make certain that it has no reason to sniff around the annexe, understand me? I know you overprescribe amphetamines; you must stop that immediately."

Baxter looked uncomfortable. "I have to prescribe amphetamines for a variety of reasons and every prescription I make is done properly, is legal, and…"

McEwan snapped, "Do me a favour and drop the blarney, Baxter! You make a bit of money on the side. *Illegal* money. Ordinarily, that doesn't bother me, but times have changed. We've got the big-guns bloodhounds in town and looks like they won't give up on even the faintest of scents. So, you need to be clean as a whistle if they show up asking questions. Only entirely defensible prescriptions for real people. You got that? Or, do I need to spell it out for you in other ways?"

He sighed while slowly nodding his head. "I understand. No more overprescriptions."

"Good. The job you offered Alice Walker - has she accepted yet?"

"Yes, she's been used twice already. Reception work so far, though. Nothing sharp end."

"*Used* is such an apt word," McEwan said. "Glad to hear it. Let the matron know too. Tell Hardcastle that Walker is as important to the annexe operations as the others who carry out the procedures." She looked away, smiled, and said to herself, "Although she doesn't know it yet." She looked back at him, her expression cold. "What else have you been up to?"

He laughed though it was obvious he was trying to mask nerves. "I have a life on the outside world. Through the masonic lodge, I've met and made connections with some high ups in the city."

"Interesting. Tell me more."

"I've been invited to become a non-executive director in a holding company being set up to manage contracts and licences for the development of Glasgow and its future expansion."

"Why you?"

"External balance. Someone to ask non-commercial questions. To be the conscience of the board." Baxter shifted in his chair and looked even more uncomfortable.

"Don't let it get in the way of our work, understand?"

"I won't."

McEwan's mind raced as she considered the recent multitude of Glasgow opportunities inherent in this news. She wondered if some of these opportunities could be exploited by leveraging Baxter's new connections. "Who are your high-level connections? Are they well known?"

He shrugged. "Someone in business, someone in law, and someone in politics."

"All secret masonic stuff, I suppose."

"For the time being yes. Nothing more to tell at present."

That'll change, thought McEwan. She placed her hands flat on the table and smiled, knowing the look was utterly insincere. "OK, we need to meet again, shortly. Away from the hospital. I like it here, so here it will be. And when we next meet, I want to review how far we have progressed with our own secret project."

CHAPTER TWELVE

On the south side of the city on the edge of a small industrial estate, Phil Groves moved quietly and cautiously through the evening murk, intent on finding the car to be torched. Only background traffic noise reached his ears. He trailed a low-light torch beam along a row of lock-up garages, peering into the evening gloom and searching for a door numbered 19. There was an identical row of garages opposite, and his head swung from side to side checking out the numerals. Some doors were closed, some partially open and clearly empty, a few padlocked. His eyes fixed on the number he sought, and he quietly moved closer to the entrance. The door was closed but not fastened. He gently placed the can of petrol he was carrying on the ground and reached up to the door handle. He pushed and the door swung up and back, the light from the torch illuminating a sleek black limousine. This is it, he thought.

His hand grasped the petrol can lid.

Just as another hand grasped his neck and yanked him backwards.

The impact of his body hitting the ground knocked the breath from him, and his ribs felt the force of boots repeatedly kicking him.

Two figures dragged him from his fallen position to a lock-up two doors further down, where a dim light was now showing. A third figure stood at the entrance. Groves was dragged inside, a sack placed over his head and again repeatedly kicked until he momentarily lost consciousness. When he came to, the bag had been removed and he realised he was in a garage that had been rigged out as a workshop with a heavy workbench spanning the back wall. His head pounded, heart racing, gut was knotting and nauseous, and fear was coursing through his mind and body as he realised that he was probably about to be murdered and there was absolutely nothing he could do to prevent that from happening. Still, he tried to make sense of things. The garage smelled of engine oil with tools and car parts scattered around the floor. Before keeping his head down in case any of his assailants thought he was trying to identify them, he dared the briefest of glances at them. None of their faces meant anything to him. He stared downwards as the room's dim light was extinguished and replaced by torches.

"Right then, sunshine. Who are you? What's your game?" This came from a man with a harsh Glasgow accent.

"Nothing, no game. I was just looking for a friend's lockup," Groves wheezed. "I'm not sure where it is and thought I'd found it."

"Who's your friend, and why do you want to find his lock up?"

"To leave this can of petrol inside. He asked me to do him a favour."

"And your friend's name?"

Groves repeated, "For a friend. Friend of a friend, really. Owe him…. Don't know the other guy's name."

"D'you think we came up the River Clyde on a water biscuit? Names!"

Groves felt the blow of a gloved fist on the side of his face.

A new voice threatened," Names. Now, or you will be wearing your nose up amongst your hair."

The pain from his ribs was now intense and Groves gasped aloud when the third man kicked him viciously in the crotch.

"We have all night pal. We're not in any hurry," the first voice said. "You want us to believe you were doing a mate's mate, who you don't know, a favour by placing a full can of petrol in the lock-up of somebody else you don't know? A lock-up which just happens to have a new car inside?"

"Yeah. Sounds stupid. I know. True… true though." Groves knew his only chance out of the situation was to appear pathetic. Right now, it wasn't a difficult act to pull off because he felt terrified and utterly useless.

The man who might have been the group's leader said to the others, "Okay, let's have him over to the bench. We'll get what we want there."

The three dragged, kicked and pulled Groves to the rear of the garage, forced him down and tied him to a chair next to the bench.

Despite the pain Groves was alert enough to pick out some words they were whispering to each other. A few times he heard the first questioner referred to as Arthur.

"Get his hand between the jaws of the vice." This came from a new voice, foreign accent, maybe Dutch or German.

Groves felt his right hand being thrust into the vice as a choke hold took grip around his neck. The captor's breath smelled of tobacco smoke. In the light spilling from the torches, he could see a hacksaw and a large pair of bolt cutters on the bench top. He was sweating now and struggling to breathe.

"First a finger, then a thumb, then the whole hand. It's your decision. Just tell me who sent you and what the petrol was for. And how did you know where to look?"

Groves was trembling. This gambling debt had gone too far. But he was terrified of the reputation of Sammy Quigley. Should he tell these people what they wanted to know? Were they just putting the frighteners on him? What should he do? How much should he say?

The decision was made for him as he felt the bolt cutters bite into his index finger. He screamed in agony and yelled, "Okay, stop! I did it for Sammy Quigley to repay a gambling debt. He wants the car burned. He told me where to go,"

The bolt cutters squeezed again.

He fainted from shock.

It must have been a while later when he came around because when he did so he had the sack over his head again and was in a moving vehicle. The vehicle slowed to a halt, the back doors opened, and he was deposited on the street with the bag still over his head and his right hand swathed in blood-soaked tea towels.

A voice from within the departing van yelled out, "Give Quigley our regards. But also tell him to stay away from the grown-ups and that we have eyes everywhere."

After an overnight stay at the Royal Infirmary, Groves was discharged and returned to the Regency Club, where his boss quizzed him on his absence and accident. He was determined to say nothing until he saw Quigley. The club manager decided to resolve that by giving the thug a call.

Quigley showed up forty-five minutes later and was enraged at Groves' failure, barely acknowledging his mutilated index finger. He listened to Groves' account of the fiasco and his description of his attackers and said, "It's the work of that bastard Arthur Burns and his north side mob. We'll send them a proper message this time." He sneered when he added, "Why didn't you do as you agreed? You're a gutless wonder. I expected you to carry out a simple task. Why didn't you?"

"They were waiting for me Sammy. They must have known I was coming."

"You mean you woke the whole neighbourhood up and they couldn't help but hear you." He warned Groves he still wanted a repayment of the debt and told him to prepare to become involved in retaliatory action. "You still owe me. And I don't care how many of your fingers you have to lose before I get my money."

Three days later and despite the injury to his hand, Groves joined up with a group of Quigley's thugs at the city's Charing Cross area. They moved westward, picking out premises they knew to be either owned or under the protection of Burns. The North Star bar on Sauchiehall Street was firebombed, two cafes near the University had their front windows smashed, several independent news agents and tobacconists on the western end of Argyle Street had paint thrown into their premises and on to their counters, and a Greek-Cypriot café on the Great Western Road was invaded and furniture wrecked, but not before the owners retaliated with baseball bats. The raids died out as the mobile patrols of the city police arrived. Groves had taken part in the attack on the Cypriot café and had sustained a leg injury which prevented his escape. As a result, he was arrested. Twelve people were injured in the chaos and the city newspapers screamed out 'Gang Warfare in the West End'.

The papers weren't wrong because that night Arthur Burns had his teams of thugs lined up to produce his own brand of havoc in response to Quigley's attacks. That was until Charlie Palmer arrived and ordered him to stand down.

"Remember what I said - low-key, scandal free," Palmer said. "The gang warfare headlines might have already gone to print, but that doesn't mean we need our names all over the news."

Burns very reluctantly accepted the warning.

Still, the city press made the most of the upheaval and laid out pages of fact and imaginative fiction, comparing the running mayhem with some of the more legendary battles which had taken place in the mid-thirties. Speculation was rife on who was heading up the gangs, Quigley and Burns' names were suggested with no hard evidence to back it up other than street gossip What had caused this latest clash of thugs was mooted, with several correspondents opting for a turf war, while a few attached the drugs epidemic to the reason behind the fighting.

Overall, the main thrust of the reporting was that the city should not, and must not, return to the lawless days of gang warfare. The city fathers needed to do much more to bring peace and harmony to the streets.

And some of them tried to do just that, even if their intentions were far from pure.

That evening, Palmer had a call from Harrison, the assistant police chief constable, who demanded Palmer use his contacts to restore calm. "I know you have influence, Charles. Use it. We can't have this nonsense on the streets. I'm being hammered by the press for action. Get a grip."

That was easier said than done because – like most gangsters – Palmer's men were an impetuous bunch, had their own vested interests, and were often prone to blood lust. Burns was no exception. Despite Palmer's earlier warning, Burns gave his thugs the green light to retaliate. Overnight, two of Quigley's pubs were set on fire, two taxis burned out, a dustbin set alight then thrown into the reception of one his taxi offices, and a lock up garage containing thousands of stolen cigarettes was set ablaze. No one was injured but gang honour seemed satiated.

When Harrison found out, the chief constable was fuming as he again called Palmer. "I told you! Calm! And then I just find out from my lads that your boys are having a bit of playtime with Quigley's plots. Maybe you're not the man I thought you were. Maybe we're not always going to be friends. Remember that."

The police carried out a round-up of the usual suspects. But, mainly through fear of reprimand only two were charged. Groves was one of them, having been identified by a shopkeeper. The names of the two arrested were published.

In the centre of Glasgow, London police sergeants Jake Airlie and Gus Bailey separately moved from café to café. Dressed respectively in scruffy, well used duffel coat, and army surplus US army combat jacket, they asked customers in furtive tones where they might buy a few pep pills. Most of the responses they were given suggested they were not wanted, but encouragingly no one seemed to suspect they were police. Confident that their covers were sufficiently robust, they moved their search to pubs in the Gallowgate. The late afternoon drinkers were similarly unhelpful, though one drinker suggested an evening visit to the nearby well-known folk club pub might be more fruitful. Having ascertained from the man that the pub was on the city end of one of the Clyde bridges, Airlie bought him a pint and bade him good day. The two undercover cops left.

The pub was packed solid by eight that evening. As planned, Airlie went in alone, leaving Bailey to watch the pub from across the street. Exactly thirty minutes later, Bailey sauntered across the street and entered the boozer. He spotted Airlie near the bar and standing close to a weedy-looking teenager holding a canvas bag. The cops locked eyes. No subtle signals were needed. In moments like this, the men could read each other's minds.

Bailey walked up to the teenager. He rubbed his face, unnecessarily looked around and asked, "Got any uppers mate? Hard cash."

The young man didn't seem bothered by the approach and question. "What're you looking for?"

"Bennies. Anything like that."

"Pound a pill. Good stuff. No garbage," said the emaciated dealer., "How many? I can do three if you want."

Bailey winced. "Just three? Fuck. Need more than that, don't I? Bunch of us going up the hills this weekend. You know. Get the booze out and down our necks, bit of a fireside singsong if the mood takes us. Hoping I might get some skirt along as well, though can't see you helping me with that. Probably don't even know what tits and arse looks like." He wiggled three fingers in the air. "But I'm bettin' you can help me with more than a poncey three pills."

"Jeez. How many?"

The detective grinned. "That's more like it. I'll take a box if you have one. There are fifteen, maybe twenty of us."

The kid looked like a rabbit caught in headlights. "That's out of my league pal. You need somebody else!"

Bailey shrugged nonchalantly. "Put me onto somebody who can fill my order and there's a couple of quid in it for you. And I'll take what you have now." He laid a five-pound note on the bar.

Quickly, the teenager grabbed the note and stuffed it into a pocket. He glanced left and right and then said,

"You can have what I've got, three left, that's all. I'll see what I can do for more, but it won't be tonight."

"Okay. I need, like, maybe fifty to a hundred. Cash on the nail. Possible?"

The drug dealer nodded. "Same time tomorrow and day after I'll be in here. On one of those days, I should have what you need."

"Good man." He half-turned, ready to leave, but hesitated and looked back. "Just you, though. Last time a supplier tried to spring an unwanted guest on me, a cop had an extended stay in hospital and the supplier… Well, the cop's pals or the wildlife will no doubt find him one day."

CHAPTER THIRTEEN

Alice was nervous when she entered the annexe for the first evening of *extra work* that she'd agreed to do for Crawford Baxter. She wasn't entirely sure why the nerves were in play, given the job wasn't particularly onerous and she was in familiar surroundings. Perhaps her emotions were unsettled because so much rested on her ability to hold down a job that provided an extra revenue stream? Maybe she was still smarting from her interview with the police, an encounter that had left her wondering whether her good nature and decorum in law-abiding society were not up to standard? No, she decided. The reason she was nervous was because there was something about her new job that felt odd. The problem was, she couldn't put her finger on why that could be.

The consulting rooms used for private examinations were on the second floor, with a staircase and a lift close to the front reception. Baxter had briefed her that morning to expect a senior midwife supervisor to carry out the procedure being undertaken. He would not be present himself. He told her that her role was primarily to greet the patient, check her appointment details, escort her to the upstairs changing rooms, take blood pressure readings, height, and weight, help the patient change into an inspection gown, and then advise the senior nurse the patient was ready.

Later, and on time, the patient arrived. The woman was in her mid-twenties and had fear writ all over her face. As instructed, Alice had almost no interaction with the patient as she carried out her pre-operation duties to the letter. When the patient was ready, the senior midwife supervisor, who introduced herself as Sadie Finlay, thanked Alice and then ushered the patient into the consulting room after telling Alice she would take things from there. Alice went back to her post at the downstairs reception desk and sat while feeling bewildered. Was this all there was to the job?

The next three occasions were identical in process. The patients had all arrived unaccompanied, entered by the front door, and left by the rear exit. Other than to re-emphasise the need for total patient confidentiality, or to pass Alice the envelope which contained her extra pay, Sadie Finlay kept herself to herself and restricted conversation to an absolute minimum. Her cold manner contrasted greatly with Alice's warm demeanour.

Alice thought the entire process seemed too clinical, too unemotional. Perhaps that's how it had to be, she reasoned. And maybe it all made sense now. Pre-natal complications were obviously a distressing matter, and it served no purpose for clinicians to become overly sympathetic or even hesitant. They had a job to do. They had to be calm, even if that meant they looked cold and dispassionate. And Baxter, who knew the process well, recognised the reality of work in the annexe meant that to the outside world its edges needed softening. That's why he brought Alice in. To soften the edges.

She wanted to believe that.

And yet, why did she still feel that something wasn't right?

In the evening of the first day of her new shift, she read a newspaper report about the dreadful gang riot. She was shocked to see Groves' name in print and mention that he was charged with assault and affray. The paper elaborated that he was thought to be connected to Sammy Quigley and might be involved in illegal amphetamine distribution. Apparently, Quigley and his gang were heavily suspected of being involved in this racket.

She realised it was time she did something about it. and decided to force the issue. She called the number Sgt Morton had left. He was not available. She left her name, said she had some information about drugs for him, and would call again in a day or so.

On her fifth extra work session in the annexe, Alice was on the second floor counting supplies in the stationary cupboard when she was interrupted by the sound of a door violently opening. She went into the corridor and was shocked to see the girl she had earlier checked in. The girl stumbled out of the consulting room, clutching a bloodstained towel around her legs and crying. Alice rushed towards her while calling out that she would help. But the midwife also emerged from the consulting room, darted a look at Alice, told her to stay away, grabbed the girl, pulled her back into the room, and closed the door.

Alice could hear the patient's muffled protest in the room.

She was saying, "I didn't want to do it. Didn't want it to happen. They. You. Not me."

There was a loud shout, possibly from Finlay.

The girl went silent.

Alice went up to the door and tried the handle. Locked. called out to the girl. Silence.

One minute later, she heard a car leave from the rear exit.

Alice was stunned, angry, and worried.

Stunned that her fears and earlier suspicions that something unofficial might be afoot were real.

And worried that if the annexe was somehow complicit in unwanted abortions, she too was already complicit in any wrongdoing, having now being a party to five incidences.

This was a moment of truth for her, and she was terrified of the implications if her fears were real. Loss of job and career would be the least of her problems. She could be sent to prison and would certainly get a criminal record. And if she was taken out of the equation that would mean that her parents would be entirely on their own.

Edith Hardcastle gave a very disbelieving look when Alice reported the incident of the girl with the blood-stained towel, and the very strange behaviour of Sadie Finlay. And she scoffed when Alice said she thought something had taken place that was not above board. Unperturbed by Hardcastle's reaction, Alice ventured to suggest it may in fact have been an attempted or a bungled abortion.

"That's nonsense, nurse. You've got a very vivid imagination. I'm certain there is a perfectly sensible explanation for what you think you saw. I'll speak to Nurse Finlay myself."

Alice was not entirely convinced, but it was prepared to accept the rebuff until she'd spoken to Baxter.

When she did so, Baxter listened carefully to her concerns, asked a few questions, then bluntly told her, "I think you don't quite understand the nature of the work we do here. Ante-natal procedures take many forms, and with any procedures there can be risks. It might be helpful if you joined Nurse Finlay and became more involved in the consulting room work. I think you need to be more professional. I expect you to put this behind you, continue your normal work in the annexe, and be open minded about the extra work."

Alice was not satisfied with the answers from Hardcastle and Baxter and suspected that her hunch was accurate. But a hunch wasn't enough to give up work and walk away, because her extra income was paying her parents' rent in their new flat. However, if her suspicions were indeed correct, she had been involved in something unauthorised, unofficial, or even blatantly illegal.

Hardcastle, and particularly Baxter, were shaken by Alice witnessing Finlay's botched procedure. She was never supposed to see that.

Baxter began to question his own appetite for continuing.

That thought remained as he and McEwan met in the out-of-town restaurant earlier than planned.

"What's the hurry?" McEwan asked. "What's up?"

Baxter nervously mentioned Alice Walker's sighting of the distressed patient, and his rejection of her concerns. His anxiety was apparent.

"God's sake man. Stop panicking and calm down. It's not the end of the world. It needs managing, that's all." McEwan made no effort to hide her impatience and contempt. "It's very important to keep her onside, and your explanations will probably not have done much to ease any fears she has." She thought for a moment, leaned forward, and said in a measured and authoritative voice, "Here's what you're going to do. Call her in for a follow-up meeting and explain to her that all the private procedures are authorised by senior medical staff, and only carried out under strict control. Some procedures are routine pre-natal, some exploratory, and some medical intervention. If viewed by a few people as on the border of legality, they are also morally justified. Get close to the truth but leave a margin of ambiguity. You got that?"

Baxter nodded and used a handkerchief to dab his face.

She watched him for a while, knowing that he required her leadership yet also cognisant that the doctor was liable to do something stupid in-order to save his skin. But he was bright and that meant she couldn't placate his fear with facile garbage. She needed to bring him into the loop of her thinking, to some extent. "There is a danger in Walker finding out the true purpose of the annexe operation. But if she thinks it is in any way illegal, she is also smart enough to realise that, after being involved in five sessions, she could be found to be complicit. She won't do anything reckless because the money she earns supports her parents. You must do everything you can to allay any fears or suspicions with a plausible explanation to the annexe's extra activities. Play the moral ambiguity card and the complexities of delicately handling unfortunate souls. Emphasise that we're on the side of good. Under no circumstances must she learn the real truth that she's fronting an abortion factory. Is that clear? Do you understand?"

"Abortion factory?" His eyes were wide. "Good lord. Hadn't thought of it that way."

She shrugged. "Conveyer belt of women and unborn foetuses. Us at the end. We take the child and the mum's cash. We move onto the next one on the belt. It's a process. A damn efficient one at that." He expression returned cold. "Do you know what to say to Walker?"

"Yes." He threw his hands in the air. "But what if it happens again?"

"You make certain it can't happen again. Review the processes from start to finish. Put in place safeguards to prevent accidental viewing, by anyone. Ensure all doors are secure and locked during procedures. And most of all, don't use Finlay again. We can't afford any more screw-ups."

"I understand. However, you'll have to find me a quick replacement for Finlay. There's an appointment scheduled for this weekend."

"Leave that to me. Now, we need to move on. While you have been allowing peeks into our operation in the annexe, I have been busy sorting the annexe's network of support. The result's based on the business model I put in place for our Liverpool and Manchester networks. But the annexe operation is considerably more far-reaching and superior."

Baxter said nothing. Inwardly, all he could think about was that – like Walker – it wasn't a straight-forward concept for him to just walk away from McEwan.

She continued. "We now have four flats in the city, on call transport in the shape of taxis, and insurance protection for the same. The links to Ireland are in place and my networks in England are locked in. The protection includes coppers giving us a blind eye, which will help when the flats are in use for drinking parties. The annexe operation must be completely invisible to all but us."

"What has the flats got to do with my work in the annexe?" Baxter queried.

"Nothing at the moment. They're for clients. But you should know how the chain works because it's likely we will have to make changes as we proceed."

"Why would that be?" asked a puzzled Baxter.

"Because of recent events, and likely future changes coming down the line."

He frowned. "What do you mean, *recent* and *future*?"

"Jeez, don't you read the newspapers? The city has been overrun by a wave of crime. The police have their heads in the sand. Even their so-called Flying Squad can't seem to do much apart from bash and crash around the city." Her expression turned serious again. "But if we push it too far, then London sends in professionals. *Real* professionals. And those guys never take prisoners. Thankfully, it's so far only deployed a small team. The hot shots will put their energies into cracking the drug problem and that will result in hospitals being put under their microscope. And what that means, Mr. Baxter, is that there've been recent changes and there will be future changes."

He blurted, "I've already stopped overprescribing amphetamines, as you wanted. Only patients with genuine needs are now supplied."

"Well done, *Sherlock*. But you miss the point," she sneered. "They will still sniff around hospitals and ask questions. We can't afford to have them anywhere near the annexe. Be ultra cautious in everything you do and take every opportunity to steer the police well away from the annexe. No mistakes." Baxter's face blanched as McEwan finished her verbal onslaught. He hated being talked down to by anyone, most of all a nurse, but the stakes in this game were enormous and she held all the high cards.

"Apologies for being slow on such matters, but what kind of future changes do you envisage?"

She didn't answer him straight away. Instead, she called a waitress across to their table, ordered sandwiches and a pot of coffee, and didn't answer Baxter's question until the waitress had gone. "There are expected changes in the law. An abortion bill is being talked about informally in parliament. It's likely to become legal sometime in the future and this will undoubtedly impact our annexe undertaking. In the US, a contraceptive pill for women is close to being marketed, I'm sure you and your colleagues have discussed this. The implications for our venture in the annexe are all negative. Additionally, gambling is on the verge of being legalised or regulated, and the licensing hours in Scotland are shortly to be extended."

"Of course, I know about impending amendments to the abortion law and what's happening in the States. But why would gambling laws and licensing hours affect the annexe operation?" asked a bemused Baxter.

"The flats we have in the networks are not only used for clients' recuperation. They pay their way as temporary drinking dens, are sometimes loaned out to illegal bookmakers, and occasionally they're used as brothels."

He couldn't believe his ears. "Christ's sake! This is all way above my head. What has all this got to do with our set up?"

McEwan knew she was light years ahead of the gynaecologist but suppressed any desire to tell him more. "Nothing to do with our set up," she said. "Forget it. I was merely enlightening you as to what I have on my plate. That way you'll understand why my nose will be mightily put out of joint if you forget to do the things I nicely ask you to do.

Baxter leaned forward and in an almost conspiratorial whisper said, "Speaking of changes, there are other vast changes coming here to the city. Infrastructure, housing, schools, roads, contracts, licences, a snowstorm of change."

"Where did you get this from?" McEwan asked.

"High level connections, which include the Lord Provost and the Assistant Chief Constable." Baxter could not help himself boasting. He also hoped it would get McEwan off his case.

"This is the non-executive director thingy you've been offered?"

"That's the one. An investment opportunity of a lifetime." He grinned. "The rewards for insiders are absolutely enormous."

"Lucky you. But just don't forget that meantime you've got to ensure what we have on the ground is safe from nosey busybodies, yes?"

"Yes," he answered meekly.

"Good. Because all your *investment opportunities of a lifetime* will mean zero if you're serving twenty years to life sentence." She checked her watch. "You should be heading back."

"The sandwiches and coffee..?"

"Are for me." She clicked her tongue and said in a no-nonsense strident voice, "You're a busy doctor. Stuff to do. Knives to sharpen. People to see. Off you pop."

Baxter stood, tried to think of something to say that might reclaim his dignity, couldn't find the words, nodded, and left.

When the lunch arrived, she ate while thinking about her next steps and adjustments she might need to make to counter recent developments. She had a far-reaching view of what the changes she had just described to Baxter would do to her business model. She was determined to take her future criminal ventures to a much higher and wider ranging level and the information Baxter had leaked would be useful to achieve her ambitions. But she would need more if she wanted to be one step ahead and control the changes and opportunities coming down the line. And she needed a deputy. Someone who could take over the leadership and management of day-to-day activities and thereby enable her to continue pulling all the strings while hidden in the shadows. She was now thinking of what attributes were needed to be the controller of not just the abortion network, but ultimately the big boss of a crime network. No doubt that person had to be ambitious, ruthless, and street-smart. She had plenty of experience managing villains in the north-west of England who fitted that bill. The problem was, she had history with them, and that history hadn't always been agreeable. More importantly, they didn't know Glasgow. She realised she that she would need someone presently in a prominent position within a local gang. She'd groom that person to be her deputy. No one else in the annexe, even Baxter, would yet be told about her plan to appoint a senior figure.

And they most certainly wouldn't be given a name.

But she had the name of a candidate in mind.

His name was Arthur Burns.

On his return to the hospital, Baxter met Hardcastle in his office and fed her the latest explanation he wanted to be given to Alice. "There is no other option. Walker must be the front-of-house face of the annexe. That's a must. We'll get her in again and give a much more plausible explanation of Finlay's screw up. The explanation and argument we will use is one of being close to the truth but covered by high level authority. Ambiguous maybe, but plausible, and Finlay won't be back."

Hardcastle shrugged. "Bye bye Finlay. Makes my life easier if we get people who know what they're doing."

Baxter liked the fact that the matron now seemed satisfied with the resolution. He said, "The sooner Nurse Walker is put straight the better. I want you to talk to her today, tomorrow at the latest. I'll follow up and talk to her shortly after."

Hardcastle met Alice the following day. Alice listened carefully to what Hardcastle had to say, asked no questions, thanked her, and left.

Later, Alice was summoned by Baxter. He repeated his earlier comments on keeping an open mind, then gave her the wider half-truths explanation McEwan had concocted. He concluded, "You need have no concerns on our private work, Nurse Walker. You're now part of a team that's making a huge difference to lives."."

She deliberately kept her response neutral "Thanks for putting my mind at rest, Mr Baxter. It just seemed so odd the way things are set up. To me it seems odd, anyway."

"Private patients have stringent demands on their privacy. We comply with their needs in that respect," said Baxter. "But there's no doubt that confidentiality does produce a rather odd air. It's normal." He smiled. "You help give confidence to clients who are often nervous and reluctant to discuss their conditions. Just keep being yourself and doing more of the same."

"Oh, I see. Will I be involved in any procedures in the future?"

"I should imagine you will, depending on how well you settle in after this little *misunderstanding*." replied Baxter. "Just keep an open mind and remember this is all for the benefit of clients who prize their privacy."

"Thank you, I'll do that. Just one more thing. I would like some more money for this extra private work."

The brazen cheek of the question took the gynaecologist completely by surprise. But he quickly saw it as a very positive thing. Even if she had concerns, she was willing to jettison that in favour of more money. He laughed. "Well, I'll consider it and let you know. Meantime, be ready to take your place when needed." He was relieved.

Alice wasn't.

She didn't believe a word and felt deep down that there certainly was something suspicious. The matron had used almost identical words to Baxter, almost as though they were being read from a script. Whatever was going on seemed to have Baxter and the matron in league.

In league with what?

She knew the answer.

Illegal abortions.

CHAPTER FOURTEEN

While arranging insurance for her activities, McEwan had regular meetings with Arthur Burns. Their discussions led her to believe he was a ringleader or deputy of a criminal organisation. She had her belief confirmed by the property developer from whom she had purchased her flats. He paid Burns protection monies and emphasised Burns' reputation as a smart and ruthless villain.

The Elder Park Library in Govan was the gift of the wife of an industrialist to the people of that borough. It was almost deserted during the day, other than for a few elderly worthies reading the newspapers, and made a perfect setting for a hushed conversation in a remote corner of the building. McEwan had arranged to meet Burns there with an incentive for making it worth his while, and Burns was intrigued to find out what a dicey middle aged property player had in mind for his benefit.

"Funny place to meet," Burns opened. "What's secret enough to meet in this out of the way place?"

She didn't care that the inclement weather outside meant that her raincoat was dripping water onto the library's nice carpet, nor that her hair was sodden and matted. "It's off the beaten track. I don't know anyone in this area, and I had a feeling this might not be your usual stamping ground." She smiled, though her piercing eyes remained locked on the gangster and were anything but benign. "Almost a neutral venue you might say. Nosey parkers are everywhere in the city and best we avoid their like."

"Sounds like something big coming up."

"There could be, if you have the guts for it."

Burns snorted his derision. "You have nerve, I'll give you that. What do you want?"

She looked around and gestured him to follow her into an empty book aisle. There, she said, "First, I want to know what's going on. These gang attacks that everyone's talking about – what's sparking them?"

He pulled an incredulous face. "How would I know apart from what I read in the papers? The rags say it's all about money, rackets, drugs probably, revenge tit for tat. Gang stuff. Reckon the papers are right."

She slowly wiped a hand across her forehead, collecting rainwater from her brow, and then quickly flicked the water onto the carpet. "Thing is, though," she looked up while rubbing her hands together to dry them off, "I *reckon* you might know a bit more than just newspaper reporting. But if I'm wrong then I'm wasting my time and your time. That would be a shame."

He frowned. "A shame?"

She nodded. "Among other things, I'm a businesswoman. I like the scent of opportunities and money."

She'd pressed the right buttons and Burns said, "So, in my world I might get to hear a bit more than the papers get their hands on." He breathed in deeply, looking at her with eyes that still retained suspicion. "Gang stuff – no idea. But what I can say is that if I were running operations, some kind of *Mr Big*, then nothing like this would have happened. I'd have dealt with things differently."

This was exactly what she wanted to hear. For him to make a comment like that to someone he barely knew, and even then, only on a passing business level, meant he was bristling about behind-the-scenes stuff. And he couldn't stop himself from making his contempt evident, even to someone like her. Crucially, it meant that if he knew who the top boss was then any loyalty Burns might have to that person might now be wafer thin. However, she could be wrong and there was risk in what she was about to say. Risk never worried her. "I want someone to work with me to build an enterprise in Glasgow. My enterprise will take advantage of every change the city will undergo in the future."

He was cautious when he asked, "What changes?"

"Licensing hours are going to increase; betting shops legalised; casinos opened; slums cleared out to make way for new estates; new transport and leisure facilities will be established to service new developments. And that's just for a start." She placed a finger against his chest. "I'm interested in angles. I think you are too. Wouldn't it be nice to control the licenses for alcohol, betting and gaming? And wouldn't it be icing on the cake to also manage the premises for these establishments?" She tapped her finger three times on his chest. "You could be living in luxury in the Bahamas in ten years' time."

He moved her hand away and said sternly, "You're off your nut, missus. How're you going to manage that?"

"I have access to inside information on all of this, including house building, new roads, schools, libraries, but above all the back door to getting the biggest earning licences and permits."

"Oh, aye, right oh." His tone was blatantly sarcastic. "You've got the council by the balls, and they will just let you have the richest pickings, because?"

Calmly, she replied, "Because I have the vision, ambition, and the experience to do this. And I have inside track to relevant information."

"You? What makes you think you're good enough to ride roughshod over the city of Glasgow?"

"*Good enough?*" She chuckled. All amusement drained out of her and was replaced by intense menace. "It's not a question of being *good enough* to run this city. I'll leave that pathetic aspiration to idiots like your Mr Big. You see, I have a brain. A damn good one. I know that information is power that's useless unless it's in the right hands. So far it looks to me like a bunch of hooligans are running around this city like headless chickens. No surprise if their boss is a dumb thug. So, I come in. With a brain. A plan. An ability to move people into positions they might not expect. I'm a thinker. And a doer. And by God, I do stuff." She held his gaze and wouldn't let go. "Does that answer your question?"

Involuntarily, Burns moved his upper body back a few inches. "And why me?"

In a blasé and matter-of-fact tone, she answered, "you bend the law, you're directly involved in crime, extortion, and leading gangs. You name it, you have probably done it. And as a result, you're an ideal candidate to work with me."

"You know this how?" Burns queried.

"I do my homework."

"Let me get this right. You pay me to keep your premises free from interference and provide cross city taxis when needed. You run shebeen drinking dens, as well as a brothel. You've come out of nowhere, and you want me to join you in some big-time scheme to take over the running of the city's gambling, drinking and leisure centres. And you want me to build and oversee more of those establishments."

"Yes. And that's just the *cheap stuff*. I have other thoughts and plans as well. And they are anything but *cheap*."

"That's as maybe. But far as I'm concerned, I'm still looking at a small-time brothel keeper. Why would I throw my weight behind someone like that?"

The comment didn't bother her. "Check out my background. There are enough guys like you in Manchester and Liverpool who know me. None of them like me, by the way. There's a reason for that. And I'll tell you this for free – to a man, not one of them will keep a straight face if you have a chinwag with them and describe me as a *small-time brothel keeper*. My advice to you is choose your words more carefully." She grinned, knowing how unpleasant the look could be. "Think it over. Don't take too long. And if you say no, I'll be relieved that I haven't wasted my time hiring someone as thick as the boss he despises. I'll find someone else. Plenty of alternatives in Glasgow." She turned and walked away while calling out, "Ta-ra, pet. I'll be in touch."

Burns watched her leave the library, but he remained where he was. He wasn't sure if the woman he'd just met was in her right mind. He knew she had a connection with a hospital on the western end of the city, having gleaned this from the property developer who had told McEwan about Burns' background. He wondered if she was working an angle with the hospital. Perhaps that had something to do with the other bigger plans she had. Certainly, she was a force of nature and right now he wasn't entirely sure what to make of the encounter he'd just had. He decided that there was probably a large element of bluster to her. On face value, it appeared she didn't know very much about Burns' background. And despite her sarcastic hints, she'd given nothing away to suggest she knew about his relationship with the city's big criminal boss, Palmer. And that would mean she didn't know he was the most trusted of Palmer's lieutenants; a deputy who knew Palmer's plan to concentrate on legitimate business dealings and leave the criminal activities to a nominated heir, one Arthur Burns.

Or maybe, just maybe, she did know his exact role and relationship to Palmer. Perhaps she had the chutzpah to go straight for the prize. He would test her boast with some people he knew down in England, and from there decide how he wanted to deal with her.

In the Saracen Head pub on Glasgow's Gallowgate. London detectives Airlie and Bailey continued their hunt for amphetamines. The place was notorious as a meeting point for young blades having a final drink before crossing the road to the Barrowland Ballroom, where they would typically spend a fruitless evening spent trying to hook up with girls. The pub sold a vile concoction of liquor under the name of *scrumpy* which, together with a glass of sweet South African sherry, was almost de rigueur for consumption on any visit. The clientele during the day were a mixture of the unemployed and unemployable, with the random curious tourist from outside the city who was keen to experience the atmosphere of one of the city's oddest attractions. Most of its patrons appeared to be under thirty, and that was why the two policemen hung over opposite ends of the bar, occasionally chatting to likely prospects and hoping for a lead. After half an hour or so, they left the pub separately and met up again a few hundred yards away at the entrance to Glasgow Green.

"Nothing doing there. Where to next?" Bailey asked with an air of exasperation.

Airlie shared his disappointment. He also knew that, like him, Bailey wouldn't stop until a job was done. "The university area and its closest cafes, drop into Buchanan Street bus station enroute, back along Argyle Street and the likeliest pubs and coffee bars. Once that's done, we'll check into the CREW room for the latest information. Then, back to the pub where we bought the three pills last week." He looked along the street. "We're getting close, my friend. No one is pushing back on us, but we need to persevere. A night out tonight in the folk club, then hang around on the Broomielaw into early morning, and finally a visit to a shebeen. That suit you?" He smiled.

Bailey chuckled. "Sounds about right. That said, I'm sick of drinking beer shandy and my feet are two sizes bigger than when we started. Do me a favour - when this is over and we're back down south, grab me a chair and pour me a real drink." He followed his colleague's gaze. "Meanwhile, let's crack on."

Arthur Burns had intended to telephone a contact he knew in Manchester to test McEwan's boasts, but an offer of a ticket to a European Cup football match at Manchester United's ground gave him an opportunity to drive down, meet the contact, and see the game.

In the bar in the Midland Hotel, Burns smiled broadly as he spotted Mick Angelo, a Glasgow Italian, long-time associate, and former cellmate in a young offenders' borstal.

"Hey, Jock. How's you doing? Long time no see," said Angelo as he hugged Burns. "What are you up to these days?"

Burns was genuinely delighted to see his old pal again. It had been such a long time. But time meant nothing for men like this. And Burns and Angelo had an unbreakable bond that had been forged when they'd both been severely punished for putting dents into a warden's skull. "Down for the match at Old Trafford tonight, and a wee break from business."

"And how is business?"

"Solid my friend, solid. Though I would like to pick your brains on something I'm interested in."

They settled down on a corner sofa and swapped news over their first two drinks. As Burns returned with glasses recharged, he said, "I need to know if you've ever heard of a player in my area. Originally, she's from this neck of the woods. Supposed to be top line. Woman called Frances McEwan."

"Common as muck surname. Even if you put it together with a Frances, you've still lost me. No bells ringing. Not to say I can't help. Tell me more."

"About forty, tall, fair haired, brown eyes, strange Scots/English accent. In Glasgow, keeps flats for drinking parties. Sometimes uses them as brothels." He hesitated. "Can't prove anything, but I reckon she's probably involved in abortions too. I came to you because she claims to have been a player in the Northwest; reckoned she ran a network down here."

Angelo thought for a moment and asked, "She got a gold tooth?"

"Yes. Well, a gold chip filling. Do you know her?"

He nodded slowly. "Has to be same person. Don't know her personally. But your girl sounds like the same gal who until a year ago was the head honcho of a network of abortionists, here in Manchester. Liverpool too. Had a score or more of blokes managing properties, taxis, even providing protection for others. She had a run in with an Irishman from Dublin who muscled in on her trade. He vanished." He shrugged. "Rumour has it that said Irishman's now propping up a support pier on the new motorway being built. If it's one and the same, your woman's an evil bitch, I'm told."

"You said until a year ago. What happened then?"

Angelo took a gulp of his beer. "She disappeared. Over the border is the guess cos she came from that way. As far as I know, her networks are still in place and being run by her people. What's your interest?"

"Think I might be talking to *evil bitch*. She's handed me a business proposition. I'm dead certain her business is good but I ain't dead certain about her. That's why I'm here. Anything else you can tell me?"

"Her main base was Liverpool. There was a point where a price was put on her head. Don't know who wanted her out of the way, but I guess there were enough who did. The thinking on the street was that the coppers shielded her for their own reasons. Then she disappeared."

"Disappeared as in you know for sure someone caught up with her, or just hasn't been seen again here and could be somewhere else?"

"My guess is she's too smart to have been brought down and will be doing what she does somewhere far from here."

"Glasgow."

Angelo nodded. "The wild west." He drained the rest of his drink. "Remember - always get a second opinion, my friend. If I were you, I'd see what Dominic in Liverpool thinks. Don't roll up and have a chat like this. He's got the rozzers all over him at the moment. Best you give him a buzz. Tell him my thoughts are constantly with him after he lost my fucking shipment and has allowed grief to get in the way of remembering that he now owes me seven thousand quid." He grinned and his tone softened as he added, "Also tell him I hope his old man's on the mend, and I'll drop everything to help while he's got the cops watching him."

Burns also finished his drink, asked after Angelo's family and general wellbeing, was satisfied his old cellmate was doing just fine, hugged him, and left.

Later that evening, after the football match, he called Dominic in Liverpool. The former inmate who'd patched Burns and Angelo up after the borstal incident was even more forthright in his view of McEwan. "That's the fucking bitch. Be very, very, careful. She's smart. Too damned smart. And even by our standards, she's got the scruples of a crocodile. If I were in your shoes, I'd be thinking about walking away. Or, walking through her, if you catch my drift."

Airlie and Bailey sat at opposite ends of the busy Silver Lounge café near Hillhead underground station, Airlie with a copy of the *New Musical Express* on the table in front of him and cradling a rapidly cooling mug of coffee. He looked at nothing it seemed, but saw everything - who came in, went out, who smoked or didn't, who waited for someone or other, and those who were just hanging around.

His colleague cosied up to a tall and thin dark-haired girl in a duffle coat and animatedly started chatting to her while never losing sight of the rest of the café. He was working at inviting himself to an art students party she had told him about. It was some kind of celebration of an award or diploma or exam passing. He couldn't be sure because it seemed she was stoned and didn't make a great deal of sense. But she made enough sense to give him a feeling that what she described was a gathering where amphetamines might be bought, sold, and consumed. He passed her a pack of cigarettes, lit one for her, and excused himself to go to the toilet. There he quickly scribbled a note for Airlie and left it on top of the high cistern lid. On his return, he re-joined the duffle-coated art student and watched disinterestedly as Airlie entered the toilet.

Airlie was in the gents' room for no more than thirty seconds. When he was back in the main café, he re-took his seat, knew that Bailey would be looking at him, didn't look back, and instead stated at a blank wall and nodded twice. It was the required signal that the message had been received. He got up and left the café.

The two undercover policemen met up within the hour at the CREW room. Now that they'd arrived, Detective Inspector Carse gave a review of progress to date.

Carse said, "In general, we have a pretty good view of what is happening across the city." He looked for signs of disagreement from his men but saw none. "Police intervention to retrieve stolen goods has been planned, and then thwarted, on three occasions. This suggests the villains were tipped off. Result - police raids found only empty premises. A similar picture emerges when raids on suspected illegal gambling and bookmaking sites turned out to be futile, with nothing illegal found. We're continuing to look for a common factor or factors across these incidents, in terms of people involved. This may lead to surprising outcomes, but for the moment we're still looking. Nothing more. The biggest issue we must address is the illegal use of drugs, particularly amphetamines. There's a ready market for them, and they're being used by all sorts, from pregnant mums to beatniks to university students, and in night clubs where parties are in swing. This is almost certainly an organised supply chain, but we don't have a breakthrough," His eyes fixed on Airlie. "Jake - do you want to give us the view from the street work you're doing with Gus?"

"Aye, why not?" Airlie responded. *"Pep pills. Amphets.* Amphetamines, to give 'em their full name. Up here, going street rate is at least £1. We've had no great difficulty in buying the odd pill, but to date haven't sourced larger quantities. We're chasing up two leads which might provide a link to the main source. Optimistic yes, but not overconfident. I'm guessing the next week or so will see whether we lift the championship trophy or not." He shrugged. "All we can do is keep at it, until we get the pusher who'll give us that bit more information." He looked at Bailey. "What do reckon, mate?"

Gus Bailey thought for a moment. "Nothing more to add really. We've become recognised in pubs and cafes, had no finger pointing that were coppers, and" he grinned, "me and Jake have kinda signed onto the dole. Least ways, looking the part. Shuffling the city, drifting, gormless expressions. And that's the cover we need. We'll use it get our target. I'm a bit more bullish than Jake. I think we're not too far away from a main source."

Carse was thinking fast. "Good work. Now, Johnny - what progress at the production, storage, and supply end of the chain."

Harper explained, "The drugs can come from three separate sources. One, directly from manufacturing plants or medical facilities that have a legal right in the UK and abroad to hold the drugs. Two, from specialised and legal distribution centres that are currently storing them in, say, warehouses. Three, and most difficult to pin down, from unauthorised labs and med centres that are illegally manufacturing the pills. Tracking the movement in the first two is straightforward but laborious. It's a paper chase of receipts, transfers, despatches and receiving centres. All movement requires authorised paperwork. The stock holdings, both actual and paper holding, are the most likely place to find discrepancies and gaps. North and South side, all of us are onto that now." He grimaced. "The illegally manufactured drugs find their way in through many different routes and are the hardest to corner. Fortunately, the demand for these would seem to be far less than for the branded pills. So, that leaves the legal amphetamines. We don't think the problem lies with the legal *manufacture* of the drugs. They're closely scrutinised and accounted for. As a result, it's more likely to be *control* of the finished legal product that's the major problem. Put bluntly, *legal* drugs are housed in *legal* distribution centres, hospitals, clinics or large pharmacies. The problem is that *illegal* bastards are getting their hands on the drugs and pumping them onto the streets. Those illegal bastards will be respectable insiders – probably drivers, factory workers, administrative staff and the like."

"Or maybe even doctors, scientists, or nurses." Carse looked at each man in his squad, his voice deep and measured when he added, "We keep an open mind. As ever, no one, repeat no one, is above our suspicion or warrants our respect simply because of title or position. No stone unturned territory. Speak truth to power."

"Power," Bailey echoed while sneering.

"My sentiments exactly." Carse nodded. "I think we're making progress at both the supply end and at the demand end of the chain. Any questions on what we've heard?"

"How do you see this progressing from here, boss," asked Airlie.

Carse moved to one of the windows overlooking the sprawling city and stood with his back to his men as he surveyed what was out there. "We stay on course. More of the same. Our approach and work to date will give us the answers we're looking for on the amphetamines issue. I'm digging into past local cop interviews to see if we can pull anything from there that might have been overlooked, or not thought relevant." He turned around and looked at his squad. "We have another review in three days. And gentlemen, that means that in three days we'll be closer to going into hunter-killer mode."

CHAPTER FIFTEEN

Airlie and Bailey left the CREW briefing room and split up.

Airlie headed to a greasy spoon restaurant on London Road where he hoped to get information from an informer he'd never met before. His only tip was that the forty-year-old man usually wore some kind of cap or hat to cover thinning hair. Aside from that, he was described as nondescript; the sort of individual who could disappear in a crowd. Airlie was not hopeful he'd correctly identify the man, let alone get anything useful from him if he did make contact.

Bailey was an early customer in the folk club pub. He bought himself a Guinness and settled down near the entrance to read the evening newspaper. The weedy looking teenager from whom he had previously bought amphetamines appeared, just as Bailey was beginning to think he'd wasted his time. He motioned to Bailey to follow him outside the pub where he stood under a streetlamp.

"What's the score?" Bailey asked as he joined him.

The teenager could barely hold eye contact, had his arms wrapped tight around his chest, and was shifting from one foot to the other. "Can't get the amount of stuff you want. Too much money. Too risky an amount."

"You're saying what?"

"You need to go to the guy who controls the stuff."

The detective rubbed his face and pretended to look annoyed. "My party's all sorted. People queued up. Good time promised and all that. Even got some chicks. Can't let 'em down." He pointed at the kid. "You were my solution. Help me create the buzz, know what I mean? But, you're no good now. Means I need to know who can help. Who's this bloke and how can I strike a deal with him?"

The kid held up his hands. "I don't know. All I'm saying is if you want to buy a large amount of the stuff, you need to get it directly from the man himself."

"Who do get yours from?"

The dealer huffed. "My business, mister. And I keep it small and tidy. Only trade fours and fives. And I get it from different places. No idea who the main guy is."

Bailey didn't believe him. "There's five quid in it for if you point me in the right direction."

The young man frowned. "Five quid. Lot of money but still only same as me punting five pills, so…"

"Oh, fuck off," said Bailey sarcastically. "Yeah, right – five pills, but let's take off how much you had to pay for them, plus how much time you have to hang around for a sale while worrying you might get nicked or stabbed or robbed, and then there's the fucking worry about payback if you accidentally slip them a pill that don't cut the frickin' mustard because it's a feckin' duff." He put on a momentary fake smile. "Five quid for a name, without all the bullshit. I'm too bright, sunshine, for your *like-for-like* shit. And I don't have time to dick around. Got to shoot in a minute to find a bloody set of amplifiers for the music.

What the fuck do I know about amplifiers?" He softened his expression, hoping the look appeared needy. "Just a name, pal. That's all I need."

The kid gestured to the club entrance. "Music shop couple of streets if you take a right out of here. Guy who runs the place will help you out. Name's Dave. Nice enough."

"Dave can get me what I need?"

"Two amplifiers. Yeah."

"Fuck's sake, pal! Look – I can sort that. What I can't sort out is your mess. Which is now my mess because I'm going to have a bunch of pissed-off party people."

The man rolled his eyes. "Alright, alright. Still don't think I can help you that much. I can take your money if you like, but all I know is that it's a gang boss."

The detective sighed, and muttered to himself, "Stupid idea to sort this party." His voice strengthened as he looked at the man and said in an overly dramatic way, "Any idea where, in this bloody enormous rabbit warren of a city, I might find a man who walks around with a sign on his chest that says he's a gang boss?"

"No, but I have a feeling it's out in the east end of the city - Gallowgate, Bridgeton and the Calton areas."

"A feeling? Oh great. What gives you that *feeling*?"

"Just street talk."

Bailey grunted his thanks and left the scene. He wasn't entirely disappointed, given his hopes hadn't been that high. But if the youth's street talk insight was of any value, the meeting had not been entirely wasted.

He joined Airlie in the greasy spoon restaurant and could tell immediately that his time, too, had not been fruitful. Keeping his voice low, he asked, "Nothing doing, pal?"

Arlie quietly replied, "Wild goose chase. I could have been sitting next to the guy but would never have known it from the lack of description given to me. You?"

Bailey wondered whether to order a coffee and food. "Something maybe nothing, I didn't expect the kid to show up with a hundred pep pills. Still, I was looking for an intro. For a fiver he told me the talk on the street is that the top dog for," he quickly glanced around to ensure they weren't being overheard, "amphetamines is thought to be a gang leader in the east end of the city. Kid was nervous. Out of his depth."

"Better than nothing. Maybe something to work on. So, last stop tonight is the duffle-coated art students party, or is that off?"

"I have an address, but not her name. We could chance our arm and try it. Trouble is, you and I barely made it through school and stood no chance of college."

"A fucking world war might have had something to do with that."

Bailey grinned. "It's a great excuse, I'll give you that. But we might just have to do a little better than that if we're going to pass as students."

Bailey laughed. "Oh, this is going to be good. Tell you what, though. Let's try to blag our way into the party while pretending to be something else. Not sure going undercover as college students is necessarily our forte."

"Pretend to be what?"

Bailey shrugged. "I don't know. Maybe something that makes us sound as though we've been out of circulation for a bit."

"Prison?"

"Don't be daft. We don't want to spook the students." Bailey thought for a moment. "What about we've been working at sea? Familiar territory for you, what with all that splashing about in rubber dinghies you did off the coast of Norway."

Airlie growled, "Oh here we go again. My adventures in the war were no more than amphibious outings with the odd gunfight, or explosives party at the end."

Bailey shrugged. "Means you know about sea. That's all I'm saying."

"Which is more than you do."

"True. I can hardly blag my way into a party on the basis that I know about North African deserts, and how to nearly break my back by jumping onto them with prototype parachutes and then leg for miles after shooting up a base or convoy."

"Bunch of fucking lunatics."

"Says the man who got frostbite in places we don't like to think about, because he swam across a fjord in December, just so he could photo a rather annoying airstrip."

Both men were silent for a moment.

Bailey said, "Something to do with sea."

"Agreed."

The party in a disused church turned out to be a gathering of what Airlie described as *beatniks*. They had no trouble gaining entrance, posing as unemployed merchant sailors, and mingling with a score of student-types who were wearing pullovers, army greatcoats, or donkey jackets. All of them seemed to be pushing towards a small bar in a corner. Bailey was wearing an army surplus combat jacket on which he'd pinned a 'Ban the Bomb' sticker. Looking the part, it didn't take him long to find the art girl from the café.

While getting bumped by passers-by in the cramped area, he said, "There you are. Lots of beautiful women in here, but you stand out." Quick as a flash, his arm moved outwards and steadied a guy's pint as the bloke holding the drink got knocked off balance in the surrounding throng. But the detective's eyes remained on the woman as he asked, "What's your name and what's your pleasure?"

Knowing the other man's drink would have gone all over her, she answered, "Thank you. I'll have a large cider, and a pink one."

156

"No name?"

"Rowena, but I hate it so call me whatever you like."

"Don't blame you. So, how about I call you Venus for the evening? And while we're at it, what's a pink one?"

She looked surprised, then laughed. "I think you've been at sea too long. It's a pep pill. Cider at the bar; pink ones from the guy in the pulpit."

"That kind of party, is it?" Bailey asked.

"Is there any other kind?"

He moved to fill the girls order, passing Arlie in the process and whispering, "guy in the pulpit."

The guy in the pulpit was startled when Airlie moved beside him, held up four £5 notes, and said, "As many as you've got mate."

Pulpit man looked shocked. "Fuck's sake, pal. You kidding me, or what?"

"Nope. And I'll have any more you can get."

Another beatnik entered the pulpit and asked for a couple of Bennies.

"We've just sold out," the pusher told the newcomer.

After the newcomer cursed and left, Arlie smiled. "Good decision. You can make a killing tonight."

157

The dealer raised his eyebrows and exhaled slowly. "I need to go out for more. Don't know if I can get them tonight. It's tough out there."

"I've just spent six months throwing up in the North Atlantic and Arctic Circle. Know all about *tough out there*. I'll go with you if you like. Be a minder for you. You get me my gear and I get your arse back here in one piece."

The dealer shook his head. "No minders needed where I get the goods from."

"Fair enough. Your call. Just so long as you're back here tonight if you get what I need." Between finger and thumb, he removed one of the £5 notes from his other hand and stuffed it into the dealer's pocket. "As a gesture of goodwill. Tell you what, though. Don't be taking that note and doing a runner on me. From fifty miles away, I can find a shoal of cod while I'm in a rust bucket that's bobbing up and down in a Force 10 and only a few hundred miles from where polar bears eat idiots who fancy catching the sights around the North Pole."

The man's eyes were wide. "I'll definitely... definitely be back."

Airlie left the pulpit, exited the church, then walked to the nearest police station where he arranged a watching party for the return of the guy in the pulpit. On his return, the crowd in the disused church had swelled. He stood near the front door, watching. Bailey was no longer chatting-up the art girl. Instead, he was alone and within a few feet of him.

The pulpit guy returned approximately forty minutes later. Strung across his torso was a small satchel.

158

Accompanying him was a thick set, scowling, hard faced man. They made their way to the pulpit. The dealer clapped his hands three times, no doubt a signal that he was open again for business.

But there was no trading to be done. Within minutes the church was surrounded by police, all exits covered, and pulpit guy and his new companion were in custody.

In the police station, it was discovered that pulpit man's satchel contained eighty amphetamine tablets.

On the Western side of Glasgow, the neighbourhood of Patrick's Dumbarton Road was similar to the area Alice's parents had left in Govan. The road was close to the river and had local shops; and it also had overcrowded tenement buildings that were inhabited in borderline slum conditions. But at least her parents' new home meant they had a roof over their heads. Moreover, Alice found it now much more convenient for her to visit them. And that meant she could look after them more regularly.

As arranged, today was her first visit to their new home and an opportunity to see how her parents were settling in.

The flat was no more than a small bedroom and kitchen linked by a short hallway. It was heavily lived-in by previous tenants and in need of some repair and refurbishment. Alice wandered around and thought she could help put the place in better order during her subsequent visits. But it was fine for now and no worse internally than their previous home. With her help, she genuinely thought she could make it much nicer.

After the initial tour, she sat down in the lounge with her mum and asked, "Where's Dad?"

Martha seemed unsure how to reply. "Had to pop out."

"You told him I was coming?"

Martha nodded but didn't say anything.

Alice was about to say what she was thinking but decided to focus on her mum. "How are you managing?"

For the occasion of her daughter's visit, Martha was wearing her favourite flowery blue dress, a garment Alice had helped her recently re-stitch when her Mum's arthritis was having a bad day. "Oh, we're getting used to it, or at least I am." She smiled though the look was sanguine. "Your father is... adjusting. Actually, he's not pleased at all." Her smile faded and was replaced with an imploring look that was direct into Alice's eyes. "He doesn't like the area."

Alice could feel anger build inside her. "You mean he hasn't found a pub he likes yet?"

Instead of chastising her daughter for the accurate yet blunt remark, Martha chuckled. "He has. There's one nearby. Can't remember what it's called. River Vaults, maybe, something like that? Who knows? All that matters to me is we've had had a serious talk and he doesn't hold the monies anymore. So, I give enough for a beer or two and that's it. Keeps him happy. Gives me a bit of time to," she looked around, "try to make things look nice."

"So why doesn't he like the area?"

"He just doesn't like change." She nodded towards the entrance. "This is on the first floor. He's used to the ground floor. The main road's nearby and traffic noise niggles him. And, to see any of his friends he has to get to the river and a ferry across to Govan."

"Dear God. He worked at terrifying heights, in a shipyard full of noise. Our previous backyard was riotous at times, so I can't see why the sound of local traffic would particularly fuss him. And as for his friends, drinking buddies more like, well they can get off their barstools and come this way, can't they?" Alice rubbed her face and didn't want to be blurting the words, but right now couldn't stop herself from doing so. "Trouble is, Dad's no longer the guy who lives within stumbling distance from the boozer and has got a few bottles that can be cracked open by his so-called friends once last orders has been called. He's become irrelevant to them. All that's left is a cantankerous bloke who lives on the other side of the river."

Martha bowed her head and said quietly and with utter sincerity, "He's old is what he is, Alice." She looked at her daughter. "We both are. And we're trying our best to cope with change."

Alice didn't know what to say. Maybe there was nothing to add to the profundity of her mother's words; the absolute finality of her statement; the terrifying reminder that a human life is irrelevant within the amoral grip of time. And within that diabolical universe, what was she to think of herself and her acerbic words towards her father? And hard truths to her mum, for that matter? Was it really so important that her dad was flawed? Did it help to remind her mum that she was married to a man whose rough life had in turn roughed up his heart and way of doing things?

Just trying to cope with change? Aren't we all, she thought. And who was she, Alice, to think she had a right to judge others given the circumstances she'd blindly walked into?

But Alice had to say something, she knew. Her mother would expect that of her. Needed that. Looked to her. Drew comfort from what little strength she had. Liked it when they sorted the serious stuff and then got back to giggling about silliness and dreaming and singing and dancing and chatting about plans and feeling free and clutching their bellies because their laughter might make them explode. "Sorry Mum, I didn't mean to be so nasty," was all she could say. But the words were real and true and straight from her soul.

Martha touched her daughter's arm. "You father was a man once. Still is, but a different sort. Even the strongest, the best, the biggest hearts... they all break eventually when life's hardest lash is constantly cracked against them. Be gentle on him now. He sips his beer and for a moment has a warm glow, I imagine. Takes him back, I bet. Warmer times. Stronger times. Me without my aches and pains. Him too plus the fear. Fear of not providing. First me. Then both of us." She looked away, a tear running down her drawn face. While looking at nothing in particular, her voice sounded distant when she said, "Let him sip his beer, Alice. Let him grumble. Let him curse and moan about traffic and say words to me that he never used to say. Makes him still feel alive, I think. Just about anyway." She smiled, gave a gentle huff, and looked at Alice.

Alice held her hand. "And what about you, Mum?"

Martha huffed again, her slight smile still on her face. She looked like she might be daydreaming as she looked at the window she'd polished earlier. As she did so, faint sunlight caused her eyes to sparkle like the film of the Clyde on a clear April sunrise. Her smile broadened. "Today is a good day. My daughter has come to see me."

"The first of so many," Alice said quickly. "I promise you that."

"That's all I need." Her eyes didn't move from the window.

Alice ever so gently squeezed her hand and said softly, "And I want *you* to promise *me* that you'll please keep the money I give you to yourself. Please. We can't let rent arrears happen again."

Martha's voice sounded so very distant when she replied, "It won't, don't worry."

Alice stood. "I'll be on my way. Thanks… thanks for wearing your lovely dress for me. And you can wear it again soon because I'll see you in a week or so."

These were the last words they would exchange.

CHAPTER SIXTEEN

As she made the return journey to the nurses' home after visiting her mother at her new address, Alice decided she needed to follow-up her earlier call to Sergeant Morton. She'd do this as soon as she got home, she concluded. That didn't happen because when she reached the hospital grounds close to her quarters, she was approached by a man.

He was in his mid-thirties, was holding his hands up to show he meant no trouble, had a slight smile, and an athletic poise that was softened by smart if somewhat old-fashioned civilian attire that included a herringbone jacket. "Hello Nurse Walker. I'm Detective Inspector Carse. Sorry to spring a surprise. I'm working with Sergeant Morton. He's busy elsewhere at present. You can take it I'm continuing his enquiries. Do you have time to talk?"

Alice glanced around, then back at him. "You have identification?"

Carse showed her his police ID.

She frowned. "Metropolitan Police? You're a long way from home."

Carse's smile broadened, accentuating the lines around his eyes. "A long way, yes ma'am."

She was about to make a flippant remark that it seemed all he knew about her was her name, given she wasn't married or widowed and therefore wasn't a madam.

But she stopped herself from saying something so churlish. In part that was because she felt sorry for the man, given Carse looked awkward in the hospital grounds, almost as if he felt like an intruder. Perhaps, she wondered, he'd become acutely aware that the gritty nature of his vocation was at odds with being in a place that healed people rather than punished them. Still, it appeared that he was at pains to disguise that vocation with a look that suggested university don or English Literature tutor at an elite boys' school. And there was every possibility that he knew full-well that she wasn't a ma'am and was simply honouring her with gracious respect. So instead, she said, "There's a small coffee bar just outside the main hospital gate. Can we go there? It should be quiet at this time, less public."

"That sounds perfect. Please - after you."

It was only a few minutes later that they were both sitting at a corner table in the café.

"So, your call to my associate Mr Morton - what's on your mind?" asked Carse.

She hesitated for a moment, trying to work out if the inspector reminded her of someone. Not someone she knew, but rather had seen. Perhaps someone in a movie. She wasn't sure. "Two things I wanted to talk about. Firstly, Phil Groves. You probably know Phil was my boyfriend."

"Was?"

"Was." For some reason she didn't feel uncomfortable that his unblinking eyes were fixed on hers. He exuded an aura of calm, she decided. Perhaps that was one of the tricks detectives learnt. "I saw his name in the newspapers recently. The report said Phil was apparently tied up with drugs or with people who are."

"The papers are correct." He remained motionless, watching her.

And still, that didn't seem to bother her. She sighed. "I don't know what else you or the papers might know. But I wanted to speak to Mr Morton about what I knew. What Phil had told me about his need for money. The conversations we had." She waved her hand dismissively. "Might be stuff you already know."

"Or maybe not. My question to you is why are you telling me?"

The question surprised her, and her garbled response reflected that surprise. "Not you. Well, yes you now. Police in general, really. I... I had a huge fall-out with Phil over all this. Not that I fully knew what *this* was. Papers later clarified that. And that's why I'm here. Sitting opposite... you."

For the first time he momentarily broke eye contact, leaned back, exhaled while retaining his smile, and said in a confident yet reassuring tone, "And I'm glad you are. I have to say, I wish more people in this city were as helpful." His expression and tone of voice changed as he looked at her again and said quietly, "It's okay Miss Walker. I'm an independent. I'm in this city for a reason and it's a big reason. But, to do what I need to do I need to have chats with people. *Confidential* chats." She wasn't sure what she thought of Carse. Aside from her recent interview, and previous brief encounters with beat cops when Dad had done something stupid, she'd barely had contact with police officers. And certainly, she'd never met

166

a real Detective Inspector before. Perhaps they were all like this? She doubted that were so. Most likely, detectives were like everyone else – some good, some bad, others somewhere in between. And that meant she had to trust her instincts on the man sitting with her. That was hard, though there was one thing that suddenly struck her. He made her feel safe. "I'd like to talk to you about the last few times I met Phil."

Carse nodded.

She spoke for nearly twenty minutes, before saying, "And that was that. Broke my heart, although I quickly realised it was the concept that broke my heart. Not the man. I was pressurised by Phil Groves to help get him money, I was shocked and declined, of course. Still, it left a sick feeling inside of me."

He cleared his throat and asked, "Any idea why he needs the cash?"

"He said he had to repay his boss for equipment he broke."

"What equipment?"

"He wouldn't say."

"And you believed him?"

"Yes. For a while, at least." She bit her bottom lip as she looked at him, while feeling stupid. "I wanted to believe him; I suppose."

"And why not?" said Carse in an authoritative and understanding manner. "As far as you were concerned, this was the man who'd proposed to you because he was in love with you. If he said he'd broken equipment, then it was perfectly natural for you to take him at his word."

She briefly glanced away and quietly said, "You're being too kind. He…" She looked at him, her eyes wide. "You see, Phil Groves isn't like you. Sorry, men *like you* is what I mean." Her cheeks reddened. "I… I knew he was a little rough around the edges. But that was okay, I told myself. He could change. Age would help, I reasoned." She shrugged. "Whether I was right or wrong on that doesn't explain the here and now. I should have realised he was, right now, the type of character who could have been trying to pull a fast one over me."

In the dying months of the war, Carse recalled thinking similar about a French woman he'd taken a shine to. His belief in her would have lost him his life had he not ultimately discovered she was a German collaborator who was operating a Nazi exfiltration route. To this day, he wondered if becoming suspicious of her was a worse outcome than dying because of a yearning to trust. "What was Groves doing when you first met?"

She pulled a face. "He was driving his boss on a visit to a hospital gala. Everything was all a bit vague at first. I assumed driving was his fulltime job."

"Can you remember what his boss looked like?"

She tried to remember. "Quite short. Foreign-looking, I'd say. Maybe Italian. I'm not sure." She held her fingers to her lips and felt apologetic when she added, "I haven't travelled."

"Ah. I wondered if it was a tall blonde man with long hair?"

"No. Definitely not,"

He thought for a moment. "Has Groves ever given you unexpected gifts?"

"Such as?"

"Earrings, bracelet, rings, anything like that?"

"No nothing like that, in fact no gifts at all. Phil Groves is no romantic spend-thrift." She looked horrified. "Don't get me wrong. I'm not that kind of woman. You know, the type that needs showering with gifts." Her expression changed. "Flowers would've been nice, though. Didn't need to spend money. There are some lovely ones that grow wild in the hills around here."

Sometimes Carse hated having to ask some of the essential questions required in his line of work. Now was increasingly becoming one of those moments. "Are you annoyed, or resentful that you have broken up?"

The formality of the question reminded Alice why she was here. For some reason she didn't like that, and her tone of voice became colder when she answered, "No, I'm not. This isn't revenge I'm looking for. I finished the relationship such as it was and, looking back, realise that I've been naïve and gullible to have been strung along by him. I don't ever want to see or hear of him again, but I accept that I'm partly to blame. As a result, normally I'd just walk away. No spite. No revenge. I'm just not that type. But then I find out… Well that there's other stuff. Not relationship stuff. Rather… legal matters." She braced herself, sucked in air, and said, "The reason why I rang back to speak to Sergeant Morton was that when he interviewed me, he asked if Groves had ever asked for drugs. I didn't reply to that."

"Because it would have been embarrassing to have replied." It wasn't a question.

She looked at him and in an instant her expression softened again. In a hushed voice she said, "Yes."

He waited.

So did she. And then she slightly slumped, as if a weight had been lifted off her shoulders, and stated, "He asked me to get amphetamines."

The detective nodded slowly. "Okay. Why?"

"To sell. He needed money fast."

"Did you give them to him?"

"Absolutely not, no!"

He held up his hands. "Don't worry. All is fine. I have to ask these things, that's all."

"Because…" She frowned then blurted, "I'm a good person Mr Carse, though I suppose sometimes even good people do bad things when love's involved. But I can assure you this is not one such occurrence. I'm a nurse. I see things. People suffering horrendous side-effects on drugs. Other awful things. And regardless of my job… Well… I…"

"As you rightly say – you're a good person." For the briefest of moments, he wanted to reach out and place his hand on hers. But he didn't do so. Instead, he said, "Phil Groves is not his name."

Her mouth opened wide. She tried to speak. Couldn't. Tried again and managed, "Not… not his…"

His expression was full of sympathy when he added, "It's Adrian Berry. And we know Berry quite well. Regrettably, and I'm genuinely so sorry to say this, it appears that you don't know him at all."

"Adrian? Adrian? Adrian Berry?" She wasn't repeating the name for the detective's benefit. Rather, she wanted to hear how the name sounded on her lips.

He knew that. "I'd like to continue this in the local police station. We can speak more freely there and not be overheard."

"God. Am I being arrested?"

"Heavens! No, no, no you're not, Nurse Walker." He looked around. "Look, I've got some thoughts. Not fully formed, mind you. I just think if it would be better if we chat away from this place. Better for *both* of us. Please."

She studied him. She was right. She felt safe with him. He wasn't a trickster. And even though he carried a detective badge and probably had to say and do things in his line of work that were not always what they seemed, right now she could tell he wasn't lying to her. He was a good man, she decided. And unlike her dalliance with Groves, she wasn't kidding herself this time. And Detective Carse had a dignity to him. She liked that. A lot. "When do you want me to come to the station?"

"Now. If that's convenient?"

She thought for a moment. "Why not. I'm not doing anything this evening."

It was only forty minutes later that Alice and Carse were driven to the police station in an unmarked police car. On the journey, she remained convinced she'd done the right thing by telling Carse about the drugs. However, a new thought consumed her, and it was one that made her feel nauseous. Should she tell the detective about her annexe fears?

In the station, Carse took her to one side, so that they were out of earshot of others, and advised her that the building was safe. However, not all the local police were best pleased that he and his men had been deployed onto their patch. And some of those men had loose tongues if they saw an opportunity to figuratively stick the knife in. As a result, that meant he and Alice needed to continue their conversation somewhere they couldn't be overheard. The best place for that to happen would be in one of the interview rooms. But, in taking her there he didn't want to disconcert her. Hence this prior conversation. She was *not* being interviewed, was *not* under any kind of suspicion, and he simply wanted privacy. To further put her at ease, he joked that it was either the interview room or a broom cupboard. She reassured him that was fine, and she understood. She was grateful, though, that he hadn't just waltzed her into the room without a prior explanation. Carse said that he'd like one of his colleagues - Detective Sergeant Kelly – to join them. He was working hand-in-glove with Carse, and it would be invaluable if she had a point of contact with Kelly as well. Again, she said that would be okay, though the prospect of meeting two detectives in one day made her feel as if everything was suddenly escalating into a world that she thought she'd never experience.

As they walked through the bustling station, primarily staffed by uniformed Scottish officers, Carse looked like a man who was in control of everything. Even though he wasn't. He called out to one officer who also happened to be the station's grizzled custody sergeant, "Harry – be a darling and get us three teas. Interview Room 1." As they walked out of the main control room and into a corridor, he said to Alice, "DS Kelly's a good man. Former submariner. Knows how to keep his powder dry and lips tight." He opened a door. "And here we are. Not exactly salubrious. But all I can offer, I'm afraid. After you."

The interview room was windowless and contained several filing cabinets, a table and four chairs, and a clean blackboard on a wall. The spartan décor was no doubt all that was needed, though it was also obviously designed to be intimidating. But Alice was unfazed because she was used to places like this. Most hospital rooms had a similar feel to them. And smell. That aroma of bleach, cheap soap, and stale human sweat.

Carse said, "Take a seat. Chairs are welded to the floor meaning unfortunately I can't do the right thing and pull one out for you." He looked around. "Miserable places, these."

She sat in one of the fixed chairs by the desk.

Carse sat down too.

But of interest to Alice was that he didn't do what she expected and sit opposite her.

173

Instead, he sat next to her and said, "Not a place to bring a lady. But as grim as this place may be, I'm glad you're here because it means I can show you some documents. Things I couldn't have brought with me to the hospital."

"I see." She looked around. "This is where people confess their crimes to you?"

He also looked around. "Not this particular room. This is the first time I have been in here. But yes, places like this."

"You must be a persuasive man."

He clicked his tongue. "I'm not sure about that. For me it's all about getting criminals to talk themselves into a corner they can't get out of. When they realise that no amount of further bluster or lying or silence will give them an escape, that's usually when they confess. Not always, mind you. Most of them, though."

She tried to ascertain how she felt with him sitting so close to her. "So, you're a thinker?"

Before he could answer, there was one knock on the door followed by it being opened and two men entering. One of them was Custody Sergeant Harry who was carrying a tray with three mugs of tea and a bowl of sugar. The man behind him was Detective Sergeant Spike Kelly, who was holding a brown police file.

Harry looked like he was fuming as he plonked the tray onto the desk. "When you're finished, make sure the mugs go back to the kitchenette. And wash 'em up."

Carse beamed. "Of course. It'll be my pleasure."

After the scowling sergeant left, Kelly sat opposite them, grabbed a mug, put the file on the desk, and extended his hand across the table. "Nice to meet you, Miss Walker."

Carse relayed to Kelly what Alice had told him in the café. "Miss Walker's been very helpful. Unsettling for her, though. I reassured her that we're here to help."

Kelly studied her for a while. Then he clapped his hands and said loudly, "Yeah. Not your fault. You didn't know what you'd walked into. This isn't your bag. I can tell." He lowered his voice when he asked, "Out of curiosity, would it have been easy to take drugs out of the hospital?"

She glanced at Carse.

He nodded reassuringly.

She looked back at Kelly. "For someone in my position, yes."

"And yet, you weren't tempted?"

This time she didn't look at Carse. "No, definitely not."

"Thought so." Kelly slowly looked left and right along the edge of the table, as if inspecting the furniture's border. Sharply, he looked up at her. "Where are the drugs kept?"

Carse interjected with a stern voice, "Sergeant – remember. Different ball game. Less direct, if you please."

Kelly smiled and nodded. "Forget myself, sometimes. Quite right, boss." His voice and demeanour were different when he said to Alice, "I worked a drugs case in the Met. Slightly different to this one. Someone was trying to copy, not steal, prescription drugs. Suspected a medical insider. Eventually turned out to be true but before I nabbed the guy, I had to trawl through gawd knows how many medical facilities. Turns out you all stash your pills in different places. No standard way of doing things. Hence my question. It would be helpful to know how your hospital runs things."

She shrugged. "It's not *my* hospital, though I know what you mean. And even within the hospital things aren't necessarily centralised. We're a big place, you see, and frequently we need speedy access to pharmaceuticals. In my wing, drugs are kept in a locked cupboard and only available under strict supervision. I couldn't access them without authority from others."

"Others such as?"

"Doctors. Where I work that would be the managing consultant."

"Who would that be?"

She hesitated. "Mr Baxter."

Kelly lifted a mug off the tray, placed it in front of her, raised the sugar bowl while looking expectantly, put it back down when she shook her head, and asked, "Have you heard of any abuse of the process controlling drugs? Any gossip of drugs going missing at the hospital?"

She sipped her tea and tried not to wince from the stewed taste. "No. None."

Carse said, "What I'm going to do now, Alice… Sorry, Miss…"

"It's okay," she said as she touched his hand. And then instantly withdrew her hand while feeling mortified. "Alice... Alice is my name. It's okay."

Carse seemed to be digesting that comment. He smiled, nodded, and pointed at Kelly, "You already know that the man who spent too long under sea goes by the first name of Spike. And I..." He looked embarrassed, or simply awkward that he was breaking convention. "Well, people who know me call me Norrie. Norman on Sundays.

Carse picked up the file and addressed Alice. "What I wanted to say is that I'd like to tell you more about the man you know as Phil Groves. This is a formal police file, containing verified data, or information we strongly suspect to be correct even if we've yet to substantiate the detail. Knowing more about the man who attempted to dupe you should help you understand that you're blameless. It may also," he darted a look at Kelly, "and I must be honest about this, aid us. Would you object if I read you some of the detail in the file?"

She shook her head.

He opened the folder and spoke. "Adrian Berry. Age twenty-five. Alias Phil Groves. Previously convicted of fraud. Also convicted of receiving stolen goods. Imprisoned for fifteen months. Released after one year. Subsequently charged with threatening behaviour to his mother and father. No evidence forthcoming. Charges dropped. Accused of violence toward then girlfriend. No evidence put forward. Accusation dropped. Known associate of well-known gang leader." He looked at her, waited, then continued while flicking through multiple sheets. "Berry has been under observation for some time, in line with a surveillance operation on his place of work. The workplace is suspected of organising illegal high stakes gambling, operating as a hub for receiving and moving on stolen goods, and lately has come under suspicion as a potential source of illegal drugs." He closed the file, stared at its cover for a while, sighed, and looked at her. "All of which gives you a flavour of the man you unwittingly became involved with. The problem might seem like its over for you, but for us it's most certainly not because we think Berry's gotten himself in deeper waters than before. Recently, a very unusual Victorian diamond brooch was stolen from a mansion in Stirling. It's been identified in the sale shop window of a city pawnbrokers. Groves has been seen regularly meeting with the pawnbroker's brother in pubs and cafes. We also believe he may have begun to look for a source of drugs, mainly so-called uppers or amphetamines as you call the drug."

Alice was motionless, transfixed, horrified, disgusted, and cross with herself. Once again, she asked herself how she could have been so stupid. Looking at a blank wall and speaking in a calm tone, she said, "I have been a complete fool." She looked at Kelly. "But, I have respect for myself and respect for good people I know. And, despite my foolery, I like to think I have a modicum of useful intellect." She looked directly at Carse. "You brought me here for more than reasons to do with privacy or a file that you could easily have memorised and recounted to me while walking alone through hospital grounds. This room." She looked around and waved her hand once through air. "Sometimes a place where people confess when they see no exit." Her eyes returned to Carse. "Not that now though. I have an exit. And I confessed in the café. Perhaps, therefore, rooms like these are also places where people are brought and given the choice of an exit. Or, of helping."

Carse and Kelly were silent.

She lowered her head, her smile bittersweet and voice barely discernible when she said, "I find myself talking myself into a corner. Clever, detective." As she looked straight at Carse, her expression was now immediate. "He was prepared to take what little money I had. Money that barely covered my living expenses. Money I was going to give to my parents. And by God, they need the money. He knew all this."

Kelly interrupted, "But didn't care because he's a…"

"Steady, sergeant." Carse let his hand linger in the air for a moment. And then he fully broke protocol, lowered his hand, and placed it on hers. Gently, he said, "Please forgive us. Kelly and I have been around the block a few times. We forget ourselves sometimes. But people like us never forget the heart of matters. As far as I'm concerned, right now there are no corners in this room. No tricks of the trade. Only three people, trying to make things better."

She took his hand and held it fully. She frowned, glanced at Kelly, then Carse, Kelly again, and let her eyes rest on Carse. "You were men once. And you still are. And… and all we're doing is trying our best to cope with change."

Carse frowned.

She said, "Gentlemen – I'm a connection to the man I once knew as Phil Groves. Perhaps you view him as a link to the bigger things you mentioned. My rejection of Groves has probably in some way forced him to take desperate measures. Hence his name in the newspapers. We're all in this mess." She half-turned and directed her next comment at Carse. "I'll help in whatever way I can."

The senior detective stared at her for a moment. Then nodded and said, "At this stage, I wanted to appraise you of what we know. That said, do you think there's any possibility that you might meet your ex-boyfriend again?"

"You want me to?"

Carse quickly replied, "I simply want you to let us know if you see him again or hear anything about him. Either way, it goes without saying that things we've discussed remain between us."

"I understand."

Kelly pulled the file closer to him. "And that's all there is to it, Miss Walker. *Eyes and ears*, as we say." He pointed at his boss. "You hear anything, he's your man. Get straight on the blower. Or come here and tell the lovely custody sergeant to find him. Me as back-up. And if you can't get hold of either of us, there's three more of us who know everything."

"Yes. The newspapers. The London men." She lowered her gaze. "There's..." God, should she do this? "There's something else you should know."

Carse and Kelly waited.

"It doesn't concern Groves or Berry, or whatever his wretched name is. It's about my job at the hospital."

"We're listening," said Kelly.

Carse was silent, looking at her.

She explained what she normally did in her job, and how she had been temporarily moved to the annexe. "As I mentioned, my parents are in a dreadful state. Money, or lack of, is at the root of everything. I asked for more work. The managing consultant and head matron in the hospital offered me a position in the annexe."

Kelly's next words might have seemed flippant were it not for the fact that his tone was serious and without any trace of being condescending. "Extra hours, new position, more money. What's not to like?"

Alice tried to smile but suspected the action had morphed into a grimace. "That's what I thought. At first. But too much money always comes at a cost. Doesn't it? They paid me more than I should have been paid for standing behind a reception desk. I was a shield, you see. Still am. Stop people seeing what they shouldn't see."

"See what, Alice?" asked Carse.

Her mouth moved but no words came out. Momentarily, she closed her eyes. When she opened them, she said, "Illegal procedures."

Carse said, "I need you to be precise. Spike and I are not physicians, obviously. But we understand illegality very well. Details please, Alice."

"Possibly…No, *probably* abortions."

"What makes you think that?"

She told them everything – more about the conversations she'd had with Hardcastle and Baxter, her front door concierge role and the lack of work involved, her accidental observation of the girl with the blood-stained towel around her waist and how her distress was handled by Midwife Finlay, the manner in which Baxter and Hardcastle had dismissed the incident and her thought that it sounded like they'd co-scripted an explanation, and finally that she'd played along with this explanation yet didn't believe a word of what was coming out of Hardcastle and Baxter's mouths. When she finished speaking, she put her head in her hands.

There was silence in the room for several seconds.

Carse broke the silence. "A lot for us to take in. But take it all in we shall. Let me have a chat with Spike and the rest of my team. Alright? I'm at the end of a phone and Detective Kelly has already explained that if you can't reach me then the entire police force of Glasgow will ensure that one of my team will know that you've reached out. And I know where to find you. Tonight, I want you to go home and rest, tomorrow's another day. I'll get a driver to take us back to the hospital. Then I'll leave you in peace."

Her hand was back on his. "You don't need to come with me. I'll be fine."

Carse shook his head and smiled. "You're not factoring in that I'm a *new boy* in town and love every opportunity I can get to take in the sights of your lovely city. The drive will be invigorating." His expression changed. "Let me get you home safe."

Quickly, she nodded.

Nearly two hours later and on his return to the police station, Carse sat at a desk in the CREW wing.

Kelly walked across the large room and sat opposite him. "What do you think boss?"

Carse drummed fingers on the desk. "We need to confer with the rest of the team. This might be bigger than we thought." His hand became still. "And I'm now wondering if Nurse Walker could be a bit more than your *eyes and ears*."

"How so?"

Carse was thinking fast, trying to piece things together. He was very cognisant that so many of his thoughts were drawn from the realm of possibilities, rather than hard facts. Still, that's what made him a detective. And a highly unusual one at that. "There are two major points of interest in what we've heard from Miss Walker. First, there might be a solid lead in the drugs investigation if she hears anything about Berry that will in turn lead us to Mr Big."

"Come on, boss. She's finished with Berry. And I believe her on that, by the way. She's got too much backbone to give up on her principles. Her parents are a massive factor. Let's be honest. Unlikely she hears anything, let alone something that'll give us a lead."

"Maybe."

Kelly huffed. "I know you too well. Normally you'd be straight in there with a tasking initiative. I noticed, couldn't help but notice, that at no point in our earlier chat did you ask her to initiate contact with Berry aka Groves. Unusual, I thought. But then I had another thought."

"I'm sure you did, detective."

"So, what are you going to do?"

"I've been thinking about little else throughout the drive back here. "I'll speak to her."

"Alright. And what's the other point?"

He wondered when Harper, Bailey, and Airlie were likely to get back to the station. It was so hard to know. Right now, he dearly wished he could be speaking to the whole team. However, he was mightily glad that Kelly was in front of him right now. He was the man who always cut through everything and with pinpoint precision. "If what she says is correct, we may have what could be an abortion factory set up in a hospital."

"Maybe. But that's not our brief. Besides, it's only her word. No real evidence." He grinned. "Like you, she could have a vivid imagination."

"Without imagination we are but one of the dull masses." He sighed. "But I take your point. That said, there's something in this that makes my copper's nose wrinkle."

"Ah! *Copper's nose*! Now you're talking my language. Makes sense."

Carse frowned. "Copper's nose; imagination; sixth sense, probably; all in the same sphere of..." His tone switched back to business-like when he said, "Anyway. I'll get alongside her again. Test the water. Carefully and gently because..."

"She's important to you."

Carse ignored the comment. "When the others are back, and if I'm not around, ban them from going anywhere until we've had a CREW briefing." He smiled. "Lock them in here if you have to."

"Got it. Thing that's still confusing me, though, is why an abortion factory has piqued your interest. It's a real bag of nails, for sure. Bloody awful, if true, but we've got our work cut out on the drugs case. Shouldn't others be looking into abortions?"

"Others are incompetent or corrupt or both!" snapped Carse. It was an outburst that was completely out of character. He composed himself. "Copper's nose, remember?" He leaned forward. "And my imagination. Here's a thing. Money, money, money. Binds so many things together, doesn't it? Damn stuff. And it feeds itself on more money. So, what if the high-end of the Glasgow drugs scene is linked to an abortions factory? Both are money-making machines. Both prop each other up in times of need. And for that to happen, here's the deal – one person, just one person, has his fingers in both pies."

"Two separate cases become one?"

Carse nodded. "The biggest one of all. Drugs and child murder."

CHAPTER SEVENTEEN

When Arthur Burns returned to Glasgow from his visit to Manchester, he telephoned Charlie Palmer. "I've some information that you might not yet know."

The response he received was unexpected, "Clown! Why did you put your mob on the streets? I told you no publicity, low-key, scandal free. What the hell were you thinking?" The line was quiet for a few seconds. "Starting to wonder if you're the right guy to handle the whole outfit when I step back."

"Christ, Charlie. They were up and away before I could get the word out. It won't happen again."

"It had fucking better not or you're looking for a new occupation sunbeam. Now, what's so new that you had to call me up to tell me?"

Burns told him about his meeting with McEwan and her boast that she knew big changes were coming to Glasgow, He repeated what she'd said about infrastructure, housing, highways, and the opportunities they'd bring.

There was no immediate answer, and for a moment or two Burns thought the line had gone dead.

Then Palmer screamed down the line, "What the fuck are you talking about? Fuck it. Never mind. Get yourself to my office now. Back door. I want to hear it all."

Burns hung up. He knew what McEwan had said to him might be explosive. And yet, Palmer's idiotic outburst said so much about the man who was supposed to be his boss. He decided to tell Palmer as little as he thought he could get away with.

Fifty minutes later, he was in Palmer's office.

Palmer had the look of a prize fighter whose wife had just been disparaged by a bunch of drunken street yobs. "Right, what have you been told and who the fuck is this McEwan bird?"

Burns knew that was he was about to say would further inflame the situation, and part of him found that absurdly funny. "She's a brothel keeper who uses our people to provide protection for her businesses."

"Oh great! A bloody brothel keeper." With no attempt to hide the sarcasm in his voice, he asked, "And this brothel keeper has suddenly got inside track on what makes my city tick?"

For some reason, the more Palmer was losing control the calmer Burns felt. "She *does* want to expand her business. That's why she wanted to meet. She said that if we worked with her, she'd count us in."

"Cheeky fucking cow. What's her background?"

"She's got several properties she uses for different purposes. Initially I thought it was just drinking dens and prostitution. Turns out it's way more than that. She has a track record in Liverpool and Manchester and she's not just flogging booze and whores. Where she makes her real money is in gang running, organised theft, and illegal abortions."

"Illegal abortions?" Palmer seemed to be calming down and now had a puzzled look on his face. "How do you know all this?"

"Had a chat with a pal of mine in Manchester.".."

"Trusted pal?"

"Damn right."

"Okay. Where does McEwan live?"

Burns wondered if the cogs in Palmer's brain were now whirring. That was the thing about his boss – typically a bull in a china shop when confronted with something that didn't conform to his way of things; but he didn't get to be where he was by being completely blinkered. "It appears she has a day job as some kind of teacher or trainer of nurses and has a place at the hospital out on the Great Western Road."

"That's ridiculous."

"Why?"

"She's supposed to be a hot shot organiser from England who plans to take advantage of the city's opportunities, and yet she currently works as a nurse and lives in a hospital?"

"Yeah. Operating under the radar, I guess. I know it's true, though. Got it from the estate agent who approached me on her behalf to provide her flats' protection."

Palmer pushed Burns for all he knew - what the woman's plans were, where she got her information from, what exactly she did in Manchester and Liverpool, and

188

whether she was a threat or just a crank who wanted to be seen to be big time. When he had finished grilling Burns, he warned him not to say anything about any of this to anyone.

After Burns had left, Palmer sat at his desk, deep in thought and expertly twirling a pen in his otherwise brutish hand. He knew Burns had his own side projects and agendas going on and therefore couldn't fully be trusted. But that was the deal with all his men. Palmer ran the show on the big-picture stuff but let his gangsters run their smaller fiefdoms with relatively zero interference from him. Unless their operations interfered with his activities and plans. And yet Burns stood out from the others because he wasn't short-term greedy. Like Palmer, he saw the necessity to expand and invest in new opportunities and not always expect immediate returns. That's why Palmer had selected him to manage day-to-day operations within his ever-growing empire. The risk in this type of ascension was obvious and precedented throughout history – a man in Burns' new position could spot an opportunity to get rid of his boss and fully take over. No doubt, Burns was smart and capable. And ambitious. To that extent, he needed to keep a vigilant and cautious eye on him. However, Burns knew that at the high-end he lacked Palmer's contacts. And that was the leverage the gang boss had over him. For now. And providing this new character McEwan didn't put ideas into his head. He wasn't particularly worried about that. Burns was old school. No way was he going to work for a nurse, and a female one at that. But he was interested to note the obvious excitement in Burns' voice when he relayed what McEwan had said. Problem was that the city opportunities she'd spoken about weren't news to him. Some of it was information that was privy to only a select few in the City Council. All of it was known to the four who attended the Dunure planning meeting.

And that meant there was a leak from someone in the Dunure conspiracy.

Not Assistant Chief Constable Harrison. He was in too deep with Palmer and knew that he'd serve a very long time in prison if some of their dealings were made public.

And not Woodhouse, the Lord Provost. He was an elected official, and the press would have a field day if they found out he had dealings with a brothel keeper.

Plus, Harrison and Woodhouse didn't have an obvious connection to the hospital where McEwan worked.

Baxter did.

And that meant Baxter was the leak.

Palmer placed the pen down and opened a small wooden box that had once contained bullets. From inside, he withdrew a cigar that had been part of a shipment that had recently arrived in the nearby docks. He rotated the cigar between thumb and forefinger while continuing to think. If the assistant chief constable and the lord provost got wind that one of Palmer's men was being courted by a brothel keeper who was getting her information from Baxter, then all the good was coming out of the four-person assembly would be undone. The officials Harrison and Woodhouse would run a mile. Their departure would be unacceptable, given their importance. Baxter was a different matter. He was simply a respectable face. There were others like him. He could be easily replaced. And replaced by someone who knew how to keep their mouth shut.

He struck a match on the surface of the desk, looked at the flame, lit the cigar, inhaled deep, blew out smoke, and returned his gaze to the flame. Though he'd need to decide how it should be done, he knew what had to happen. Baxter and McEwan had to be silenced.

He placed his fist around the flame and squeezed tight.

Alice was in a staff meeting in a conference room in the main hospital when she was called for by the senior registrar. She immediately thought it was connected to the visits of the police, and that thought seemed confirmed when the senior registrar ushered her into his office where a uniformed policewoman was waiting.

In soft sympathetic tones the registrar said, "Sit down please, Alice. I'm sorry, I'm afraid I have very bad news for you."

She had the briefest of moments of feeling utterly stunned. Then it was as if her life's backstory rushed her brain and was squeezed until the juice of irrelevant memories were gone and all that were left were two or three thoughts that no doubt – no doubt whatsoever – had to be the shortlist contenders for why she was being asked to sit down by a man who normally barely gave her the time of day. There was no other possible reaction. Not *bad news*, such as she had to move out of her nurse accommodation or even that she was being sacked. Instead, there was the dreaded insertion of the word '*very*'. That word changed everything. Her eyes swivelled from the registrar to the policeman and back. Both didn't seem real.

The registrar did not sit. With a sober yet nervous expression, he glanced at the police officer then fixed his bespectacled eyes on Alice. "I am sorry to have to tell you that there has been a dreadful fire overnight at your parents' home address. Your father is very seriously ill. He has been taken to the royal infirmary where he is in intensive care."

"Fire? Father?" Her words felt like they were leaking out of her mouth, as if she had no choice in the matter. "Mother?"

The police officer said, "I'm so very sorry. Your mother is dead."

Alice let out a harrowing scream. "No, no, no!"

The policewoman moved across to comfort Alice, held her hand, and repeated how very sorry she was to give out such horrific news.

The registrar went to the door and called into the corridor, "A nurse, please. And sweet tea and water."

Alice's hands were shaking violently as she rocked back and forth in her seat, her eyes clenched tight. She wailed, "No. Not true. Can't be. Dear God. Please. Not true. Just this one time. Please. Not true."

The registrar stood to one side as another nurse entered the room and sat next to Alice and whispered words that Alice was vaguely aware of but couldn't decipher. The policewoman still held her hand. The nurse held her other hand.

The policewoman's words suddenly became distinct and comprehendible, as if a radio dial had been minutely adjusted to block out static and other interference and enable a clear airwave. "It's too early to be certain. The fire brigade is still assessing the cause but from their first estimates it appears a fire broke out in the hall of your parents' flat. The brigade says the fire took hold quickly and smoke engulfed the flat in a very short time."

The nurse said quietly, "We're here."

From across the room, the registrar said, "Our thoughts are with you, Alice."

Alice dropped her head, tears running down her face and cascading onto the scrubbed floor. "My father? Seriously ill? *Seriously*? Another bad word."

The registrar took possession of drinks that were handed to him at the door and went to the small group. "We don't yet have up-to-the-minute news on his condition. I'm in direct communication with the hospital where he's been taken. They've been very helpful. We're making arrangements for you to go to him."

Alice took the mug of tea that was handed to her. But the shakes were so bad that hot liquid splashed over the floor.

The nurse took the mug from her and said, "Tea can wait. Let's get you to the hospital so you can see your Dad."

In the Royal Infirmary, Alice was shown along corridors to an area of high activity which she knew from signage was the intensive care section. The nurse from her own hospital accompanied her there and then told Alice that she was in good hands and would not be alone. After the nurse left to attend to her other duties, Alice waited in the corridor until a doctor approached and asked her to follow him to a small room off the main passageway.

"How is he, doctor?" she asked in a wavering, frightened voice.

"His chances are slim, I'm afraid. The next twenty-four hours will be decisive. He suffered massive smoke inhalation. And it's notable that his general condition is not very robust."

She nodded slowly. "He's had respiratory issues for some years, and recently was diagnosed with Alzheimer's disease."

"We know. We'll do our very best to get him through this, but it would be wrong of me to give you false hopes. I'm sorry."

"*False hopes*," she echoed. "False?" She frowned, shook her head again to try to shake out her muddled thoughts, cleared her throat, and summoned some kind of memory of what she sounded like when in control. "Yes. I know you will do everything you can. I'm very grateful for your help, doctor."

He looked at her for a moment, no doubt assessing her condition. "We'll keep you updated on his condition." He handed her a slip of paper. "Call this number. It's the line into the intensive care unit."

"Thank you. Thank you so much." She unnecessarily folded the paper into a small square before secreting it into her pocket. "My Mum… mother…"

"She is elsewhere. Your hospital is taking care of matters. The registrar is the person to liaise with."

She left the doctor's room and walked down the corridor, feeling like the walls and floor and ceiling were shifting. Her legs buckled. She grabbed the handle of a nearby medical trolley and nearly spilled its contents as she steadied herself. No one came to her. Perhaps she was alone? Or maybe she wasn't but so what if yet one more person in this place had lost their footing or become incapacitated with complete and utter grief?

She'd experienced deaths in her work as a nurse, but never in her personal life. Presumably, this is how it should be. The dislocation from reality. Dreamlike state. Arms and legs tied to string and moving at the whim of a spiteful child puppeteer. Crazy thoughts. Snapshot memories. Her gut churning. Taste of blood. Taste of vomit. Smell of bleach and rot. Needles in her eyes and pliers yanking at her teeth. And the regrets that wanted to take the real Alice back in time and order her to do things differently.

She stood for a moment, gripping the trolley, letting its clammy metal rail send a message to her brain that she was here. This was happening. Everything was real. Even though the reality was twisted and horrific. She breathed slowly and deeply - like the mums did during contractions, like she did when she was a kid and preparing for a race in school sports, like she did when she was asked out on her first date.

She had to move.

Make it to the end of the corridor.

Keep walking.

Get the bus.

Go home.

Somehow, she did all that. Had to. Had to be strong for her father.

The following morning the registrar came to her accommodation and told her that her father had died during the night.

The next days passed in a blur for Alice, and it was sometime after the joint funerals before she felt she was able to face the world. A world vastly changed.

The report on the fire confirmed the early thinking that it had started in the hallway, and it was caused by faulty electrical wiring. The report added that an earlier fire safety inspection had instructed the property owner to immediately replace unsafe wiring.

On the day of her mother's death, and when faulty wiring was one possible explanation for the fire, one of the thousands of chaotic thoughts she'd had was what she should say to dear Frances McEwan, given her flatmate had gone out of her way to save her parents after eviction. Frances would be devastated to know that she'd unwittingly helped secure an unsafe place for Alice's parents. The report today changed everything because it named the property owner. And that owner's name was Frances McEwan.

Carse was oblivious to Alice's tragedy. In the CREW room, his team were buzzing with expectancy as they gathered around a table. "Ok gentlemen, keep the noise down. Our fellow lodgers might think we're on to something," cautioned Carse with a smile. "We're heading in the right direction with our efforts so far, but no need to advertise it, not yet at least. Let's start first with progress on identifying the leaks." He passed copies of an organisation diagram to each. "There has been a total of eight raids against suspected criminal activities in the past six months, only two of which have been successful. And those successes resulted in nothing more than recovery of low-value stolen goods, mainly clothing. The others, the unsuccessful ones, were aimed at high-value consignments of spirits and cigarettes, stolen cash, and drugs. The diagram shows the areas, the police teams, and the planners involved in all raids." He put his finger on a wall map of Glasgow. "The successful raids were planned and carried out by teams in the west of the city, and near the airport. They appear to have been rapid, ad hoc raids, on the back of word from informants." He moved his finger. "The unsuccessful were more deliberately planned and aimed at premises in the north and south of the city. The substantial amount of manpower required for some of these had to be agreed at a high level, and this brought in more people than perhaps needed to know." He moved into the centre of the room, looked at his men, and said, "We've unearthed the high-level common factors that link all raids. Those factors are three names. Three men. *Very important* men. One of them could very possibly be the source of leaks. This is a far cry from having the proof to bring anyone down, but it is a move forward. We keep on."

The team exchanged looks but said nothing.

"Now. Drugs. Specifically, amphetamines. Our last update gave us some optimism. The latest objective is closing in on the street supplier. Jake, please."

Airlie briefly repeated detail about the trawl he and Bailey had undertaken which resulted in the arrest of the pushers in the disused church. "When interviewed, the two in custody have sought to having their charges reduced by admitting their guilt and informing on their source. The name they both independently gave me and Gus was Sammy Quigley," He ended with a grin.

Carse was pleased. "Well done you two, but we're not out of the woods yet. We'll have to prove it, and we still need to find where the drugs originate from. Anything new Johnny?"

Inspector Harper walked the team through the detailed search he and his men were carrying out. At two distribution centres there were notable discrepancies between paper inventories and actual stocks for a variety of items. These items included drugs, but not amphetamines. "The control of items is slipshod. There are a vast number of SKUs to house and record and so…"

"Whoa, Johnny," Bailey called out. What the blazes is an SKU?"

"Sorry gents. Stock keeping units. Things on the inventory list."

"Oh right. We knew that lads, didn't we," Bailey laughed.

Harper continued, "So, the task is not difficult, but is time consuming. We can't rule out the source being a distribution centre, nor can we say it isn't somewhere else. The work continues."

Carse thanked the team. "Gus, Jake - I want you now to split your time between pursuing evidence against Quigley and helping Johnny and Spike in the search for the amphetamine sources." He continued, "As Spike knows, I've interviewed a nurse who had a relationship with a villain linked to Quigley. She agreed to help further if she can. That interview brought out another possible crime scenario that I want to share with you." He briefed the team on the conversations he and Kelly had with Alice Walker, her links with Groves aka Berry, and her suspicions of abortions in the hospital annexe.

"Bloody hell boss." It was very rare for Airlie to look shocked by something, but he had such an expression on his face right now. "Are you serious?"

Harper added, "Serious stuff if true. Murder in anyone's book today." The seasoned investigator frowned. "Any real evidence?"

Carse shook his head. "No, but something's telling me this should be followed up. I raise it because it's not in our current brief. That said, I think we should be all over it."

Bailey argued that any attention taken away from their current task could jeopardise their objective. Harper said nothing. Kelly backed Carse and reminded the team that real progress had been made on the drugs front. Airlie was the last team member to contribute. "I reckon we drive ahead on the drugs brief and probe the abortion suspicions at the same time. Can't see one getting in the way of the other."

It's what Carse wanted to hear, but nevertheless he asked, "How so?"

"You've said the nurse will help. If she's right, she can test her suspicions with our aid. We're searching for illegal drugs. We've an authorised brief to go where we think we need to. Under the guise of searching for illegal drug distribution, we could raid the annexe when the nurse tells us there's an abortion taking place. If we find nothing, we're just doing our job. If we find something, it's something we unearthed during our investigations."

"That's more than a bit iffy Jake," Harper said.

"So is illegal abortion," Airlie countered.

The team threw the suggestion back and forth, some supporting, some testing, none outright against. Finally, Carse asked for a team view. He got consensus.

Carse said, "This will need full detailed planning, a fall-back plan, outside support if needed, a painstaking walk-through, individual roles and responsibilities, and a communication plan which Nurse Walker will need to trigger."

"What if she pulls out?" asked Bailey.

"Then the deal is off. But she won't back out." Carse looked at Kelly. "Spike - get the plans of the annexe and the surrounding area. It would be invaluable if we built a scale model."

"Anything else boss?" asked a bemused Kelly.

"Yes. Gus and Jake - sketch a walkthrough of approach, positions, alarm, entry, take down, and exit. I'll talk to Miss Walker and take her through the help we can give her." He was about to tell his men to set to work, but hesitated. "Gentleman – there's something else I wanted to share with you. Two things. One, a suspicion; the other rather more a personal observation. The suspicion, and I must stress it's only a thought, is predicated by a question. What if money made from illegal abortions is linked to drugs being stolen from hospitals? If that's the situation, we're dealing with a senior criminal with fingers in both pies. The cases are not only linked. They are in fact one case. And..." he hesitated, because what he was about to say to these robust men was something from the heart and not something he'd typically share with such officers, "my personal observation." He looked at each of them, made a decision, and continued. "Manufacture, theft, shipment, and widespread distribution of illegal drugs is one thing. One *major* organised crime thing. In itself, it justifies us being here and tearing up this city. But now we have something else – the possibility that there is a fixed location whose sole purpose is to systematically murder unborn children." He looked at Bailey. Then Harper. Then Kelly. Then Airlie. "Some of you liberated places like that, at the back end of matters. All of us mopped up the pieces and made sure that the devils responsible were hanged, drawn and quartered. I'm guessing we all thought we'd never see the like of such abominations again. But people are people and devils continue to walk amongst us. Some may be in an annexe in a hospital in Glasgow. We need to go in there. Just like we did in another place in April '45. But, and there is a but, when it comes to horror – true horror – you've faced up to more than any man should have to confront. As a result, it will not be a slur on any of your names and careers if you decide to walk away from the annexe case. I, of all people, will respect that decision." He waited.

No one spoke.

Then Harper said, "And with the greatest of respect to you, Norrie, it would be impossible for me to walk away."

"Damn right, me an' all," said Kelly.

Bailey laughed, "Fucking devils. Here we go again." His expression turned cold as he stared intently at his boss. "And up and fuckin' at 'em."

Airlie looked at Carse. "You see. We have to. No matter what it does to us." That's all he said. It was all he needed to say.

Alice had taken time off work to arrange her parents' funerals, register their deaths and complete the seemingly endless tasks associated with life's final chores. Frances McEwan was away from the hospital base for the entire time. As was often the case, she was probably visiting another medical centre and training staff. Probably. Alice didn't know what to think anymore.

Alice was in her accommodation when the door opened.

It was McEwan. She looked like she was aghast as she closed the door behind her and went up to her flatmate. "I've only just heard. Been off the grounds, you see. Just got back. Oh, Alice." She placed her hands on Alice's arms. "I'm just so very sorry. So very sorry."

Alice stepped back and out of McEwan's embrace. "Not sorry enough to have ensured that the flat they lived in was safe! Not sorry enough to tell me that the property was yours and it had fire risks. Why did you tell me it belonged to a friend? I trusted you. Believed you. How could you?"

McEwan said nothing.

"If you had had the repairs attended to, my parents would still be alive!" Alice spat out.

McEwan broke eye contact, looking left and right, clearly trying to think fast. Her voice was imploring when she said, "This... this is not what you think. Look, I know... Well, this is a horrible time." She looked at Alice. "I'd only purchased the property the previous week. From a friend. Sort of a friend. That'll change. But there was no time to have the repairs carried out before they moved in. The work was scheduled for next month, and you had a desperate need for a rapid move for your folks. I did this to help you out. Remember?"

"Or make some quick cash."

"Alice!"

Alice huffed and looked at her coldly. "What? You're offended by that comment? Forgive me, but I'm offended that my parents were put into a flat by someone I trusted to make them safe. Least ways, it never occurred to me that you would overlook that they'd be spending a month in an unrepaired flat that was in fact a death trap."

McEwan sat in a chair, held her head in her hands, and stared at the floor. Quietly, she said, "I have to... think this through. Because you're right. Damn friend I bought it off. Still my fault, though. Knew repairs were delayed by a few weeks. Not my decision." She looked at Alice, her eyes wet and cheeks flushed. "I thought it would be alright. Chances of anything happening almost zero. And... and you were so desperate. I wanted... wanted to make you happy. Wanted your parents to be secure." Her head slumped again and she stamped the floor as she said, "Stupid, stupid, stupid!"

Alice watched her. "Did you not have any other flats?"

"No!" She was evidently frustrated as she threw her arms up and exclaimed, "And if I knew of anyone else who had one that was... better, I'd have told you. Had a word with them. Sorted things. Please. This wasn't anything to do with money. It was all to do with..."

"My happiness." Alice walked to a window and looked out, across the hospital grounds and beyond. She looked back at McEwan. "I know that you tried to help. I do know."

CHAPTER EIGHTEEN

In a private dining room in the University of Glasgow, the four members of the Dunure group met after a short supper and reviewed the progress of their plans. Charlie Palmer confirmed he had set up the holding company named as West Coast Holdings and registered himself as secretary and director. A launch budget was agreed, and all verified their own capital commitment, after which the meeting broke up. As they were leaving, Charlie Palmer asked for a word with Crawford Baxter, and they stayed behind in the dining room.

"One of the worries I have about our venture is the absolute need for secrecy. Don't you feel the same?" asked Palmer.

Baxter looked impatient. "Of course, its paramount."

"Do you think the others are security minded enough?"

"I certainly hope so, don't you? Why do you ask that?"

"If the information we have gets out it will completely ruin me. And I've worked my backside off for too long to fail at this. I just want to feel confident that all of us have this nailed down tightly and no leaks."

All trace of impatience in Baxter's face was gone, replaced by a sudden pale visage. He stuttered, "Do you think I, or any of us, would give out that knowledge?"

Palmer shrugged, "I might be being a bit paranoid, but I have a worry that there might be a leak."

"Leak? How? Why? And what are you going to do?"

"How? People talk, or nick stuff they shouldn't. Why? I find money or being shit scared for their own skin are the usual reasons. And as for the *what to do* bit," his voice sank to a whisper, "I for one would trace the leak and end the involvement of that individual. Both with the project, and with life."

Baxter stepped back and shook his head in disbelief. "Why are you telling me this? Forget…" he held up a hand. "Forget I asked. I *know* why you're telling me. And I can assure you I'd never, ever, consider giving out our secrets. For God's sake – like all of us, I've got too much to lose."

Palmer smiled, half-turned, and made ready to leave. "All about weighing up pros and cons, isn't it? People who've got a lot to lose also have to consider if they've got even more to gain by opening their gobs. Catch you soon, *sunshine*."

As he walked away, Palmer felt sure that he had his man. He would instruct Burns and his men to sort that out.

Baxter walked from the Dunure Group meeting to his flat, his mind reeling from what Palmer had said. Did he know what he was getting himself into? Was it too late to drop out? Could he really continue with this charade of non-executive director in a business he felt was illegal? He didn't know Palmer very well. Baxter's introduction to the business project had been through the Lord Provost, Woodhouse, as a thank you for Baxter's help in procuring an abortion for his granddaughter. And that was the first time he'd even heard of Palmer, let alone met the man. Still now he didn't know much about the chap beyond he was a businessman and freemason. And Palmer's comments weren't the only thing troubling him. In many respects, his biggest worry was McEwan. She was ramping up the activities of the annexe and that meant that any form of police intervention would most likely bring with it a life sentence in prison for anyone involved in illegal abortions. So much rested on McEwan, but could she be trusted? During his last meeting with her, he felt she was getting far too big for her boots, and he loathed the way she spoke to him. Did she care that the Dunure information he'd given her might somehow have got Palmer on his case? Once again, he wondered why he'd felt the need to boast to her. He knew the answer. He'd done so out of fear.

The next morning, Baxter was in his annexe office when he received a phone call from a police officer who told him that he was carrying out routine checks on hospital staff who had control of drugs. The officer said that he'd like to talk to Baxter in person and wondered if it was possible that they could have a chat in his hospital office in an hour. Baxter agreed and waited for the visit, while in a state of panic.

When that hour was up, the police officer was shown into Baxter's office and introduced himself as

Sergeant Angus Bailey. The cop was wearing everyday street clothes, rather than smarter attire.

The look surprised and confused Baxter.

"Good morning, Mr Baxter," Bailey said while showing Baxter his warrant card. "No doubt you've been alerted to the flood of drugs on the streets. Papers are full of the detail." He smiled while shaking his head. "Can't say your local rags are making the job of blokes like me any easier." His smile remained but his unblinking stare was intense. "Never mind. There are still some lines of enquiry that we can keep away from the noses of reporters. That's why I'm here. I'm working with colleagues to interview medical staff in positions of control of drugs. Lots of staff. You're one of them, I'm told. So, a quick routine chat with you, if that's alright? Quick because I've got quite some medical staff list to get through today. And that means that you'll have to forgive me for diving straight in. Have you experienced any problems controlling the drugs in this place?"

"Please sit down, sergeant. Would you like some tea or coffee?" Baxter's voice was a little strained.

Bailey sat and said, "As I say, on the clock. Suspect it won't be until teatime until I get my hands around a nice brew." He raised his eyebrows. "Control of drugs? Also, what kind of drugs?"

Baxter replied, "There are a wide range of drugs here. Do you have anything you particularly wish to know about?"

"I'd like to know the process for the receipt, distribution and recording of drugs issued. Is there a logbook or something like that?"

"There is a daily drug register,"

"May I see it please." Bailey knew he was pushing things a bit. He didn't care.

"Just a moment." Baxter went to a metal cabinet fixed to a wall, unlocked it, took out a book, returned, and handed Bailey a thick hard-backed register.

Bailey riffled through the log. It was current, entries having been made that morning. "Do you dispense or prescribe amphetamines regularly?"

Baxter felt confident to answer, "Yes, I do. Many of my patients are pre-natal and suffering psychological alterations that are causing them distress. Amphetamine is effective in countering depression." His voice grew deeper as he added in an authoritative tone, "All perfectly legal and above board. If Scottish police, or indeed police in London, have a problem with that I suggest you take it up with the National Health Service and the highly respected body of medical science that it relies on."

Bailey waved his hand. "Do I look like a man who's got a minute to spare to have that kind of chinwag? Anyway, we don't have a problem with that. It's the stuff that goes missing from hospitals that bothers us. And right now, top of the list are amphetamines. They're causing us no end of problems on the streets. Means I wouldn't mind knowing if any *scientifically approved* amphetamines have gone missing from your annexe wing?"

"Missing? What do you mean?"

"When you come to reconcile what you had, against what you have prescribed, are there any discrepancies?"

He could feel a small tic start in the corner of his mouth and placed a hand to cover the affected area. "No. None."

Bailey asked the consultant to walk him through the process of how the drugs under his control were ordered, by whom, and how they were received and stored. Baxter answered him fully before explaining to him how a drug was typically issued to a patient.

Bailey took notes throughout the meeting, thanked Baxter for his help, apologised for taking up his time, smiled as he said good-bye, and left.

It took Crawford Baxter the rest of the day to regain his composure. He called McEwan and asked for an early off-site meeting with her. His nerve was cracking.

They met in a property McEwan had recently bought close to the main Great Western Road. Baxter was impressed when she let him into the flat which was as luxurious as his own flat. He wondered what McEwan used it for, given he knew she didn't live there. He was brought back to Earth by McEwan asking, "What the hell do you want that needs an urgent meeting like this?"

He wondered if she'd guide him to a seat in the lounge, but so far, she seemed to want to get this over with and stayed in the hallway. He answered, "I'm worried about the information I gave you on the future opportunities in the city," For some reason her suddenly felt like a naughty schoolboy who'd told tales about his pals. "I shouldn't have done that. It was highly confidential material. And it came from people I've come to think of as friends."

"*Friends*, ha!" She chuckled but her look was antagonistic. "You'll secretly think you're smarter than them. They'll secretly think you're a gullible fool who might be able to tell one body part from another but doesn't have a clue how to work business angles. You'll all have your private opinions about each other. And given money's your common denominator, I guarantee none of you will be friends." She looked quizzical, though her eyes suggested she was anything but puzzled. "Are you worried what I will do with the information?"

"Well, if it fell into unscrupulous hands who knows what could happen."

"Unscrupulous hands?" She held up her own. "Like these?" Her expression was now challenging.

So much so that he suddenly had an urge to leave. "Wrong choice of word. I meant…"

"Whatever you meant you're clearly now unsettled. Maybe that's the surgeon in you? Realising you're having to rely on someone else to make the incision. Is that what's happening? Loss of control and unwarranted faith in others?"

"All I'm saying is that I regret saying what I did. It's happened and I realise there's no turning the clock back. However, what I previously let slip is all I can do to help on this matter. Doesn't affect our other arrangement. But on this one I'll need to keep my mouth shut going forward."

"No."

The blunt nature of her response added to the sense that it was a mistake to come here. "I... Look, if you plan to use it, at least let me know how, so I can be prepared for any questions that come my way."

"Sounds like your associates have doubts on your reliability."

He tried to calm his breathing. "They are naturally concerned that confidences are maintained."

"That's your problem. You just keep passing me the goods and all will be well. Understand?"

Anger now accompanied his sense of unease and nervousness. "It's inappropriate for me to be spoken to in this..."

"Things change though, don't they?" she said in a drawling tone. "Once upon a time you were the important man. But thing is, there's always someone else out there who might be more important." She moved so close to him that her mouth was now only centimetres from his. In a deliberately husky and sexy voice, she said, "And guess what? That person is me." She laughed as she took one step back and clapped her hands. "Events are already in train. Unstoppable. You pass me juicy information. I do something with that. I make money. And that means you make money. It's as simple as that. So, no. You won't be coming to me, in places like this, now or at any time in the future, to tell me that, going forward, you'll need to keep your fucking mouth shut." She looked away and put her fake quizzical expression back on. "Actually, that could happen. And your mouth could stay shut." She looked straight at him, her eyes black. "People I know could help that happen. Put your head in a box. Mouth shut."

His heart raced fast, breathing erratic, and his stomach felt like something very strong was gripping it hard. He had to deescalate this. Not least because the woman standing in front of him had transformed into something else altogether. And he believed every word of her threat. He sucked in air, nodded, and said, "You might not be surprised to learn that I value my head. And you've given me clarity on your position. All I ask is that, going forward, we tread delicately so that my position with my business associates isn't compromised. If we don't protect my access to their information, then we lose that information. Would you agree?"

She looked like she was in reluctant agreement when she huffed, nodded once, and said, "That's the only thing you've said that makes sense."

He tried not to sound relieved when he said, "One other thing I wanted to discuss. Hardcastle and I have independently spoken to Nurse Walker to quell any fears she had over annexe operations. The two-pronged tactic seemed to work. Walker accepted the explanation and," he smiled while shaking his head, "the brazen young thing even said she'd be happy to continue the private work providing I raise her pay. I'll do that, though not by much."

She waved her hand impatiently back and forth through air. "Yes, yes, all good with Alice Walker. But Hardcastle - you say she spoke to Alice independently? What did Hardcastle say?"

"It was no different from my explanation."

"How do you know?"

"I briefed the matron, and she took notes as I did so."

Her brow was furrowed. "Is there any way that Hardcastle could know the explanations came from me and that you and I have our connection?"

"No. As far as Hardcastle's concerned, she and I run the annexe operation. The explanations were mine as far as she knows."

"As she ever heard of me, even under other circumstances?"

He shrugged. "I can't be sure, but certainly she's never mentioned your name to me. Nor have I overheard her mentioning your name. It's possible she has some passing professional awareness of you. Most likely not, though. You move around a lot. Not as if you work in the wing next door. But even if she did see you come into the annexe, so what? Just one of the dozens if not hundreds of changing nurse faces that come and go."

"Good. Now, given *Fuck-Up* Finlay's the reason why we've had to play Walker and Hardcastle, what news on Finlay's replacement?"

"The name you put forward will come in to see me when she arrives from England, but she can only stay in Glasgow for a month."

"I'll arrange an extension, if need be." She grabbed her coat. "Have you tightened up on the procedures at the annexe yet?"

214

For a brief moment, he wondered which procedure she was referring to. No way was he going to mention the visit from DS Bailey this morning and his questions about missing drugs. He realised she was referring to Finlay and the young woman in her care. "I have. The last episode can't happen again."

"It had better not. Now, I'm busy and need to go. Anything else?"

He recalled the man who'd showed him ID belonging to the Metropolitan Police, the newspaper report that said an elite squad from London was in town, and the look on the detective's face that superficially suggested amiability but covered something else altogether. "Nothing else."

Baxter chose to walk home so that he had time to think. The exercise helped in some ways, but not with his mind. That was still in turmoil. He loathed McEwan and if he could be rid of her his problems would vanish. He knew her for the venomous and vindictive woman she was, and the hold she had over him gave her licence to do as she pleased. However, he also had two other huge problems. Namely Charlie Palmer and Sergeant Bailey. If Palmer discovered he was disclosing information to McEwan, there was every possibility that Palmer would be joining the queue to put Baxter's head in a box. If the detective thought he was lying to him about his lack of knowledge of how drugs could go missing, the detective might probe further. And if that happened, then he'd be standing on the doorstep of the abortion factory.

He walked the streets for hours, lost in his misery.

When he arrived home his desolation was further deepened by sight of a crop haired, heavily built youth waiting at the door of his flat.

The young man went right up to him and placed in hand firmly on Baxter's upper arm. "A message for you from Mr Palmer. No leaks, if you want to see your pension," the youth whispered.

God almighty. This confirmed that Palmer was way more than just a legitimate businessman. But he didn't know what to say to the ruffian other than, "Understood." He opened his front door, entered the luxury apartment, and closed and locked the door behind him.

He poured himself a stiff drink and slumped into an armchair while rubbing his temples. Think, think, think, he told himself. He sipped his drink while absent-mindedly staring at one of the many bookshelves containing modern and old volumes about medical science. These were books he'd read as a student and still referred to as a qualified doctor. And as a student, he'd quickly realised that to be a successful doctor one didn't need to have an inclination towards science; instead, what was of paramount importance was a razor-sharp logical brain that could solve problems. And that's what he needed to do now. Get the measure of things and solve problems. And to do that, as with being a doctor, he needed to strip everything down so that each part was easily identifiable and therefore malleable. He nodded. Like all good physicians, he needed a working hypothesis. Without that, he was doomed to a state of submissive inactivity. So, who were his working parts and how should he move them? He decided to construct shorthand labels for each. Even if those labels weren't wholly accurate, they'd do for now and for the most part would be accurate enough for him to make the right decision.

Walker – naïve, no threat, and motivation nothing more than to make a few more measly pounds, shillings, and pence.

Hardcastle – bitter woman yet completely at Baxter's mercy.

Scottish police – overstretched, or corrupt, or incompetent, and most under the control of Assistant Chief Constable Martin Harrison.

Bailey and London colleagues – a huge problem, but only if they got close to the annexe.

McEwan - deranged yet clever and utterly calculating, though a new person on the block compared to the established Glasgow players.

Palmer – a man who sat at the top table of the Dunure Group and who Baxter was now convinced was some kind of gang lord.

Baxter imagined they were chess pieces on a board, waiting to be moved by his hand. And he had to decide which one posed the biggest immediate threat to him. The answer was now obvious.

Palmer.

He resolved to tell McEwan nothing more of value that came out of the Dunure Group plans. This would require careful management on his part because she'd still require something. He'd just have to make sure that *something* was information that could have come from elsewhere. Of paramount importance was Palmer realising that secret information wasn't leaving the Group. And there was every possibility that McEwan would lose interest in Baxter's association with the Group once the money really started flowing in from the annexe operation. And flow it would because he was already required to arrange procedures for three more clients who were in need of the annexe private services.

And that thought reminded him of his last job of the day.

He needed to put his staff on standby for the first of those clients.

A client who was going to have an abortion.

Whether she wanted one or not.

He reached for his diary and moved the adjacent telephone closer to him as his finger moved down his list of annexe staff and their contact details.

And within that list there were names that had a red asterisk next to their names.

They were the ones that comprised the inner circle.

The individuals that ensured the smooth running of the death factory.

His finger stopped on Alice Walker.

He picked up the phone.

CHAPTER NINETEEN

Carse knew nothing of the bereavement Alice had suffered and was jolted to find she was on compassionate leave when he'd tried to contact her. He left a message for her to call him if she could. He heard nothing for days, before she got in touch and told him what had happened.

He drove to the hospital after arranging to see Alice. In the same nearby café where they'd met before, they spoke for a while, with the detective offering his sincere sympathies and any help from him that she may need "This must be the most distressing time for you. If you like, we'll put our meeting off to a later date."

"No, please don't. I need to be busy. I'm trying to get my mind back into what is now, not what was."

"Is there anything I, or we in the police, can do to help you?"

"Thank you, no. The funerals have been and gone. Their affairs, such as they were, are tidied up. And I now want to pick up my life."

"I understand. But if you feel it's too much at any time, let me know."

"I'll be fine. What do you need me to do?"

"A few more questions first, then maybe we can look at next steps. Our main purpose in Glasgow is to get to the bottom of the drugs explosion here. I have my people looking into both ends of the supply chain. We have suspicions that the drugs are being sourced from hospitals, or major pharmacies, so that's why we are here in Ardengrange. You've said you have never seen, or heard, of any drug abuses here, either missing drugs, or abuse of process control."

"Yes, that's right. Never."

"Before Groves asked you, had anyone else ever asked you to get drugs for them?"

"No."

"Never ever had any suspicions something funny was going on?"

"No never, other than the private work in the annexe I told you about."

"Ah, the annexe work. That has given me a dilemma, Nurse Walker."

The nurse looked at Carse and said, "Please call me Alice. Remember? Is it still okay to call you Norrie?"

He smiled and said softly, "Of course, Alice." In a work situation, no one called him Norrie. This was a first. "Your concerns over the annexe had me thinking hard. My team and I have a clear objective to identify the source of amphetamines. We can't take our eye off that ball. And that means I must be very careful not to jeopardise our chances of success by diverting time and attention to a suspicion. Particularly when we have no hard evidence of wrongdoing. Do you see what I mean?"

"But I'm absolutely sure there is something illegal going on there."

"I don't doubt your certainty, but we need more than that. If we are to do anything, and I say if, then there needs to be hard evidence."

"Isn't abortion a major crime?" she asked.

"It certainly is, and that crime is exponentially more serious if the mother is forcibly made to have the abortion against her will. Then we are looking at murder."

"You need hard evidence. Maybe I could get what you need. Then there'd be no more suspicion. Instead, pure facts. No time or resources would be unnecessarily diverted. Your eye would be firmly on the ball. Because after all, you'd be investigating one of the most abhorrent crimes on the planet. That of…"

"The murder of a child who a mother wants to live." Her offer to help in a proactive way was exactly what he wanted to hear. And yet, why did he wish she'd not made the offer? "You seem to be certain on this. Are you?"

She briefly looked away, deep in thought. "At first I was unsure, but the more I have thought about what has happened, the more convinced I am."

Carse hesitated for a moment and said, "Okay. There may be a way you can help, in fact help solve both our concerns. It would however put you in a difficult position if things went wrong."

"What difficult position?"

"If the police were to interrupt what we suspect is an illegal termination, you could be seen as a participant, even if you were not in the room."

"Would I be arrested? Prosecuted?"

"You'd have to be arrested. Otherwise, it would be obvious that you were the source of the information leading to the raid. We'd arrest you to protect your involvement with us. Prosecution? No, because we wouldn't charge you after arrest and therefore matters wouldn't progress to court."

"How would you intrude on a medical procedure? What excuse would you give for doing that?"

"Our separate drugs case is the key to that. If a nurse helping with police enquiries suspected there was, say, an abuse of the drug process taking place on her patch, we could use that as justification."

"I would be that nurse I assume?"

"You would be the ideal person."

She thought it through. More for her benefit, she said, "If there was nothing illegal, it would be just seen as a follow up from a tip off, by people doing what they are supposed to be doing?"

He smiled and nodded.

"How would it work?"

He leaned closer to her. "If we were to intervene in the annexe, it would require you to play a key part. You would have to be the one who triggers the intervention. Can you do that?"

"I think so, but I need to know exactly what I am expected to do."

"We've covered enough for now. I want to be entirely convinced in my own mind, and to have my team totally convinced too. I'm meeting them later this evening, after which I'll get back to you." He rubbed the side of his face and looked away. "I just... just need to be certain about things, that's all."

Carse reflected on his latest meeting with Alice. He had a growing concern that there was something there pulling at his sixth sense of detection. He was taken by her sincerity and conviction that something awful was going on in the annexe. And despite lack of evidence, his copper's instinct told him he should pursue the suspicion. The very clear sincerity and concern which she exhibited when describing her experience cried out for follow up. Ultimately, he realised his next move would define the sort of policeman he was. Was he a safe, play it by the book copper? Or a law man who risked his reputation to take down criminals on the strength of his experienced copper's hunch? Also fighting for space in his mind was a feeling of attraction he was developing for her. Carse cautioned himself to keep his mind on his task.

He rounded up his team and briefed them on his conversation with Alice Walker. "The more I speak to the nurse, the more I think she is right that there is criminality taking place in the hospital annexe. She's nervous and concerned she might get caught up in the aftermath of any raid we make on the place. That's a possibility, but I think her cooperation would be a mitigating factor. She's willing to take part, but we need to be very clear on how we go about this."

"Sounds like you made a personal commitment, boss?" Harper queried.

"Yes. A commitment that we go in. I want everyone here for a full walk through in the morning. We'll look at detailed plans of the surrounding area, the building, access and exit areas, positioning of participants and their roles, trigger point for launch, communication mode, the works. You all know the ropes. We've been here before."

"What about the hospital authorities? Are they in or out," Airlie asked.

"Out for the moment. We would not pre-warn if this were a raid on a drug bust. We take the same approach with this one. If the stuff hits the fan afterwards, it's down to me."

"And the local uniforms?" again from Airlie.

Carse quickly replied. "Leave that to me. I need to pull a few strings."

"The '*Go!*' signal?" This from Bailey.

"I'll sort that soonest. It's all on the nurse and the information she can give us."

"Plan B?"

Carse wagged a finger. "Still work in progress. But a back-up plan must be available soonest. It'll depend on us having all the walkthrough information. That, and the nurse's input."

As part of a liaison task, Carse had a weekly briefing set up with the Chief Constable of the region. It was more of a polite courtesy than detailed reporting, but he kept the top policeman informed on the broad progress of his team. He said nothing of the annexe suspicions, or the suspected leaks. Instead, he made the amphetamines the main topic. The Chief Constable was keenly aware of the weekly political dance he had with Carse, but astute enough to understand the importance of each supporting the other. During their latest face to face meeting, Carse was pleasantly surprised to hear from the head policeman that another raid was scheduled, this time on the Regency Club, and there was a possibility this could be helpful to Carse's team in their search for drugs.

He remembered that Alice Walker's ex-boyfriend worked in the Regency and asked the Chief Constable to be kept informed.

Early next morning, across the city two police teams with search warrants entered and searched the Regency Club, and also the pawnbroker's premises.

In the club, the accounts and the daily tallies were taken, together with cash receipts, cash in hand, and membership logs showing subscriptions and personal details. The gambling room showed nothing out of the ordinary, but in the living accommodation and under a bed, police found a canvas bag containing several watches, rings, bracelets, and necklaces. Some of the items were adorned with precious stones. The manager gave no satisfactory explanation for their presence, other than to say it was the room that was used by Phil Groves. Groves had recently been released on police bail and was still working at the club, though was off work that day.

The club owner, a small man of Mediterranean extraction, was brought in during the search and questioned. But he too couldn't give satisfactory answers to police questions. Groves' room was thoroughly searched but nothing more unearthed. After the owner and manager were interviewed and released, the club was closed pending further investigation.

The police put out an alert for the arrest of Groves.

At the pawnbroker's premises, the storeroom was searched, the safes opened, and the contents logged. The two brothers were interviewed, both pleading innocent of any wrongdoing. The search found several items which – because there were no loan notes or sale receipts - could not be traced back to the owner. The brothers were independently quizzed on their relationship with Groves. Both denied knowing him. But eventually the brother Doug admitted knowing Groves when the police told him they had often been spotted together in a pub. Doug remained adamant that he knew him only as a regular in that pub. The police closed the pawn shop and began a detailed analysis of the inventory held, plus the available accounting paperwork.

Groves had been visiting friends that day, having been released from custody on bail following the gang riots. He returned to the club to find two policemen at the door entrance. He was again placed under arrest on suspicion of handling stolen goods and questioned in the station by a city crime team investigating the jewellery thefts. He denied any involvement in theft and protested that the bag with the jewellery found under his bed had nothing to do with him. And when probed, he also denied any involvement in drugs. However, he admitted that from time to time he heard rumours that someone at the club was selling stolen goods but did not know who. He claimed he was being set up. He also denied knowing any of the pawnbroker brothers, or meeting either of them. The detective leading the interview reminded him that he was being questioned under caution, and lying would be seen as obstructing justice. That reminder didn't deter Groves from continuing to deny any knowledge or involvement. That was until he was informed that the pawnbroker Doug had admitted he knew him from the pub they used. Doug had elaborated that he'd put a stolen brooch up for sale in the pawn shop and that Groves had supplied him with the brooch. It was simply bad luck that the brooch was identified by the owner from whom it was stolen.

The canvas bag found under his bed was currently being checked for fingerprints, as were the contents of the bag. His fingerprints would be compared. Groves then changed his answers, saying that occasionally he would deliver items to the pawnbroker on behalf of club members. But he was adamant he never stole anything. He could not remember everyone who had asked him to take goods to the pawn shop, but under interview pressure admitted he had been doing it for some considerable time. He was then charged with handling stolen goods and remanded in custody pending further investigations.

Carse was informed of this development within hours of it happening. He pondered how he could use the news to draw out Sammy Quigley. He now knew he had a solution.

That evening, the local news bulletin commented on the police raid and announced that an arrest had been made in connection with drug theft and illegal distribution.

The information from the drug pushers in the disused church, and his Regency connection, resulted in Quigley being taken into custody and questioned on suspicion of drug offences.

In the CREW room, the London detectives had positioned two tables end to end, and on the tabletop had fashioned a model of the annexe and its surroundings. A rough cardboard mock-up of the building was central, showing roads leading to, from, and around the building, and the undergrowth and nearby trees in relation to the entrances and exits. Large scale copies of the building's plans were laid out, with key points of windows, fire exits, stairs, elevator, passages, and rooms, together with their uses and probable occupants, all marked in red pen. The team studied the target, made some minor alterations, then discussed timings for moving into, and out of, the building if needed.

Finally, they satisfied themselves they had enough to take down the annexe under almost any circumstances.

The one remaining element centred on Alice Walker. None of the planning was worth a sweet wrapper if she could not carry off her part. Was she steeled for her role, and what signal would she give to start the party?

"I've an idea which could work as a signal," Bailey said. "I was in the building yesterday, interviewing Crawford Baxter, and had a good look around. Along the corridors at regular intervals are fire alarms - the little red box type where the breaking of the glass gives access to the alarm. If the nurse broke one of these when she was sure, we'd have no difficulty hearing it."

"That sounds a goer," Kelly said. He looked at his boss. "What do we think?"

"Providing the alarms are working, I agree, it seems good."

"What happens if the nurse breaks the alarm and there's nothing illegal going on?" Harper asked.

Carse replied, "That's part of the role Miss Walker will be asked to play and might be the stickiest part for her. Making certain an illegal act is under way is a judgement call. She needs to be coached on how she deals with it. I'll ensure that she's fully briefed."

The rest of the team agreed with the signal plan, with the proviso that the alarms needed to be proven active at least one day before the team's raid.

Carse nodded. "Maybe that's something we can get Miss Walker to establish. I'll chase that up. We need a final brief with the nurse, here, before we can say we're all set."

Carse arranged for a minibus to pick Alice up and bring her to the CREW room. After she arrived, he explained the plan he and his team had developed, and walked her through the process, using the model on the table to emphasise the key elements and the roles of each of his team.

"That's about it, Alice." He lowered his voice when he asked, "Are you ready to help? To alert the force positioned outside when you feel sure an illegal procedure is under way?"

She answered with honesty. "All very daunting. Frightening, really. And my life? Are you sure I won't be prosecuted?"

Perhaps he shouldn't have done so but he placed a hand on her shoulder. "You've brought this to the attention of the police and are helping to end a criminal act. If there's a crime in progress, in relation to you matters will develop exactly as I've previously mentioned. You'll be arrested, but not charged. After all, to the outside world we've decided that you're merely a receptionist, with no direct involvement in what happened. And no charge means prosecutors don't have you in their case files. Also, that means the press don't get hold of your name. Don't worry. I'm protecting your name. I'm protecting you, full stop."

She digested what he said. "And so, all I need to do is brace myself for an arrest?"

"Yes."

"Will you be the arresting officer?"

"Maybe." He called in the rest of his team to the CREW room, and they gave Alice further detail about what they would be doing and every step she would have to take. They explained their cover of searching for stolen drugs. Her task was to identify the date and time of the ambush. With the event timetabled, she was to ensure the fire alarms were operational and ready to be used as the go signal. And on the day, she needed to be mentally prepared for the possibility that she'd be arrested with anyone else on the premises.

Briefing over, Carse drove Alice back to the hospital. It was dark and rain was lashing the windscreen as he stopped close to the hospital's main gates and said to her, "Unmarked car but to drive in might bring attention. Trouble is," he pointed at the roof, "it's not exactly great out there? I don't suppose you brought an umbrella?"

She shook her head. "I should have looked at the forecast. A lot on my mind, I suppose. But don't worry, I'll be alright. Just fifty or so yards and then I can use most of the inside hospital to get to my block."

He leaned over his seat, rummaged in his coat that was on the back seat, and then leaned forward. In his hand was a small, extendable umbrella. "Take this."

She hesitated, then took the item that was sheathed in a canvas cover. "Scottish police issue?"

He felt embarrassed. "Mine. Actually, it belonged to my grandfather. He told me to never trust the wireless reports when it came to the weather." He smiled. "Probably he was trying to tell me about life itself, the umbrella being symbolic. Mind you, that thing's done me alright while I've been standing around for hours on end in London and elsewhere and watching wrong-uns. And whether he meant it or not, the umbrella's proved more useful with the weather than the wireless."

She laughed. "I can't. It's yours. Your family's."

He waved a hand dismissively. "I'm fairly sure you're not going to do a Groves on me and nick it." The moment he said it he regretted the cheap joke. "Sorry, I…"

But she was unfazed. "It's okay. Plus, theft is a tad old fashioned. It appears that pawn brokers are the way forward these days." She beamed.

231

So did Carse. "Take it anyway please. It'll make me feel good if you do."

She lowered her hand and rested the umbrella by her side. "Your men deeply admire you."

His lips reverberated as he blew out. "I suppose they do. And that responsibility rests heavily on my shoulders."

"Responsibility?"

He shrugged "We're not *yesterday's men* yet. We don't have the luxury of meeting up for a beer and swapping stories about the old days. We're still in the days. And that means it's vital that our respect for each other only extends to how we performed in our last job. Lives depend on that mindset because one day we become someone who's not quite as good as he used to be. Happens to everyone, no matter what. The man by your side needs to know that he's not reliant on that bloke when his day's come. And the weight I feel is because I have four sets of eyes that are looking at their boss while wondering, Is today the day? I have to make sure it isn't." He shook his head and was apologetic when his tone changed and he said, "I'm rambling, and you need to get in and get dry."

She touched his hand. "When that day comes, you'll have other things in your life. And you'll be a stronger man in different ways."

He looked at her. "Do you think so?"

She nodded.

CHAPTER TWENTY

The annexe facilities were serviced by a central hospital maintenance team. Alice phoned this team and, on the pretence of her being new and needing to check out the building equipment, asked to have the lift, lighting, and fire alarm tested. At the end of the day, and with the annexe virtually unoccupied, a workman appeared with a check sheet listing the inspections carried out. The lift and lights had been certified as serviceable in the past month. The fire alarm had not. As a favour to the bright young nurse who asked him, the workman carried out a test on the fire alarm there and then. The short burst of the alarm lasted no more than five seconds, the workman declared himself satisfied, amended his check sheet, and left.

In his annexe office, Baxter finalised arrangements for the next client - a wealthy Englishman and public figure who said he had a university student in his care and that she was carrying a child that wasn't wanted. The procedure had been agreed.

Baxter called Alice into his office, asked her to sit down, and enquired how she was.

She lied, "I'm fine Mr Baxter. My family tragedy is behind me. For the time being, anyway. It helps being back at work."

"I'm very pleased to hear that, Alice. You're an important part of the team here." He opened a file in front of him, placed his reading glasses on, and said while he read the folder's first page, "I'd like you to be available for the next private consultation. It's been scheduled for three days' time. Saturday at seven in the evening, to be precise."

Her heart skipped a beat. This was it. The day and time it would all happen. "That's fine. I can be there. Which consulting room?"

"Usual room. Just make sure you're there in plenty of time," Baxter said briskly.

"Okay, but isn't that a little late in the day for a consultation? For a Saturday anyway?"

Baxter rolled his eyes and said, "Private practise, Nurse Walker. Our patients set the times to coincide with their diaries. We comply."

"I understand. Of course. Any other instructions, Mr Baxter?"

"Nothing specific. Just make sure you carry out your normal procedures for new patients. Oh, and be aware that there'll be a new senior midwife supervisor on site for the procedure."

She remembered Carse telling something about attack being the best form of defence and to play up to Baxter's view of her. "Will I be paid at the end of the procedure? And do I get a raise?"

Baxter smiled. "I find that people who're motivated by money are usually the ones who can be relied upon to do a job. Yes, I've approved a raise for you and as usual you'll get your cash at the end of the procedure."

She stood. "Thank you. And I agree with you about people and money. Certainly, the job's all I have now, so you won't see me letting you down."

As she walked out of the hospital grounds, Alice was surprised that she had carried off her conversation with Baxter so calmly given she felt anything but calm. She found a public call box and called Norrie Carse. He was unavailable, out on a task she was told. She asked the recipient of her call whether he was part of Carse's team. He wasn't. She told him to tell Carse that she'd called and said the matter was urgent.

By the time Alice finished her regular shift, Carse was waiting for her at the nurses' quarters.

"News?" he asked.

"Not here," she said in a near-whisper. They went to the detective's car and sat inside.

Doors closed, she blurted out, "I've got the next abortion date."

"Wait a minute. We don't know if it's abortions until we have the evidence,"

"You know what I mean. Baxter has asked me to be ready for a procedure this coming Saturday. In the annexe. Same consulting room. At seven in the evening."

"Seven in the evening? Good. It'll be dark then. Anything else?"

"Yes. I've had the facilities people test the fire alarm and it's working."

"Excellent. Who will be in the building besides you, the patient, and the person carrying out the procedure?"

"There's an annexe porter, but I am not sure if he works weekends, or if he will still be there at seven. He has a small office next to the reception. No one else should be in the building, although anyone may unexpectedly come in. Like the matron or Baxter."

"We can cross that bridge if we come to it. We're ready to go after one last briefing." He looked around, his expression earnest when he returned is attention to Alice. "One other thing. The girl? Young woman? The person who's having the appointment? Do you know if she's attending through her own free will?"

She raised a finger to her mouth as if she was about to chew a nail, then quickly dropped her hand. "Baxter didn't say. Why would he?"

There was an expectant hum in the CREW room as the team gathered round the tabletop with the model. Alice was in casual attire and had been picked up earlier to join them.

Carse kicked off proceedings. "The task is on for this Saturday. Nurse Walker is ready to play her part. She is fully briefed by me and knows exactly what to do. I now want to take a final walk through of the plan."

A murmur of approval went through the room.

Alice felt that the atmosphere was charged.

She'd never experienced such a sensation before.

Just like she'd never experienced the grief attached to the death of loved ones.

Until a few days ago.

From grief to exhilaration. Within such a tiny space of time.

Somehow, she needed to find time to make peace with herself for having such contradictory emotions.

Now was not that time.

The Saturday of the planned procedure dawned.

Alice Walker went through the motions of her daily tasks. She was scheduled to finish at four in the afternoon, but as the day wore on her nerves became more difficult to control and she emotionally tried to push the day back. It seemed an age before the end of the shift arrived and she returned to her room to prepare herself for what lay ahead. Her roommate was out, probably away on a visit somewhere. Since their altercation following her parent's death, Alice had distanced herself somewhat from McEwan. She was civil and collegiate, but less friendly. She imagined that time would help heal their relationship. After all, in her heart she knew that Frances had just been trying to help.

She cast her thoughts back to events over recent weeks - her parents' financial plight; Groves and his marriage proposal; Groves and his deceptions; her new job at the annexe; Baxter and Hardcastle and their cover up of what she was convinced was criminal; her introduction to

Norrie Carse; McEwan's lies about the flat her parents moved into; Groves' arrest and the newspaper reports; her parents' deaths; and now her role as an insider for the police in what could be one of the biggest criminal cases in Scottish history. She could hardly believe what had happened in such a short time, how much her life has changed, and what lay ahead of her.

She stiffened her resolve to carry out her part in what she hoped would bring closure to a grim period in her life.

Saturday evening had a chilly feel to it.

A low cloud base carried rain in its shrouds, and a northerly wind blew litter around the streets and pathways.

Alice walked along the internal road to the annexe, her thoughts focused on what she was about to do. She knew that Carse and his men would be placed around the building, in the evergreen shrubs and trees which surrounded the annexe, but she could see no one. She could hear the rumble of traffic from the Great Western Road which skirted the rear of the building, and strangely felt that this would give some added cover to what was about to happen. In addition to Carse's men, she knew there would be uniformed police in the vicinity, but again, saw no one. As she approached the building, she made out the figure of Edith Hardcastle coming towards her.

"Hello Alice. Working tonight, are you?" she asked.

"Yes. Another one for Mr Baxter. All helps on the financial front." Alice suspected that Hardcastle probably knew full well what was going on that night.

They went their separate ways. When Hardcastle was out of sight, Alice stooped, picked up a stone from the path, and then continued to her destination. She entered the annexe at six thirty PM, just as the porter was locking his office door and preparing to go home.

"Evening, George. You're here late."

"Evening, Miss Walker. You've caught me just finishing off moving boxes up to the laundry room." He smiled while stretching his back muscles. "Been a long day. I'm looking forward to a quiet pint of beer and the evening paper to tell me how much I've won or lost on the horses today." He pointed at the stairs. "The cleaner's just finishing mopping the floors of the downstair offices and will be off shortly. Oh, and the senior nurse is upstairs. Haven't met her before. Must be new."

"Thanks, and good luck with the horses."

George left, heading back down the road Alice had come from.

She thought it would make sense to introduce herself to the new midwife and went up the stairs to the first floor. The consulting room door was ajar. Alice put her head around the door and called out, "Hello. Anyone here?"

A woman in her fifties turned from the bed where she was smoothing out sheets. She was wearing a nurse uniform of a type and colour Alice had not seen since her training days in England.

"You must be Nurse Walker," she said. "I'm preparing the room for procedure. What do you want?"

"Just thought I'd introduce myself before the patient arrives," Alice said with a smile.

"No need," said the older nurse, curtly. "When the patient arrives, carry out the usual blood pressure, weight, height checks and inspection of garment fittings. Then, advise me when you're finished. I'll take it from there."

"As you wish," Alice replied. She retrieved her reception file from a chair and returned downstairs, busying herself by checking diary events from that day, the information on future appointments, and the schedule of routine tasks to be carried out. She found it very interesting that the newcomer upstairs had talked of a *procedure*, not an appointment or health check.

At six fifty, the office cleaner said good night and left, just as a car quietly pulled up outside the entrance.

Alice stopped what she was doing and moved to the annexe entrance to greet the arrival. She could see the car had three occupants - the driver and two passengers. The car was not the run-of-the mill type she had often seen on the streets of Glasgow; this was possibly foreign, she thought, and very expensive.

The passengers got out and approached Alice. One was male, middle aged, in an immaculate suit, and had the haughty look that Alice associated with privilege. He was gripping a young woman who looked to be in her late teens or early twenties. By contrast to the man holding her, she was in unremarkable casual attire and her immediate proximity to the man looked odd.

"Hello, I'm Alexander Smythe, Mr Baxter's client. I am expected?" he asked in a refined English accent.

"Yes, yes of course you're expected Mr Smythe." She frowned as she looked at the girl.

Noting her gaze, Smythe said, "The patient. Confidential. Baxter's aware."

This is private practise, she reminded herself as she forced a smile and looked back at the man. "Welcome to the gynaecology annexe. I'm Alice Walker, I'll see to it that you are comfortable while you're here. The consulting rooms are on the second floor of the building. We have a lift. Or would you prefer to take the stairs?"

"Lift," came the blunt reply.

Alice tried to make welcoming small talk on the way to the consulting room, but it became clear that neither the client nor the patient had any wish for that. On exiting the lift Alice led the way along the corridor to a changing room. The internal configuration of the upstairs was unusual in that a corridor ran its length, giving access to each room but there was no downstairs exit at the far end of the corridor. Each room had a door leading from the corridor, and in each room an exit door leading to a parallel corridor on the opposite side. Alice presumed the upstairs layout was previously designed so that much smaller rooms could be accessed from either corridor. Post-war, the internal walls had been removed to provide much larger rooms. Now each room had a separate entrance and exit.

In the changing room, Alice asked the man to leave. He told her that he would do no such thing, and that Baxter was aware that he would remain by the girl's side at all times during the procedure. Alice didn't like this at all. But she could easily imagine Baxter shouting at her if she deviated from something that had obviously been agreed upon between client and consultant. She told the girl to put on a medical inspection gown. When the girl had done so, Alice weighed her, took her height, temperature, and her blood pressure readings, then asked how she was. In a brusque tone, the man answered on her behalf, saying she was fine, and it was best to just damn well get on with this.

At seven-twenty PM, she escorted the girl and man to the consulting room and introduced them to the new matron. As she did so, she deliberately placed the file she'd been carrying onto a side-table. And she did that in a casual, absentminded way.

"Thank you, Nurse Walker," the nurse said. "It's all mine now. If we need anything I'll call for you. And don't forget to take your file with you." She addressed the patient. "How are you, young lady?"

Alice didn't hear the girl's response because the door had been closed quickly. But before the door fully shut, she'd noticed that the bed was now in the centre of the room. Alongside the bed had been placed a chair and a stainless-steel table which held an array of surgical instruments, a kidney shaped bowl, cotton wool, and a several towels. She decided not to loiter but had seen enough to convince her that her suspicions were true.

The room was being set up for invasive surgery.

Given the reason why the woman was here, that meant an abortion was about to take place.

She was annoyed that her subterfuge of leaving her file in the consulting room hadn't worked. She'd hoped it would have given her the chance to interrupt proceedings to retrieve it and see what was happening. However, the new nurse was obviously of an orderly type and a stickler for privacy. That didn't matter now.

She knew that the next minutes were critical. How long did it take to carry out an abortion? She didn't know but guessed at least half an hour. She quietly waited in the upstairs corridor for a few minutes but heard no sound from the consulting room. How long should she hang around? She made up her mind. In exactly twelve minutes, she'd go downstairs and break the fire alarm and set off the '*GO!*' signal.

Twelve minutes.

That time duration might as well have been twelve hours.

Because that's what it felt like.

As beads of sweat took an age to trickle down her back.

And the silence in this part of the hospital allowed her to hear the slightest creak and groan from the old building.

Tick.

Tock.

And then the final *tock* meant she had her own 'Go' signal to attend to.

She tried to move silently to the stairwell, cursing the sound of her work shoes against the floor of the hollow hallway. Once downstairs, the distance from her reception desk to the fire alarm looked to be a long way, but she covered the distance in a few strides. From her pocket, she withdrew the stone she'd picked up from outside and used it to break the glass and set off the alarm.

The next moments were a blur to her.

Kelly and Bailey hurtled into the reception area. Each were followed closely by a uniformed policeman. Kelly raced along the ground floor. Bailey headed upstairs, taking the steps two at a time. What she didn't see, but knew was happening, was a similar scene was being enacted at the opposite end of the building, with uniforms supporting Airlie and Harper.

And then it happened.

Just like he'd promised.

Carse appeared at the front entrance and formally placed Alice under arrest for aiding and abetting a suspected illegal abortion.

Outside, uniformed police watched each side of the building from its surrounding foliage, intent on ensuring no escape from windows. Inside, the consulting room had to be forced open. Within the room, the nurse, client, and an ashen-faced girl looked aghast at Bailey and his police support.

"What's happened?" the nurse asked in a cracked voice.

Bailey lied to the occupants.

"A fire? Where is it?"

The girl was lying on the bed, her legs open, a surgical instrument by her thighs. She began to cry, then to wail. "Please! Please!"

Standing at the head of the bed and with his hands pinning-down the girl's shoulders, Smythe glared at the police officers and bellowed, "God damn it! You have no right to barge in here, no matter what. I'll ensure that…"

"What are you doing nurse?" the young policeman in uniform challenged.

The matron said nothing.

The girl continued to sob.

Bailey said, "What they're doing, constable, is what they call an abortion. And it's what we call an *illegal abortion*."

"Is this true?" the policemen asked the girl.

She nodded her head and whimpered.

The constable looked uncertain and glanced at Bailey.

The seasoned detective nodded once. "Ask her if she's here of her own free will."

The constable was wide-eyed and perspiring as he spoke to the girl. "Did… did you want this to happen?"

The girl seemed confused, maybe terrified. "No… No…He…"

"Shut up, bitch!" shouted Smythe.

Bailey ignored the man and asked the girl, "Are you hurt? Have you been operated on yet?"

The girl shook her head.

Bailey muttered to the constable, "Girl needs lots of care. Gloves off with the other two."

The constable breathed in deep and addressed Smythe and the matron. "I'm arresting you both on suspicion of taking part in an illegal termination of a pregnancy. An abortion in other words."

The midwife cursed. A deluge of tears burst out of the girl's eyes. Bristling with rage, Smythe moved away from the bed and towards the constable, his fists clenched.

Bailey made three paces, placed two fingers on the man's throat, simultaneously swept his leg against the man's ankle, and kept hold of him as Smythe flipped backwards and onto the ground. While keeping one hand on the client's throat, Bailey used the other to grab the man's balls. He tightened the grip in both hands, leaned forward so that his face was close to Smythe's face, and said, "Best not. 'Cos what the young constable didn't mention is this isn't just an illegal abortion that we're looking at. My eyes are looking at murder of an unborn child and without mum's say so. Forced termination. The real deal fucking horror show. And that means I'm liable to do what I do and take matters into my own hands. Understand?"

The building was searched by more officers. All other rooms and passageways were empty or locked. No one else was found inside. A car waiting at the rear of the building was blocked from exit, the driver arrested, and he joined Smythe, the midwife, and Alice in a black maria van.

The girl was attended to by female officers and medical specialists who'd been specially drafted in on the grounds that something like this might happen. The girl was taken to the police station where she was to receive further care and submit a full statement when she was fit to do so.

Under police escort, the black van also went to the same station. Its arrested occupants were offloaded and put in separate cells.

And meanwhile, Carse and his team were searching for Baxter, given there'd been no sign of him at the annexe. In order to cast the net wide, Carse had arranged a national warrant for his arrest. All of Scotland's police had authority to look for and apprehend Baxter. But it was Carse who found him on the same evening as the raid and took him into custody, having surprised the doctor leaving his golf club where he'd had dinner. The senior detective interviewed Baxter under caution. The consultant was clearly rattled but denied any knowledge of, or involvement in, the abortion factory, or in illegal drugs. Carse obtained a written statement from him and knew exactly what he was doing when he released Baxter, pending further investigation.

Carse instructed his team to probe deeper into Baxter's background, his past roles and contacts, present affiliations and known associates. That evening, a few well-placed phone calls and well-posed questions got results. The CREW team unearthed his Liverpool practising background and his later inappropriate-behaviour charge by the regional medical board. They also ascertained he was a freemason, with influential associates within Glasgow. Though perfectly legal and seemingly above board, the latter reveal interested Carse.

However, the only thing Carse had on Baxter being involved in illegal abortions was Alice Walker's word.

The situation with Frances McEwan was far worse. An arrest warrant was also put out for her. But she'd vanished, and as yet there wasn't the slightest lead that could help Carse's team track her down.

It was nearly midnight when Carse returned to the police station for the third time since the raid at seven PM. Harry, the custody sergeant, told him that a doctor had examined the girl and she was physically fine and able to supply a statement. Smythe, his driver, and the matron had been charged, and were still being held for interview.

Carse went to the cell containing Alice. Though perhaps he didn't need to, he apologised for the indignity of her arrest. "That was a remarkable thing you did today. The investigation has a long way to go before it is all over. But in your case, I'm going to move things fast and get you out of here within the next couple of hours. One of my officers will take a statement from you. And then that's it." He looked at her with utter admiration and meant every word when he said, "I'd like you to know that it took guts to do what you did."

She didn't like it when he spoke to her in his formal voice but held back from saying so. He had his work cut out right now. Plus, there was the major fact that he'd just risked his career and reputation on her word. More accurately, on her in general. "Will I have to do more than be interviewed?"

"Once you're out of here and in slower time, you'll certainly have to talk with the hospital authorities. But don't worry - your part in bringing this crime to book will be a credit to you. I'd like to keep in touch though, if you don't mind? There may be things that still have to be ironed out."

"That's fine with me," she said with a smile. That's not what she thought, though. The prospect of Norrie Carse staying in touch with her was significantly better than just fine.

The interviews of Smythe, the midwife, and the driver, supplied important information.

The driver protested that he had only been hired to pick the girl and her escort up from a classy city centre hotel, drop her off, wait, and then take them to an address in Bearsden, in the northwest of Glasgow. He knew nothing about why the girl was there, nor the purpose of his trip to Bearsden. He was not a party to whatever had gone on at the annexe, he claimed. He identified the person who hired him as a forty something landlady, about five feet eight, light brown hair, an odd accent, and a gold filling in a tooth. She had hired him before, to pick up people from ferries, or bus terminals. All of them were female.

The midwife's description of the person who hired her to carry out the procedure was the same as the driver's, with the addition of a name.

Ruth Cohen.

The midwife added that Cohen had recruited her before, in northwest England, and confessed that she'd had earlier involvement in similar activities.

By contrast, Smythe had a solicitor at his side within half an hour of his arrest. He made no comment.

Later that night Alice was escorted into a police interview room. Carse and Airlie were present, but it was Detective Inspector Harper who took a statement from her and then got her to sign the document.

She was now free to go. But before that happened, Carse spoke privately to her in the empty hallway of the station.

In a low voice he told her, "The midwife has confessed to intent to carry out an abortion. An abortion that was against the will of the poor expectant mother. The midwife has named and described the person who hired her to do it. The name she gave was Ruth Cohen."

When he gave her the person's description, Alice realised he was almost certainly describing Frances McEwan.

This was impossible, Alice thought. Frances could not, would not be involved in the annexe abortion activities. Then again, there was the flat that her parents had died in. She told him what she was thinking.

"We'll find out soon enough," said Carse. "I've urgent enquiries underway with forces in the northwest of England. I've asked for everything and anything on a Ruth Cohen. Now, I'll add the name Frances McEwan into the mix. And if McEwan's got a maiden name that's she used for anything suspect, that won't get in the way of our enquiries. Put bluntly, if McEwan and Cohen are one and the same, we'll make that connection." He sighed and muttered, "It's finding her that seems to be the trouble." He looked sharply at Alice. "Goes without saying – a sighting or peep out of McEwan, call me immediately."

"Of course." She shook her head in disbelief. "Just when I thought things couldn't get stranger." Her mood however changed when the thought occurred to her that, for the most part, she'd played a significant role in this evening's events and had helped thwart the annexe operation. And that meant she was now free to think about better things. Things that maybe, just maybe, her future may contain. She readily smiled and felt relaxed as she looked at Carse. Her association with him, she now realised, would now be different. Alright, he'd stay in touch with her on minor-detail police matters. But for the most part, the real reason to stay in touch would be for other reasons. Non-police reasons. And how did that make her feel? He was eight years or so older than her, tough, smart, and a successful detective with a way of holding the loyalty of his men. All of that was good but of more importance to her was that he was tender, sympathetic, and crucially it was obvious that he liked her. No. His attraction to her went way beyond that. When she was in his presence, it was almost as if he'd been searching for something and had now discovered what he was looking for. And yet there was a sense in his eyes that he didn't know what to do next. She wondered if he had surviving family, or a large network of friends. Something about him suggested he didn't. Perhaps he'd come home from the war, the same war that he didn't talk about, and realised there was no one home. And if that was the case, could she change that? Should she be the one to change that? And was she getting ahead of herself? She tried to sound matter of fact when she said, "Perhaps we could meet up in a day or so? I'd... be keen to hear more about the police case, of course. If you have time, that is?"

Carse smiled. "I think that would make perfect sense."

The news of the raid on the annexe spread quickly. Local, regional, and national newspapers ran various editions containing breaking news about the daring and controversial takedown, fattening their reports in evening editions once further information had come to light. Central to all reports was the insistence by the police that it had acted on a drugs tip off and the hospital raid was in line with the pursuit of illegal drug thefts and distribution.

McEwan was in Stirling when she heard of the raid. She made several calls to Baxter without success. The reason she was in Stirling was to meet Arthur Burns and continue her attempt to recruit him. But Burns didn't show up. This didn't overly bother her beyond the inconvenience of being out of Glasgow, an inconvenience that now transpired to being a blessing given the raid. What she didn't know was that the reason Burns wasn't with her was because right now he'd been summoned by Charlie Palmer.

They were in Palmer's office. The air was thick with cigar smoke which usually meant that Palmer had spent the preceding hour either celebrating a success or plotting someone's downfall. Palmer was behind his desk. Burns was sitting opposite him, the ankle of one leg resting casually on the opposite thigh. Both men were in their *day-job* clothes, a look that got them into smart establishments but also was cheap and robust enough to absorb spilt beer and blood.

Palmer stubbed out his cigar and cracked his knuckles. "This woman could be much more than just a nuisance to us, if what your findings say are true. We'd be better off with her gone."

Burns raised an eyebrow. "Totally gone? Written off?"

"Disappeared is the word I prefer. Make it your priority."

"Before or after Baxter?"

Palmer scowled. "Priority means first. At the top of the list. Ahead of anything else."

Burns shrugged. "Okay. But don't worry about Baxter. That's sorted. I'll concentrate on the woman."

Following his police interview, Baxter had not gone home. Thus, there was no reply when police officers called at his flat to take a statement. Their phone calls were also unanswered. And neighbours told officers they had not seen him.

He was in a late-night café near Glasgow Central railway station, seated in a corner, writing. His plan to manage McEwan and ensure Palmer was placated had gone wrong. Maybe it would have worked. But then the raid happened and his shocking arrest at his prestigious golf club. That had been awful. The interview with the police had fully broken the limits of his nerve. And he should never have allowed his nerves to be tested in this way. His overprescription and illegal distribution of amphetamines; conspiring in the illegal scheme with the Dunure Group; recent threats from Palmer; establishment and management of what amounted to an abortion factory; blackmail and disparagement by the sneering Nurse McEwan. Once he was a respectable doctor. Somewhere down the line he'd made a wrong decision, taken a wrong turn, and realised too late that he was completely out of his depth. And while there was no going back, there was also no route forward. No hope. No solution. Nothing for him because any resolution he might once have had was now utterly crushed.

When the detective who introduced himself as Carse released him on bail, he'd said the temporary release was due to lack of current evidence and the need to conduct further investigations. That may have been true. But it was the look on Carse's face when he released him that bothered Baxter. He would have expected a cop in his shoes to be annoyed, or at least overly professional and formal in an effort to mask such annoyance. Instead, Carse seemed calm. Perhaps he was hoping that Baxter would lead him to incriminating evidence? Or was it something else that could account for the expression that could just as easily be interpreted as belonging to a man who knows exactly what's going to happen next? Whatever Carse was thinking, Baxter knew his own mind. And that mind told him it was only a matter of time for him before matters ended.

He hated McEwan, loathed her and wished her dead, but he also knew he was the architect of his own downfall.

He wrote a long letter, addressed to the Chief Constable of the City. In it he confessed to illegal drug sales, illegal abortions, and his participation in the high-level conspiracy involving the Lord Provost, the Assistant Chief Constable, and the businessman Charles Palmer. He named no one else. When he finished, he wrote a shorter second letter, after which he went to his car in a nearby street, then drove off into the night. He stopped briefly at a block of flats near the university and posted the second letter into a personal mailbox at the entrance. He then continued his journey.

He was not going home.

At seven in the morning, an early dog walker found his body at the edge of the ninth green on his local golf course.

CHAPTER TWENTY-ONE

Inspector Johnny Harper's supply chain investigation of pharmacies and medical distribution centres had narrowed the source of drugs leakage down to a specialist central receipt and distribution point, midway between Edinburgh and Glasgow. This was a transit centre where drugs were received from manufacturers, cross-docked to waiting vehicles, and dispatched to hospitals, clinics, and surgeries. This was a non-standard service, set up to meet emergency requests. The drugs, including amphetamines, were not stored but simply received and redistributed almost immediately.

The accounting of these items bypassed the accepted methods and was carried out daily by site managers who compared receipt notes against demand notes for incoming goods; and receipt notes against despatch notes for delivered goods. Spike Kelly and Harper had found that demand patterns for incoming amphetamines increased significantly when certain key employees were on shift, but no incoming receipt notes met the volume demanded.

Manufacturers sent items to meet false requisition orders, which then vanished in the transit centre.

Amphetamines topped the list.

Three employees were linked with increased amphetamine activity when they were on shift, and each had an important responsibility in the chain. The employees were a shift operations manager, a receipt and despatch manager, and an inventory manager.

In a paper-strewn, untidy, and cramped office, Harper met the operations manager and asked, "Can you tell me about your job."

The manager answered, "Not a lot to tell really. The outstations - hospitals, surgeries, pharmacies and so on - don't always get their forward planning right, so they're often asked for emergency top ups of medicines, drugs, et cetera."

"How does that work?"

"Their request comes through to us. We put a red flag on it and chase up the suppliers who speed up the request and deliver to us within a day. We gather all items for the same destination and dispatch at once."

"So, your team puts in the order?"

"Yeah, at the request of the outstation."

"How often does it go wrong?"

"We have good control here. The supplies always get to their requesting destination in the required timeframe."

"Sounds slick," Harper commented.

"Yeah, well, we're pretty much on top of things."

"How often do you lose things, or they go missing in transit?"

"Oh, hardly ever. Why?"

"You never have any shortages or, what do you call it, shrinkages?"

"Occasionally, very occasionally. Nothing's perfect, yeah?"

"Do you record the losses? The missing, or whatever you call them?"

The manager's eyes narrowed, and his body stiffened slightly. "Yes, we have a register of those."

"Can I see it please?"

The manager handed a battered, hardbacked ledger to Harper.

The detective glanced at its contents and said, "And a similar register for outstation requests?"

"Eh, yes. Around here somewhere."

"I'd like to see that too, please. I'm sure you'll find it."

A quick riffle through the pages of the ledger told Harper that the losses were more frequent than the manager would have people believe. But there were no discrepancies with amphetamines. Anywhere.

When the manager returned, he handed Harper a ring binder file. "Requests register. Everything in there's faxed requests."

The detective opened the file. "Who controls these registers?"

"I do. I'm the manager. It's my job."

"And how do you keep tab of what comes in against what is requested from the suppliers?"

"We have an end of day review of that and of despatches against requests."

"Who's we?"

"Myself, the inventory manager, and the despatch manager."

"And the results of those reviews are recorded?"

"Well, not always. There's often nothing to report, so we don't make work."

"I see. But you do have some reports?"

"Yes, of course, somewhere around." The manager smiled as he gestured at the state of the office and the chaotic mass of papers. "Somewhere."

"Good. You've been most helpful. Please find them for me. I need to take them, and the registers, for a day or so to finalise our own review. Who are the inventory and despatch managers and where can I find them?"

"They'll be on the shop floor currently. I'll take you there."

Harper was shown onto a noisy, bustling warehouse floor and introduced him to the inventory manager and despatch manager. The inventory manager explained the layout and said it was simple - one end received the items, the opposite end housed a line of vehicles, and in the centre the small boxed incoming items were broken into their respective outstations and moved across to the right waiting vehicle.

"As I said, a simple cross dock operation," said the inventory manager, after he'd shown Harper around.

A brief conversation with the despatch manager and look at the incoming items told Harper much the same story.

Harper looked around at the hive of activity and back at the three men. With the registers and end of day reports under his arm, he made ready to leave and said, "You've been very helpful. Thanks. We may need to talk with you again. Do you have any problems with that?"

Their voices said, no problem. Their faces told a different story.

Kelly had been wandering around the perimeter of the transit centre while Harper was inside. He met Harper at their car and swapped findings. Harper scratched his head and said, "It's a shambles of a paper chase operation. The control of the movement internally must be a nightmare. Or a golden opportunity to steal." He talked Kelly through his meeting with the operations manager and subsequent walk around the warehouse activities. "I have the actual registers they use to track the order, receipt, and despatch of the goods. For this shift, we'll need to check out any other shifts. It shouldn't take us long to analyse the information. What did you sniff out?"

Kelly shrugged. "On the face of it, all looks quite normal. Boring, even. Vans and trucks come up to the inbound security gate, get stopped, flash papers to the guard, then get waved in. The outbound vehicle movements are much the same - flash papers, then get waved out. The only exception was a motorbike rider with a rear pannier on his bike. I didn't see him come in, but he stopped at outbound security, showed some papers, and was let out."

"It looks like the action is all inside the building then," Harper said.

Back in the stations' CREW Wing, the paperwork taken by Harper was analysed and discrepancies found when the operations, inventory and despatch managers were all on shift.

Amphetamine discrepancies.

The three men were arrested and brought into custody.

Separately interviewed under caution, they could not satisfactorily explain the inconsistencies, and eventually confessed to their individual part in illegally ordering and disposing of amphetamines.

In transpired that the thefts had at first been spur of the moment opportunistic events, until they realised from the buyers that they were overseeing goods that had huge value on the black market. After that, the three managers simply met the demand.

That demanding voice was Sammy Quigley.

He developed a simple method of daily motorcycle pick-ups from the transit centre, with false invoices provided by the internal accomplices to pass the outbound security staff. This had increased to become the main source for illegal drug distribution throughout Glasgow.

No leakage from hospitals was found.

The admissions of the transit centre employees and their incrimination of Quigley, together with the evidence obtained by Airlie and Bailey from their work on the streets, provided a strong case for prosecuting Quigley.

Guessing correctly that the police would be looking for her, Frances McEwan steered clear of the nurses' quarters and moved into the flat where she had last met Baxter, on the Great Western Road. She knew she needed time to find out what had happened at the annexe, who was involved, and what had happened to Baxter. And Baxter was her biggest concern. He knew it all. She could put distance between any allegations of involvement if Baxter kept quiet. But would he, she wondered. His recent nervousness did not give her confidence. She decided her plans of widening criminal enterprises with Burns must, for the time being, be shelved.

After a few days of being unable to contact Baxter, she found a phone number for Edith Hardcastle and called her. "Matron, its Nurse Frances McEwan here. I've been trying to reach my associate Crawford Baxter. Could you tell me where he is?"

"Nurse McEwan? Your name doesn't ring a bell. Should do if you know Mr Baxter. Do I know you?"

McEwan put on her most amiable voice. "Happens all the time in my line of work. I'm a nurse trainer. Can't remember the last time I had a workstation or pretty much anywhere called permanent. But I'm fully recorded with your hospital. Doctor Baxter is one of my clients. I run training sessions for some of his staff. Not all of the time.

Not for a while, actually. Hence why I'm trying to get hold of him. Just trying to drum up business, if I'm honest."

"Ah. That would explain why your name hasn't crossed my desk. I just do clinical work and don't really involve myself in other matters. Mr Baxter is the one who deals with people like you." She grunted. "You obviously don't read the news."

McEwan frowned. "Not recently."

"Not today, for sure, because it seems that you're trying to drum up business from a man who this morning was found dead on a golf course." It was hard to tell if she was being sincere when she added, "Terrible, just terrible."

"What! What's happened? Do you know? Accident or what?"

"Police statement to the papers seemed a little ambiguous to me. Accident, assault, or whatever. Not really clear."

"Dear God. That's awful," McEwan said. "Are you at work? Can I come in to see you? I'm sorry. This must sound very callous of me. It's just that I've got a full training program lined up and one of the things we're really proud of is showcasing the application of a new pain relief drug that's been proven to minimise anxiety to both baby and mother during birth. The drug's just been nationally approved. I'd love to tell your nurses all about what we've been doing. But, I need someone in your part of the hospital to sign me up. Someone who's not…"

"Dead." Hardcastle was silent for a moment. "I'm off to Edinburgh for a two-day conference this afternoon, so today's bad. If you still want to, or need to talk, I'll be

264

around at the end of the week. Maybe things will be clearer then."

"Thanks matron. I think it would be a great idea to meet."

"Alright. And onwards and upwards. Hopefully we can put this… terrible, terrible, news behind us."

After she ended the call, McEwan tuned into the local radio station. When the news came on, she listened carefully to the broadcast police report on Baxter's death. Hardcastle was right - details were terse, with cause of death still being investigated. When questioned by a reporter at the police press conference, the police declared that it hadn't ruled out foul play.

The death was welcome news to McEwan.

Palmer and Burns were nowhere nearer to finding their supposed gangland colleague O'Hara. No one on the streets was saying anything, which they felt was ominous.

"He may have just legged it, boss. Scared of your anger at his stupid attempt on Quigley," Burns suggested.

"Or he may have been taken care of by Quigley's team," Palmer said. "Either way, he's out of our game. We need to find a rising star to take his patch. O'Hara is a now a former employee."

"Understood. I'll talk to my team and get a name for you," promised Burns.

Palmer grimaced, grabbed Burns' arm, and yanked. "We have a more pressing problem to sort. This bitch who wants to rule the city - what do we have on her whereabouts? You've had plenty time to find her."

"Nothing definite yet."

"Nothing yet, boss," mimicked Palmer as he let go of the arm. "What have you done to find her?"

"Don't worry. I'll sort it. We'll find her."

"You'd better fucking sort it. What have you been wasting your time on? Do it now, or I'll get someone else to do it for me. Understand me?"

"I understand you perfectly," whispered Burns, repressing an angry retort.

Carse was at police headquarters for a scheduled progress review meeting with city's Chief Constable. He covered progress on the drugs search, the success at the transit centre, and the questioning of Quigley.

"Good progress, Inspector Carse. That will help blunt the edge of the people in the networks pushing these drugs. For now, of course. What about the leaks? Overall organised crime? Any news?"

Carse admitted that they had been less successful, with only a handful of potential names, and no concrete evidence. He turned the conversation to the suspicion of illegal procedures in the hospital annexe, uncovered because of the drugs trawl, and gave the top policeman an inside-track report of the raid and arrests.

"I was surprised to learn of this, Inspector. How did you come upon it? And why did you pursue it? It wasn't in your brief to do so, was it?"

"You're quite correct sir. No, it wasn't part of our brief. But this is a crime that goes to the heart of society. I doubt any experienced policeman could ignore such a thing. My team were briefed and given the chance to opt out. I'm proud to say they all opted in. Our progress on the drugs front was, I believed, sufficiently advanced to take on this additional task. Ultimately, it was my sole decision."

He omitted the significant role of Alice Walker, saying simply they had some assistance from staff.

At this point, the top cop said that he had some news but would be returning to the matter of Carse's flagrant breach of police standard procedures. He told him about the death of Baxter and the contents of the letter found on his person. Carse frowned.

As the Chief Constable forewarned, the subject then returned to the annexe raid. Carse was severely reprimanded for deviating from his brief. He was warned to expect a written censure, but also warmly congratulated on his success.

"You made the right call when it mattered," the Chief Constable concluded.

Carse wasn't surprised at the contradiction. That was the way of police forces up and down the country.

When he was back in the CREW room, Carse gathered his team and briefed them on Baxter's demise. They immediately suspected dirty work until he told them of the letter found in Baxter's jacket pocket addressed to the Chief of Police. It was a four-page confession, explaining his reasons for ending his own life. His part in the annexe abortions was of most interest, since it raised even more questions.

"Where does McEwan fit into this, boss?" Kelly asked.

"Like a hand in a glove, I think. Almost every hour we're getting new information about her. We still haven't got the full picture, but it's beginning to look like she was a key player in a similar abortion set up in the Liverpool area." He glanced at a map on the wall showing the British Isles and wondered where McEwan now was. "We don't yet know what her full involvement in the annexe was, but one of the arrested has made a positive identification of her and confessed to a previous association in the north of England. Local, regional, and forces elsewhere are continuing to search for her. She's a key individual in all this, I believe." He frowned. "Correction. I'm starting to wonder if she's *the* key individual."

"Didn't she share a room with Nurse Walker? Have we had any input from her about McEwan?" Bailey asked.

Carse nodded. "I've asked Alice Walker to tell us everything she knows about McEwan. I'm going to see her this evening. We may build up a better picture from that."

"Are you taking her a nice bunch of roses," asked Airlie.

"With immediate effect," Carse picked up a file, "back down from that line of questioning, detective

268

sergeant." He had a stern expression when he looked at Airlie. Then he smiled.

When he met her as planned at their increasingly usual spot that was the café, he asked her to think back to anything that might give him and his team an insight into the person they sought.

Alice thought for a moment, her eyes searching the ceiling, brow furrowed. "She seemed so welcoming, kind, helpful to me. She got me a room transfer from a noisy dormitory to share a twin room with her. She listened to my problems with my boyfriend and me moaning about the need to get money for my parents. And she persuaded me not to leave nursing." She looked at Carse. "She was like a big sister, counselling me. But we weren't always in each other's pockets. Her job often took her away. There were times I didn't see her for two or three days. But when she returned, she was always the same - chatty, helpful, friendly. She calmed me down when the police came to see me. Encouraged me to take extra work within the annexe. And was there when my parents were evicted. At short notice she arranged a place for them to go to." Her expression changed. "It was shortly after that when things changed. You see, I found out later that she owned the property. The flat that…"

"Your parents died in."

She was visibly trembling as she sharply nodded. "I confronted her about the faulty wiring and her ownership of the flat. She gave an explanation that sort of made sense, though she couldn't fully explain why she didn't tell me she'd bought the property and hadn't told me that it was deemed a fire hazard. We made peace, but it was a turning point. Certainly, our friendship wasn't the same after what happened. But we still lived together, spoke and all that. And I genuinely felt that our relationship would get back to normal in time." She rubbed her arms as if that might stop the shakes. "Then the annexe happened, and you told me about a woman with a gold filling."

He slowly extended a hand and held hers. Softly, he asked, "Why do you think she was so kind and helpful to you?"

"What do you mean?"

He was treading carefully with his words when he elaborated, "Did you ever think she had a special reason for her kindness?"

"No, I didn't. Do you?"

He breathed in deeply and exhaled with a sigh. "Unfortunately, yes, I do. If it turns out, and I think it will, that she was heavily involved in the annexe depravity, I believe she saw you as the ideal front of house. The professional, open, and friendly nurse to welcome all clients. She kept you onside, and in her sights, to use you for that very purpose. And that means she targeted and groomed you from day one."

"Dear God!" Her eyes were now moist. "How could she... how could anyone be so cold blooded? And manipulative?"

He rubbed his hands against hers. His voice was still gentle, but also firm when he said, "Bluntly, I think she saw your naivete and exploited it." He waited, expecting her to pull her hand out of his and scold him.

She did neither. Instead, she looked away and said, "I grew up in poverty and with wonderful people and played in the streets with kids who were from families just like mine." She smiled at the memory. "You know what it's like when people are thrown together. All the good and the bad. Laughter and tears. Stuff we don't like to think about. Other stuff we want to bottle and cling onto forever. All the talk, the chatter, the information that goes back and forth like a million airwaves. All of us trying to get along. Not even survive. We didn't think of it that way. Not when we were young, least ways. And there's me. Quiet. Watching it all. Absorbing, because I'm not really a chatterbox and like learning by listening. And so I do learn." She raised his hand to her cheek and smiled as she felt its warmth against her skin. "I saw the good things. But that didn't mean I was unaware of the bad things. I heard them. Knew about them." She lowered his hand but kept it close. "I'm not naïve. Never was. It's just... just that I like the good things. Why waste a life by paying attention to the bad things?"

He nodded. "I wish I could be the same."

"You are. I think the bad things annoy you. Given any opportunity, you'd dearly like to click your fingers and make the bad things go away. By contrast, I'm sure there are some detectives who are defined by what they do. Crusader types, I suppose. Take away the bad people and those detectives are left with nothing. You're not like that at all." She wiped her eyes and now had a ready smile on her face. "You're a dreamer. Just like me." Her smile faded. "I do accept, though, that we cannot always be in a pleasant dream." Her expression steeled as she stated with deliberation, "Frances McEwan deliberately set out to exploit and manipulate me?"

He hated hearing her repeat back what he'd said about McEwan's agenda with Alice. "Yes. Her longer game might well have been to enmesh you and involve you in the actual terminations. Home grown if you like. After four or five sessions, you might be held to be complicit. And then, why not exploit you further? After all, she knew you needed money. Rather, your parents and Groves needed money."

"Where is she? Do you know?"

"No, we don't. I'm hoping to find out if there is anything else you know about McEwan that can help us track her down. What do you know of her outside interests, friends, relatives, regular habits, clubs, or pubs she might visit?"

She narrowed her eyes while racking her brain. "Frances kept her cards close to her chest. She said she had some relatives in the area, but not who or where. When she went out, she was usually smartly dressed, very fashionable I'd say, but I don't know where she went. When it comes to her private life, I can't really help. Sorry."

"You're doing fine and every little helps. If there is anything else you think of later, please call me."

"I will. And thank you. You've been very kind to me in all this." She reached into her handbag, withdrew an object, and held it out. "Your grandfather's umbrella. It's stopped raining."

"For now. Please keep it."

She frowned. "But you? Your family?"

"Just me. And," he leaned forward and caressed her hair, "this is more important than what I have or don't have."

CHAPTER TWENTY-TWO

The evidence pulled together by the CREW team was at the heart of the drugs charges laid against Sammy Quigley. He denied involvement in all of it, but the prosecuting authorities were very confident of a conviction which would keep him off the streets for a lengthy period. Drug abuse was, however, still a prevalent crime and removing one player helped but did not remove the blight.

For his part in handling stolen goods, Phil Groves was imprisoned for fifteen months.

Charlie Palmer was in a hotel room, dressing for an evening black-tie dinner at an old Victorian hotel in the city centre, when he heard the radio report put out by the police about Baxter's death. After a string of curses, he called his garage and had a car bring Burns to his hotel room. He had wanted Baxter silenced, but not permanently.

Palmer launched into his visitor as soon as he entered the room. "What the bloody hell have you done, you fucking clown?".

"When? What…what do you mean?"

"I wanted Baxter's mouth shut, not his air supply shut off."

"Baxter? He's been sorted. As you wanted."

"I didn't want him dead." Palmer took a step closer and said between gritted teeth, "I have a fucking nightmare to deal with now."

"He's not dead. He was warned off. Severely."

The gang boss threw his arms up in exasperation. "He's dead! Brown bread, you idiot. Dumped on the golf course."

Burns couldn't hold his tongue any longer. "Don't call me an idiot. You're the idiot if you think I had anything to do with killing Baxter. He was only leaned on. Heavily leaned on, I admit, but that's all. And he got the message."

Palmer's face was flushed, the veins in his neck protruding. "You've screwed up well and truly this time. He's dead and I want to know who killed him. Was it you? Or that maniac Dutch guy you have in your team? I can't trust any of you fuckers to carry out simple instructions."

"Are you thick or something, Charlie? If Baxter's dead, it wasn't by me or my lads."

"Lies! You and your team are out of control, Burns. You don't even know what they've done. Fucking idiots. Clowns." His rage got the better of him. He stepped in close to Burns and delivered a vicious headbutt to the bridge of the younger man's nose.

Burns staggered, clawed at Palmer's shoulder, and shook his head, splattering blood across Palmer's dress shirt and on to the bed beside them.

Palmer grabbed a bedside lamp and swung it at his opponent, landing a glancing blow on his head.

With the bitter salt taste of his own blood in his mouth, Burns recovered his wits and aimed a wild kick at Palmer's crotch. The kick missed and landed on the boss's midriff.

The two lost complete control and launched; punching, kicking, gouging, and grappling each other. Blood streamed from their faces, as they jockeyed for advantage across the spacious hotel bedroom. The noise was horrendous, as furniture and mirrors became collateral damage in their increasingly ferocious attempts to end each other.

A break in their struggles allowed Palmer to stand back for a second. He saw Burns on the floor and rushed at him. In a reflex action Burns reached up, put his foot in Palmer's stomach, and launched him over his body. The momentum of the gang boss's rush carried him across the room. Palmer screamed as his body crashed into and through the flimsy original Victorian features room window and down to the street sixty feet below, scattering pedestrians and halting traffic.

The preceding fracas had been going on for three or four minutes, alerting the hotel staff. In turn, they alerted the police who were quickly on the scene.

Burns was arrested and taken to the central police station for questioning.

In an interview room, sparsely furnished with only a table and chairs, two non-CREW detectives questioned Burns.

"Arthur Burns - did you murder Charles Palmer?"

"No, I did not."

"How did he leave the room you were both in and die sixty feet below?"

"It was an accident. Straight up. An accident."

"He accidentally jumped out of the window?"

"No. We were struggling. You know. Grappling. And he accidentally went out the window."

"If you were struggling why didn't both of you go out the window?"

"Well, we were fighting. He rushed me and just went past me and out the window."

"Why were you fighting?"

"Stupid trivial thing. Arguing about nothing."

"What is, or was, your relationship with Charles Palmer?"

"I'd worked for him on and off for years, in his garage and on his construction teams."

"Did he owe you money?"

"No. It was just a stupid argument that got out of hand. Can't even remember what it was about."

"You had an argument with someone who jumped out of a window, and you can't remember what you were arguing about?"

"No. Not like that. We were battling, you know, punching and kicking. He had given me a rollicking for something I'd forgotten to do for him. And slagged me off.

Called me all sorts. I wouldn't take that, so I pushed back. And we started fighting."

"Were you on good terms with Mr Palmer before today?"

"Yes. We didn't have any problems."

"In all probability he was dressing before attending a black-tie dinner. Why did you go to his hotel room?"

"He called for me. Sent a car. Asked me to do something for him."

"What did he ask you to do?"

"He never got round to telling me. He started having a go at me as soon as I walked into his room. Within a minute we were fighting."

A second detective took over the questioning. "I must be a bit hard of thinking, so help me. Can you explain why he sent a car for you, while he was about to join others for a formal dinner in a very public place, but then didn't tell you why he wanted you? Presumably you weren't expecting a fight. If you did, why would you have got into a car? And yet he tore into you as soon as you arrived, and you can't remember what the argument was about apart from it was some trivial thing to do with something you'd forgotten to do. Have I got that right?"

"I know it sounds crazy, but that's the way it was."

"You need to think hard again, Burns. You can't give us a sensible explanation for why you were in that room. You've admitted that you were fighting with Palmer for reasons you can't really remember. And you were in the room when he went out the window. I don't believe you.

You need to get your memory revved up, because now you are looking at a charge of premeditated murder. We'll give you some time to think about things. We'll take a short break."

The detectives left Burns to his thoughts.

Outside the interview room a detective inspector told the interviewers that the Chief Constable himself was interested in this case because of Palmer. The inspector didn't elaborate why there was such high-profile interest.

The truth was that Baxter's confession was having major repercussions.

Arthur Burns wasn't new to police interviews. He thought he could tell when he was on a winner and when he was not. The problem Burns had right now was there were things he didn't know. One of those things was the suicide letter holding Baxter's confession. And even though he now knew Baxter was dead, he'd only found out today when Palmer had accused him of Baxter's murder. Nor did he know that when the police had broadcast the finding of Baxter's body, they had deliberately reported that investigations were continuing, and that foul play could not be ruled out. Unfortunately, Palmer hadn't waited for final confirmation of cause of death and assumed that his orders to put the frighteners on Baxter had been over-stepped. Had Palmer waited for a further police report on Baxter he would have heard that Baxter's death was suicide. He wouldn't have gone for Burns. And at this moment he'd be enjoying a black-tie dinner with his motor trade associates. Instead, he was on the way to the city morgue.

If found guilty of premeditated murder as threatened, Burns knew he was at best, facing a very long time in prison. To have any chance of a lesser charge, he would have to open up and tell the police everything. Accidental manslaughter looked his best hope, and over the following days he gave the police details of, and the reasons for, his fight with Palmer. He'd decided to hold nothing back and divulged everything - his long time and close relationship with Palmer and his criminal empire and his role in running key parts of Palmer's empire.

He named his now deceased boss as crime's mysterious and low-key. Mr Big.

And he told police about the plan to hand control of the crime network to Burns.

The police response to his disclosures were sceptical.

"So, you and your boss had a fight because he thought you killed someone who committed suicide? You haven't told us why. What was the dead man to your boss? Did you know the dead man? Did you kill him? Charlie Palmer was Mr Big, and you were to take over, eh? You'll need to do better than that."

Burns realised that Palmer's short-tempered rush to judgement had collapsed their whole house of criminal cards. He was not sorry Palmer was gone, but it was of no benefit to him. He couldn't go back to his gangland ways after blowing the whistle on the organisation. The only choice he had left was to give the coppers something they didn't have. He revealed the full extent of police bribery and corruption he himself had set up. Names and ranks. From beat coppers to senior officers. The whole kit and caboodle.

The assembled police at the interview said nothing in response, but abruptly closed the interview.

Arthur Burns was charged with the murder of Charlie Palmer and held in custody pending further investigation.

Reflecting on Burns' allegations, the senior detective said, "This is going to hit the fan if it's true. The force is already under enough pressure with drugs, robberies, and extortion. Together with the allegations in the suicide note, we now have this."

"Do you think Burns had a hook into any of us? Do you believe him?" his colleague asked.

"Who knows? What I do know is that I'm clean. But we're all going to be under the cosh until this is cleared up. The brass upstairs won't let these allegations lie. Happy days!"

The bribery allegations were handed to a team from the Edinburgh force for investigation.

Back in her nurses' quarters, Alice Walker busied herself with cleaning and tidying the living accommodation. While the physical activity was welcome, her mind was swamped with the events of the past few weeks. She sat down at the dressing table and gazed at her face in the mirror.

Her eyes showed the trauma she'd experienced. They were sad, unfocused, and had a faraway look that said she wanted no more. Yet, within her heart she was a little gladdened. She seemed to have the support of Detective Carse. Not just support. Maybe something else. Maybe. For sure his kindness had touched her and engendered a warmth that she welcomed.

A feeling that was in direct contrast to that which she felt for Frances McEwan.

The animosity and repugnance she now had in her heart for McEwan shocked her. She had never felt like this, about anything or anyone, and she didn't like that feeling. It was a feeling that didn't belong to her. If McEwan was responsible for just a tenth of what the police thought she had done or could do, how could Alice not have seen that? How foolish, how trusting, and unsuspecting she had been. Was she still that gullible? Had she learned anything?

She looked around the room and fixed her gaze on at McEwan's locked wardrobe and dressing table. What secrets did they hold? She fought back a mad impulse to break them open and take revenge on anything she found that would give her some kind of emotional satisfaction. Leave it all to the police, she reasoned.

She forced her head back to face her own mirror, picked up a hairbrush and started to vigorously brush her hair. Funny how little attention she really paid to herself, she thought. I'm twenty-seven, my biological clock is ticking. Where am I heading? Since she had finished with Groves, she'd not thought of a night out, a day in the city, or even a picnic in the park. Too many other events had closed in on her. The other nurses she knew were work mates, colleagues, fellow travellers on a treadmill of care. They were not night-out pals who could be banging on her door to join them in an evening of frivolity. And what did she have before that scoundrel Groves? Hardly any form of meaningful young-adult life. Her only real challenge was to make sure her parents had a resupply of butter or sugar.

So much water had passed under the bridge since then.

Today she felt that she really didn't know what challenges lay ahead. Had she abandoned any idea of marriage, children, a new family? She knew had to get a firm grip on her life or it would leave her behind, like the last bus disappearing into the night. The police had yet again asked to see her. More statements. Maybe news of developments with McEwan. Or would she be charged as an accomplice in the abortions? Morning would tell.

The Lord Provost and the Assistant Chief Constable of Glasgow met for lunch at the Rogano Oyster Bar in the city centre, a regular haunt of theirs. In an upstairs corner booth, they discussed the recent shocking events.

"Palmer is dead. As is Baxter. Do you see a connection in the deaths?" whispered an agitated Lord Provost.

"Palmer was murdered," responded Harrison. "He had close connections to gangland figures. A known criminal has been charged. Why he was killed is still under investigation. Baxter committed suicide. He left a note. It's with the coroner. Foul play is not suspected. I can't see any link between the two."

"God's sake, man! Keep your voice down." Woodhouse said while looking around with a look of panic. Satisfied they weren't being overheard, he looked back at Harrison and said quickly, "No link, other than the fact that they both were privy to our scheme for taking advantage of the major rebuild of the city and its environs."

"That doesn't fill me with joy, given they're no longer here and for the moment we are," came the glib response. "Do we replace them, continue on our own, or abandon the scheme?"

"That's three sixty-four-thousand-dollar questions, Mr Harrison. To answer them we need to know if their deaths are connected to us."

Woodhouse squeezed his podgy hands together. "I think for the time being we shelve it, say for six months. By then we should know."

"That could be the death knell of the project. But," the senior police officer sucked in air, "I agree that the current risks far outweigh stubborn resolve. In the absence of a better plan, we'll shelve it until year end. Agreed?"

Oliver Woodhouse nodded fast, mopped his flabby face with a napkin, ran perspiration-covered fingers through his silver hair, and said," Yes. Agreed. For now."

The requested information on Frances McEwan started to further mount. It came from Manchester, Liverpool, Leeds, and - with the aid of the Irish police - from Dublin. Her file thickened, grew into a second, and a third, and there was every chance of more volumes given more intelligence was still arriving.

Carse gathered his team together in the Wing to brief them on the intelligence they had to date. He wanted their views on the best way to flush the woman out.

"This would appear to be one sharp cookie were dealing with," Bailey said. "She's no fly-by-night brothel madame."

"And she must have upset some big players," Harper said. "There was a contract out for her elimination. That's heavy." He looked at the others. "Do we know if it's still in force and who put it out?"

Carse shook his head. "Don't know, and don't know, in that order. And we have no real lead on where she's gone to ground. We'd do well to check out her contacts, past and present. Those contacts are many, so we'll have to get help from the uniform."

There was a groan from the team at the mention of uniformed help.

He held up his hands. "I realise that we have infinitely superior experience, capabilities, and intellect, coupled with dogged determination, an utterly incorruptible disposition, charm, and rugged yet dashing good looks." He dropped his arms, darted at look at one of the men, and said in a low and confidential tone, "Not you on the last bit, Airlie." He smiled as he resumed his louder address to the team. "So, what I suggest is that the four of you do door, to door, to door, to door, to every blessed door in Glasgow."

He nodded, his grin wider. "That way we don't need to groan at the mention of uniform."

Kelly grumbled, "Point taken, boss."

The rest nodded and murmured like naughty schoolkids who'd been caught and knew they were in the wrong.

Carse's expression and tone were different when he said, "McEwan is our number one target. Remember what you saw in the annexe. Make no mistake about the nature of the person we're looking for."

"Have we pulled out all the stops with informers on each side of the border?" Airlie asked. "Shouldn't we be on the streets looking for her, chasing up anything that looks favourable?"

Carse raised an eyebrow. "You might want to rephrase that, Jake. But yes, and uniform and local plain clothes have got that covered. There's a small bag of gold being dangled in front of informers. Their information might be invaluable. What we don't have right now is a recent photograph of McEwan." With a flat hand, he pointed at each man. "It's *divide and conquer* time. Harper and Kelly – I need you to pour over and assess incoming information. You get a nugget, we all mobilise. Airlie and Bailey – time for you ladies to get your *glad rags* back on and start hitting the streets."

Ten minutes later, Carse got into his car and set off to meet Alice. He needed to give her the news about Baxter and answer a few of her questions.

He picked her up from the hospital and drove to a spot out west towards the beginning of the West Highland

Way. The reason for the drive was because he sensed that a change of scenery, outside of the city, would help clear her head and do her the world of good. He also thought it might do him some good as well. Once deep into the countryside, he spotted an empty bench overlooking the start of the arduous but wonderfully picturesque trek. He pulled the car over and stopped by the bench. Nothing else was on the high and deserted country lane save for a mobile café a couple of hundred yards away. They got two coffees from the café, took them to the bench, and sat next to each other while looking out onto the stunning scenery.

"The information we have on McEwan so far is bewildering. She has tentacles everywhere, it would seem." Carse blew on his steaming coffee while continuing to take in the vista. "But first I have some other news. And if you haven't heard it already, please brace yourself." He looked at her. "Crawford Baxter is dead, found early in the morning on a golf course near his flat."

Alice placed her coffee on the bench while shaking her head. "What is happening?! Is this all… connected? Was he murdered?"

"No. It was suicide. Massive barbiturate overdose. He left a lengthy note in his pocket, confessing to overprescribing and selling amphetamines, and to managing the annexe as a clinic for private illegal abortions. You were right, Alice."

"Did the note mention anyone else involved?"

"No. No one else."

Her eyes widened as she continued to shake her head and look at scenery that was now no longer registering. "Wow. Increasingly these days, I simply don't have the words."

"An inquiry is being set up by the hospital and you will very likely have to give your evidence to them in the same way as you have to the police. But you have nothing to fear. If anything, prepare yourself for the possibility for a promotion, more pay, and a civilian commendation for bravery."

She frowned.

He shrugged. "Just a letter I wrote. To Scotland's Chief Medical Officer, or whatever he calls himself."

"Norrie!"

"I carry quite some sway with him from back-in-the-day mucking around stuff that he and I found ourselves embroiled in. Still, that's not why your appearance before an enquiry will be the opposite of a grilling. That'll be down to you, my dear."

CHAPTER TWENTY-THREE

The allegations in Baxter's confession came under review at a top-level Police Board meeting to which Carse had been invited. Chaired by the Chief Constable, the attendees were present purely on a need-to-know basis.

"The main agenda point of today's meeting is to review the recent death, by his own hand, of a well-known gynaecologist found dead on a golf course," the top policeman said. "Crawford Baxter is the name of the deceased. As well as confessing to the running of an illegal abortion clinic and selling stolen amphetamines, he alleges that he was involved in a high-level conspiracy to fraudulently use inside information on the massive redevelopment plans for the city. With the help of senior city officials placed in positions of discretionary authority, a cartel of suppliers would illegally obtain the most lucrative contracts, and hence profits. The letter named two of the highest city officials and an eminent businessman. The implications for the integrity of the council, and indeed the law, are enormous. The names are all well known to you, but at this stage are to be kept top secret until an investigation into the allegations has been carried out. Inspector Carse will add to what I've just said".

Carse stood up, moved to the head of the table, and joined the Chief Constable. He looked around the room, cleared his throat, and said, "Crawford Baxter ran an illegal abortion service from his hospital facilities. This was discovered by my team while pursuing stolen drugs. I will return to those two matters in a moment. In regard to high-level conspiracy, we knew nothing of his conspiracy allegations until the suicide letter. The businessman he names as involved in the conspiracy was killed a few days after Baxter died. A suspect is in custody accused of the businessman's murder. To have the charges against him reduced, that suspect has confessed to a wide range of criminal activities, including widespread police bribery. He says that the businessman was in fact leading a double life and was the Mr Big of the crime network in the city. The extent of the bribery allegations, and conspiracy plot, has for obvious reasons, been handed to colleagues in the Edinburgh force for independent investigation." He studied the men and women in the room before continuing. "The work my team carried out was focussed on the illegal supply and sale of drugs and was successful to the extent that four people are in custody, accused of managing the supply chain in the Glasgow and West of Scotland area. During that work, we were made aware of the high likelihood of illegal abortions being regularly carried out in one hospital. We decided to investigate and interrupted an illegal abortion in mid-procedure. The abortion was unwanted, and I very much doubt it was the first of its kind. Put bluntly, a poor woman was dragged there so that the baby inside her could be butchered. And butchered by so called respectable members of the Scottish and English establishment. No doubt that woman would have suffered trauma for the rest of her life. However long that life would have been. On the day of the raid, my men and I entered a murder factory." He paused, recalling going with other British soldiers into a village in Europe and pointing guns at the residents while forcing them off to a place just thirty minutes' walk away. Young, old, male, female, the villagers' task was to pick up the bodies of people that they knew were being massacred nearby. It was a severe yet necessary punishment, given they'd turned a blind eye to the systematic horror on their village's perimeter. With a cold and deliberate voice, he said to the senior Police Board representatives, "This happened under your noses and on your watch."

"Inspector!" shouted the Chief Constable.

Carse ignored him. "The mother received our medical care and support. She is still receiving support. The scum involved in the abortion attempt were arrested. One of those pieces of scum was the unit's managing consultant, Crawford Baxter. I interviewed him. But he was not in the vicinity of the incident and so I released him, pending further investigation. He then disappeared." A trace of a smile was on his face when he added, "Disappeared with the thoughts I knew he'd be carrying." The smile vanished. "Death was due to a heavy barbiturate overdose." Carse sat down.

The room was silent for a moment.

Chief Constable stood and addressed the assembly. "Detective Inspector Carse's team have all but finished their work here. I'm sure you will all join me in thanking them for their superb work."

Nods of approval accompanied him as Carse was shown out of the boardroom.

One hour later he joined his team in the CREW room. to noisy quips of "How did it go, boss?" and "Do we still have a job?"

"It went as I expected and there was never any doubt about our jobs. But there's unfinished business. McEwan's still missing and I want her found."

McEwan was not in the best of moods. She picked at her food, watched television news reports, and cursed at the lack of information on Baxter's death. She also felt she was in limbo and making no progress right now. Hardcastle had to be met, but the woman was currently away. And after Burns had not turned up at their planned meeting in Stirling, McEwan couldn't track him down, even to tell him to put their plans on the back burner. And yet, despite her black mood, she felt secure. No one knew where she was. The only person who had ever been in this sumptuous new flat had been Baxter. And he was gone. The coward took the easy way out.

She reached into her overnight bag. Beneath £1500 in banknotes, she touched the small hard backed books. One British, one Irish passport. If things became too hot, she planned to lie low for a while in Spain, journeying there on her Irish documentation, via Dublin. She reasoned that in a year at most, things would have quietened down, and she could return.

Still, all this waiting for others to show up was frustrating. She drummed her fingers while deep in thought and decided to grab the bull by the horns and be proactive. After pulling the telephone close to her, she dialled a number. A woman answered.

"Matron Hardcastle speaking."

"Oh, hello Matron. Its Frances McEwan. Do you remember? You said we could perhaps meet to talk about the terrible death of Mr Baxter? I mentioned my training course and the need to get authorisation. I'd still welcome your guidance on who I should now approach in the hospital. Also," she faked a sigh, "it's quite important that I know a bit more about Mr Baxter. Just in case there's any scandal that might negatively affect any work I do in his part of the hospital."

"Where are you now?"

"Glasgow. In my cousins flat, as it happens. I have some days off and am looking after her place while she finishes a contract in Carlisle. She's an interior designer."

"I don't care what your cousin is. Can you come into the hospital?"

She sighed again. "I could, but not until next week. You see, I promised I wouldn't leave my cousin's place before her new furniture arrives. Would it be possible for you come along to see me? It's only a short walk from the hospital. I could make some lunch or something like that?"

There was silence for a few seconds. "I suppose it would be alright. In any case, it'll count as work for me, given it's a work matter. Means I can claim out-of-hours overtime. But it would really have to be an evening and not for long. This evening will do if it's not too short notice? No food though. Can't be long."

McEwan smiled. "That would be great, Matron! Thanks ever so much! How does seven PM sound?" She gave the address of the flat.

When the call ended, McEwan felt like the spider who had just talked to the fly. She needed to know everything Hardcastle knew about the annexe raid, and more importantly how much the matron knew about her set up with Baxter. Was she in the dark, as Baxter had said? Or did she know of McEwan's integral role? Had she been interviewed by the police? What did she know about the investigations?

These were life or death questions.

If Hardcastle knew enough to incriminate McEwan, the matron's life span was about to be dramatically shortened.

As forewarned, the matron's evening visit was brief. With little time to spare, she quickly covered the events as best she understood.

She was not in the annexe when the raid took place. Nor was Crawford Baxter. Three people were arrested, one being Nurse Walker. "I was astonished when I heard the news of the raid. It never occurred to me that the annexe, my annexe, could be used for something so evil."

McEwan knew she was lying about the use of the annexe but realised that it also told her that the matron probably didn't know of her arrangement with Baxter. If she did, why would she pretend she knew nothing of the annexe's role?

Hardcastle continued, "I know nothing about why Baxter committed suicide. Our relationship was purely professional and even in that realm we didn't have that much contact. I've had no idea about his personal life."

For sure this was another lie, but on balance McEwan believed Hardcastle didn't know why Baxter killed himself. "Didn't the police ask about Mr Baxter?"

"No. They haven't spoken to me. Anyway, I couldn't really help them."

"All together a dreadful episode. And now I have no one to sign me up for the training course I'm offering," McEwan frowned. "As I've mentioned, it would be good to know who I could approach. Who might have the authority."

"Can't help you there. That said, you could try our registrar. I doubt he'll have signatory authority, but he's worked in the hospital since the dawn of mankind. Why don't you pick his brains. If I think of anybody else, I'll let you know."

Their brief conversation was over in ten minutes. McEwan offered some refreshment, but Hardcastle said she was pushed for time and had to leave.

After she closed her door, McEwan pursed her lips, looked at her watch, and felt hungry. Always a good sign she thought. On balance she decided she had nothing to fear from Hardcastle. One less chore to attend to. However, the information about Alice Walker was unnerving. How much did Walker know? Was she a threat? Walker had questioned Baxter when a client procedure was messed up and she had seen things she was not meant to. Had she seen more? Looked for more? Would she have to be put out of the way? McEwan needed to find out. But if Walker had been arrested, was she still in custody? How could she get to her? Should she even try, or simply vanish again and let time fade memories and heal? She made a decision. It was becoming too difficult to get all bases covered. Too many spinning plates.

And that meant she'd make something to eat.

And then completely disappear from all matters Glasgow.

Edith Hardcastle left the flat after her short visit to McEwan and headed back to her office in the annexe. She locked her door, sat behind her desk, and took out some papers from a desk drawer. She sat for a long time, alternately looking out the office window at the darkened sky, then turning her attention back to the papers. She gave a soft huff, returned the papers to the drawer, and locked it. She knew what she wanted to do, what she had to do. She just had to make it happen.

Word that the Edinburgh Police were tasked with investigating suspected bribery and corruption in the Glasgow Police force was leaked a few minutes after it was announced at the Police Board meeting. Within a week Martin Harrison, the Assistant Chief Constable decided to take early retirement. He left the Glasgow City force and in doing so raised no eyebrows within the higher echelons of the force. And he left with the self-penned valediction, "The demands of leading our law enforcement teams have increased dramatically in recent years. It has become very much a job for a younger man, and I happily step aside to make way for fresh blood. I do so after a record of which I am truly proud,"

But the Edinburgh force was having none of all that. The force already had him high on its list of interviewees.

McEwan's flight from justice was meticulously planned. Her belongings were packed, the hired car had been delivered and fuelled up, the ferry passage from Holyhead to Dublin arranged by phone, and a stop for a short break on the three-hundred-mile journey south picked out. The hired car could be dropped off at Dublin airport and she could stroll to the departure terminal for her Aer Lingus flight to Malaga.

She sat on the floor in the middle of the plush flat's lounge, checked everything for a third time, and decided she'd prepared everything correctly and was ready to go. She'd even put on a cream floral dress for the occasion of travelling to warmer climes. She intended to drive overnight, when the traffic south was lighter. She would leave at exactly ten PM.

At half past seven her door buzzer sounded. A puzzled frown appeared on her face as she went to the door. No one knew she was here. She used the spy hole in the front door and recognised Matron Hardcastle, wearing outdoor clothes and carrying a holdall. Though she was confused by the unexpected visit, she wondered if the matron had suddenly got a brainwave and knew someone who could sign off on McEwan's fictitious training course. She unbolted and opened the door and was about to welcome her.

The welcome never happened.

Because Hardcastle used a lead cosh to viciously hit McEwan on her head.

McEwan slumped to the floor. Hardcastle dragged her body inside and closed and bolted the door.

When McEwan came to, she found herself securely tied and bound to a heavy chair. Her face was a red mask from the bleeding head wound, her mouth stuffed with cotton wool and tightly closed by black tape.

Hardcastle was glaring at her as she sat on a pouffe, her holdall open at her feet. "Wondering what the fuck is going on, eh?" She smiled, though her eyes were intense and flickering. "How does it feel to know you're not getting away from your past, you slimy bastard? Not this time."

McEwan's eyes rolled in pain. She hopelessly struggled against her bounds; her head shook from side to side; all to no avail.

Hardcastle reached into her bag and withdrew a barber's cutthroat razor.

McEwan's widened as she stared at the object. She struggled more violently, but with the same futile effect as before.

Hardcastle wafted the razor through air while keeping her eyes fixed on McEwan. "This is not a two-way conversation. You will listen until you can't anymore. I have been looking for you for a long time. Why? Because you're a heartless bastard." She momentarily looked around. "Quite clever of you to vanish into this snug little bolt hole." She looked back at her prisoner. "Thing is, though, nobody knows where you are. Except me of course.

Seems you're not as smart as you think you are." She rose, walked to a kitchen area, removed a sheet of kitchen roll, and returned to her seat. In front of McEwan, she used the razor effortlessly slice off thin strips of the paper. "How easily the blade cuts through. Can you imagine it taking off an ear? Or opening a new mouth beneath the nasty one you have?" Her voice remained measured, icy, and venomous. "By the look of your bags, seems you're all packed and ready to fly the coop." She opened McEwan's overnight bag and tipped its contents on to the floor. "Well, look at this. More money than you can wave a stick at. And what do we have here? Of course. Two passports!" She shook her head while smiling. "You won't be needing these where you're going." She took the razor and deftly drew its blade along the material covering McEwan's arm. The material began to change colour as the blood seeped through. "That's the first of many. It's not really painful at first, is it? It's the horror of knowing what I'm doing that's the kicker. That said, and as I go along, it will get painful. Very, very painful."

McEwan tried to scream. All that came out was another barely audible sound. She instinctively wanted to move away from the blade and the woman holding it, but she could barely move her body an inch.

Hardcastle positioned a dining chair in front of her victim and sat on it. She was now at eye-level with McEwan. From her holdall, she withdrew a sheaf of papers, placed them on her lap, and whispered, "I'm going to read you a story." She read from one of the sheets.

"Once upon a time, in a land far from here, a beautiful young girl fell in love with a handsome prince. He was everything she dreamed of, but like many love stories, it ran

into difficulty. The prince made her pregnant. But he denied responsibility and left her to fend for herself. Her mother didn't know what to do for the best. She asked a relative for help. That relative wasn't really much help, and turned to others who could help. They said they knew what they were doing and took money for it".

Hardcastle picked up another sheet. "And now I'm going to read you a letter. A real letter. Pay attention." She proceeded.

"I have no regrets in writing this. I know you will use the information contained here to right a wrong which should have been put right a very long time ago, and if not righted by you personally, then by your agent. The person who wronged you and your family has been hiding in plain sight. The one you placed a contract on long ago is among us. She has changed her name and lives by blackmail and threats of exposure. I am culpable in not having enough courage to unveil her before now. You see, she has blackmailed me for a very long time. Now that I am gone, her power has too. Ruth Cohen, or Frances McEwan as she calls herself now, completely bungled the abortion you niece underwent in England. She is the one you have sought for a long time. Do what you would have done years ago."

Hardcastle said, "That was left for me by Crawford Baxter the night he took his own life. He knew, because I had told him, that my niece died in excruciating pain. From sepsis. Two days after you performed a barbaric procedure and called it an abortion. He knew it was you who did it. But for his own reasons didn't tell me you were now masquerading as someone else. He also knew that I had put a contract on your head, after my distraught sister could no longer live with the loss of her only daughter and took her own life. I've thought about this moment for a very long time." Her eyes glared. "And I'm going to make you feel the same kind of mental and physical suffering my family endured."

McEwan writhed but to no avail.

Hardcastle leaned forward and slid the razor along McEwan's shoulder. Once again, the material changed colour. From her holdall, she removed a small glass pot and held it above the first cut in McEwan's arm." She looked at her victim. "I did warn you about the pain." She sprinkled the pot's contents onto the wound. The salt bit in almost immediately.

McEwan strained against her binding and violently shook her head from side to side.

The razor moved again over McEwan's thigh. Then across her forehead. Then her ear. Salt was applied to all the lacerations.

McEwan again thrashed violently. The cream floral dress she was wearing had now become a red and brown mass of material, with only occasional glimpses of its original colour.

Her torturer rummaged through McEwan's packed bags and saw the flight tickets and ferry pass. "You won't be needing these now, given you're going nowhere nice." She placed the tickets in an ashtray, found matches in the kitchen area, and set the tickets alight. She pulled a look of sympathy and said in a tone that mirrored that fake expression, "Oh, poor you. All dressed up and ready for the excitement of travel. Don't worry though, sweetie. It's not so dull here. How's about we spend the next thirty minutes doing something *really* exciting?"

She leaned forward.

And spent thirty minutes slashing McEwan and pouring salt in the wounds.

The floor was covered in McEwan's blood.

McEwan was still moving.

Hardcastle slashed some more and waited.

McEwan was still.

Hardcastle searched for a pulse.

She found nothing.

She pressed the edge of the razor hard against one side of McEwan's face and slowly and deeply sliced downwards.

No movement.

No murmurs.

Nothing.

But Hardcastle again checked for a pulse.

There was nothing.

Probably McEwan had died a while ago.

But now there was no doubt.

Hardcastle nodded and whispered, "Bye bye. And where you're going you won't be seeing my niece."

She stood and looked at the savaged mess that once looked human. She'd sated her need to inflict abject pain on McEwan. Through Hardcastle, her family had gained revenge. Honour was satisfied. The matter was now closed. It was time to go.

She deliberately didn't waste time cleaning anything up. She wanted to leave a message. And my goodness, what a message it would be for anyone who entered this chamber.

She took the money from McEwan's bag, the car keys for the hired car, and left. It was past midnight when she drove away.

On a piece of waste ground near the Forth and Clyde canal in the north of the city, the hired car was found in the early morning hours. It was minus registration plates, torched and abandoned, a quarter of a mile from the nearest bus stop.

The identity of the owner was found from the engraved engine block number, tracked to the hire company.

And that eventually led to the discovery of McEwan's body in the blood stained flat.

In Liverpool Lime Street railway station, a 57-year-old spinster got off the main line train from Glasgow, hauled her suitcase to a taxi, and headed for a lady's hairdressers in the centre of the city. Later, the now blue rinsed senior booked into a bed and breakfast, where she stayed until the following day when she agreed a deal for a luxury flat on the city's southern outskirts.

Norrie Carse, still intent on finding the whereabouts of McEwan, was formally taken off the hunt by the Chief Constable. "You and your team are due kudos for the work you have turned out on drug abuse, I will personally tell your men so. The diversion onto the illegal abortions set up, and the raid on the hospital equally deserves praise, but I am formally telling you that your involvement in following up that crime ceases, as of now."

"Why, sir? What's happened," queried an indignant Carse, "McEwan and Hardcastle are still at large." The Chief Constable looked around him, inclined his head towards Carse and said, "Not anymore. McEwan's body, or what's left of it, was discovered in a flat on the western exit roads from the city. She had been slashed repeatedly, all over, and bled out. A salt cellar was found on the carpet, and it appears that salt had been used to magnify the pain from the cuts. The room is like an abattoir."

"God almighty, that sounds extremely personal. Fingerprints?" Carse asked.

"Some. My teams are working on it, and working extra hard to find Matron Hardcastle. There's no need for you and your team to linger. Understand?"

"That's very disappointing, sir. My men deserve to be in on the final act."

"We'll just have to agree to disagree, inspector," the senior cop said, emphasising the difference in rank. "That's the way it will be."

CHAPTER TWENTY-FOUR

The CREW team gathered in a small conference room in the central police headquarters for the formal address by the Chief Constable. They were winding down their operation and preparing to leave, after completing all necessary reports and evidence statements.

His remarks were predictable. Good job, well done, difficult times and so on. What did nettle the team, despite the Scottish chief's accolade, was his criticism for diverting from their task to make the annexe raid, and the patronising way he delivered his comments.

When he finished and left, the CREW remained in the room, some sitting on tables, others lounging in chairs, all loosening ties and sipping coffee or smoking. Carse then broke the news that McEwan's mutilated body had been found, the local police were hunting Hardcastle, and that their involvement was no longer required, or wanted.

"Fuck's sake, many thanks Jock," spat Kelly.

"Settle down men, it's the name of the game." Carse soothed.

Carse checked the door was closed, sat on a desk in front of his men, and spoke earnestly to them. "We've done this a dozen times in as many places. The big chief pats you on the back but adds a bummer. Not only did we successfully complete the job we came here to do, but we also went the extra mile."

"And then some, boss," said Kelly.

"And then some," Carse repeated. He looked at each man, wondering how many times they'd risked their lives for others in the team, him included. He'd lost count. But he knew them so well. Airlie and Bailey bickering at each other like an old married couple and then always doing the right thing when things around them turned sour, Harper never tiring of telling Kelly the blatant falsehood that it was his submarine and no doubt his torpedo that sunk a top secret reconnaissance craft he was on, Kelly frequently positing that Harper was turned in Colditz and was a German spy, Airlie occasionally taking his boss to one side and asking if he needed tips about women, all of them constantly at each other's throats and laughing about silly stuff because, hey, their life expectancy now was little different than what it had been in the dark years of a world war. They were cynics, and they deserved to be. And they were a joy to be around. But he knew they relied on him so much. For all their banter and wise cracks, they listened to what he had to say. They drew from his strength. And that meant there were times when he had to cut through the chatter. They expected that of him; needed that from him. Now was one such moment. He said, "Gentlemen. We bang up the villains. More spawn. We grab the drugs. That's no bother for buyers because there's plenty more drugs on tap. So, what are we doing? What difference do we make? Probably not much. But I reckon enough. What we did, what you did, was to plug a very serious leak in a major pipeline. You got people off the street who belong behind bars. In the course of that, we were asked to make a professional decision. Ignore a potentially very serious crime or stick to the brief we were given? I'm proud to say you did both and did them very professionally." He smiled.

"The brickbat from the top man here in Glasgow is more to do with the fact we're outsiders, and his own people missed something seriously criminal in their own backyard. That's why they want to keep it to themselves now." He stood and said in a commanding voice, "Well done, gentlemen. The beers are being lined up as I speak. My final order of the day is that you are to report for duty next door in the Grant Arms pub."

"With immediate effect?" asked Airlie.

"With immediate effect, sergeant."

The following lunchtime, Carse had arranged a final meeting with Alice. Officially and typically in situations like these, he'd have wanted the meeting to give his thanks for all her help and show his team's gratitude with something like a bouquet of flowers. It seemed odd to want such a meeting with Alice. So instead, he invited her for lunch. He'd chosen an unpretentious restaurant in the west end of the city, not far from the hospital, and didn't know how he felt about the possibility that Alice might misconstrue the reason for lunch. Not that he really knew the reason. Except – that he wanted to see her, and also to impart some dire news.

The early part of lunch stuck to discussion on the annexe case.

Carse had the difficult task of telling Alice that McEwan was dead. "She was murdered, viciously and violently killed. I'll spare you the details. The local police have a lead on the killer, and my team and I are no longer needed on the case."

"Murdered?" she gasped. "By whom?"

"Person or persons unknown, as yet, but I think the local police have a handle on the culprit."

"Good god almighty, what next? Will this ever end?" Alice shuddered and wrapped her arms around her shoulders.

Carse steered the talk away from the news which had clearly upset her, and pushed neutral conversations about what each of them was going to do next in their work lives. Carse said with some resignation that he was returning to an employment environment where he was comfortable and pretty much knew what he would be doing. Alice said she was intent on leaving her personal nightmare behind but did not know much else. It was only while empty plates were being cleared away by a waiter and coffees were delivered to their table that they looked at each other after a rather embarrassing moment of silence and no doubt realised what each of them were thinking – that they'd just wasted the last hour. They smiled at each other. They relaxed.

She asked, "When do you think I will be free to leave Glasgow?"

He frowned. "You're free to leave anytime."

"I mean, from the memories. Don't you find memories sometimes have a bit of a hold?"

He huffed. "What good memories do you have of this city?" His face reddened when he realised what he'd said. Alice did have good memories of Glasgow. Many of them would have been with her parents. He felt awkward and stupid. "I'm sorry. What I meant was that you'll find a life full of new experiences that will help you to overcome much of what you've gone through."

She nodded. "I told you – dreamer, just like me."

"What will you do?"

She thought about the letter she'd once received at the nurses' home, encouraging nurses to apply for assisted passages to work overseas. That letter seemed a lifetime ago. "I want to get far away from the memories for a start. Under their help scheme, I'm applying for a nursing position in Canada."

His stomach tightened. "Canada? That's getting away from Glasgow, no mistake."

She chose her next words carefully. "There's nothing to keep me here. At least not here in Glasgow." She looked out of the adjacent window. Outside a fine rain was hitting the city. "Not entirely bad memories. But the spirit of your sentiment is correct, Mr Carse." She looked at him. "Even good memories can become bittersweet."

For a man who was used to outsmarting even the canniest of criminals, right now he didn't really know what to say. He blurted, "Maybe there's something good for you outside of Glasgow but still in the United Kingdom." He tried to smile though sensed it looked forced. "Big enough place. Plenty of new faces. Job opportunities galore for nurses of your calibre, I'm sure."

She reached across the table and touched his cheek with her finger. "New faces." She nodded.

"It would be good to meet…" he could hear his voice stuttering, "good to meet and, you know, chat in places like this. Regularly. Canada's a..." he placed his hand around hers and could feel the emotion welling up inside of him, "long way... long way, to visit. I don't mind though," he added quickly. "Come to see you in Timbuktu if needs be."

The comment made her laugh. While a tear ran down her face. "Wherever it is, I don't think you'll need to get on a slow boat to Timbuktu." She leaned across the table and gently kissed him on the cheek.

But she didn't then sit back down.

Instead, she stayed there.

Her heart beating fast.

He slightly moved his face.

So that his lips were closer to hers.

THE END

Printed in Great Britain
by Amazon